Dead Man Dancing

(A Maddie Fitzpatrick Dance Mystery)

by

Kate O'Connell

For information, email **Cozy Cat Press**, cozycatpress@aol.com or visit our website at: www.cozycatpress.com

COZY CAT
P R E S S

ISBN: 978-1-939816-73-3

Printed in the United States of America

Cover design by Paula Ellenberger
http://www.paulaellenberger.com/

1 2 3 4 5 6 7 8 9 10

This book is dedicated to my parents Mark and Barbara Harrison. For 47 years of love and support, some of them spent holding your breaths, thank you.

Special Thanks

Thank you to the supportive staff at Cozy Cat Press, especially Patricia Rockwell and Galina Velgach, and to Julie Seedorf for helping when technical difficulties struck in South Africa. Thank you to my writing girls @Suki Jakes. You continue to amuse and inspire. And as always, thank you Paul and Eden for getting onto the dance floor.

Prologue

The man shuffled through the garden intent on reaching the wooded area before the sun set. He didn't want to draw attention to himself and relied on his slow gait to render him unnoticeable to any prying eyes. Shuffling was the way he moved through his days at the retirement village, so shuffling would be the way to attend to this business as well.

While he crossed the well-tended lawn without running into anyone, he hadn't been able to shake the feeling of being watched. The sensation had distracted him so that he tripped over a forgotten hose snaking its way across the grounds. He steadied himself, instinctively patting the package in his pocket, grinning as he confirmed that it was still there. The one person he didn't want spying on his business had been dealt with. That thorn in his side, an annoying reminder of the past he hadn't expected to ever see again, had been inconvenienced in his room. He'd made sure of that before he left the building.

The old man took a final step in the fading sunlight and continued into the shade of a tree then on into the gloom of the small wooded area at the back of the grounds. When he reached the spot he'd found the day before, he bit down on the toothpick clamped between the remaining natural teeth in his mouth then spat the two broken pieces onto the sodden ground. He cackled more loudly than he probably should have and, unable to hold the excitement of his adventure inside any longer, he followed the outburst with a hoot of joy.

"This'll show that lousy imposter."

He felt a surge of energy he hadn't felt in years as he bent over the gnome lying listlessly at his feet, its face distorted by mud, its hands broken off years ago. Taking the small trowel he'd stowed under a pile of rotting leaves, he started digging. It didn't take long because it didn't have to be buried deeply, just deeply enough. Completing the task, the man took the slim package from his pocket and dropped it in the hole, then covered it with the loose soil he'd unearthed. After throwing the trowel as far as his arthritic hands could muster, he turned to the Shadylawn Retirement Village and headed back to whatever inane entertainment the staff had concocted for them that evening.

Satisfied, he retraced his steps, passing an ancient maple towering over the rest of the trees. From behind it, a shadow glanced at a photograph one more time to be certain. *Yeah, this was the guy.* The photo showed the old man in a suit and he was younger by a lot but it was the guy. Also satisfied, the shadow put the photograph back in his pocket. *The old geezer was going to be an easy target; he probably couldn't run more than five yards without collapsing*, he thought. The shadow frowned. He liked a bit of a challenge. But a job was a job and the money was too good to mess this job up. He'd find the old guy later tonight.

The shadow waited until the sun had sunk behind the grand buildings, then walked to where the old man had flung the trowel and went to see what the old crackpot had been up to.

Chapter One

Maddie Fitzpatrick stood with her back to the full-length mirror, her weight on her left side as she swung her right leg in an effort to relieve the stiffness in her hips. She'd taught four back-to-back Argentine Tango lessons, and the day wouldn't be over until she finished with a class she'd agreed to teach at the Shadylawn Retirement Village.

The two students in front of her, Lydia and Joy, had spent the last hour dancing while simultaneously arguing about who was going to lead and who was going to follow, literally changing roles every five minutes. Joy would invariably acquiesce with a disgruntled sigh, before the urge to lead overcame her again and she would forcibly spin Lydia to face the opposite direction and take over. The problem was that in each of their bids to lead, neither woman was listening to the music, and both were growing increasingly frustrated. Maddie walked back to a table, picked up her iPod and lowered the volume.

"Okay, let's stop for a minute." The women sprang apart from one another, then turned and looked sheepishly towards Maddie.

"We did it again, didn't we? Both of us were trying to lead."

Lydia was the taller of the two women, her toned body told Maddie she worked out, probably jogged as she had the long lean calves and sinewy arms of a marathon runner.

"It was because you weren't listening to me. Why don't you just let me lead?" replied her partner.

Joy was shorter by several inches and heavy in her hips and legs. She looked to Maddie as if she would have made a good model for a statue of a South American fertility goddess. As Joy gazed at Maddie, her face became increasingly pinched and Maddie imagined she was about to stamp her foot in frustration. Maddie held a conciliatory hand up.

"Okay, the two of you need to decide who's going to lead and who's going to follow. And for the time being, I'd like you to make a decision and hold to it for the entirety of our next class. You two dance fluidly together and I know I said that the lead and follow are roles that can be played with, interchangeable at some point, but not quite yet."

Apart from their inability to agree on their roles, the two women did move well together. Maddie could often tell how it was going to go within the first Argentine Tango class. Couples either did, or didn't, listen to one another and it came down to communication. Not verbal communication, which she hadn't been able to quiet between Lydia and Joy from the moment they walked into their first class, but a corporeal communication, which couldn't be heard unless the dancers actually shut up for five minutes.

"Okay, we have time for one more dance. Now, who is leading?"

Lydia simply opened her arms to invite Joy to enter the embrace. Joy shrugged and wafted into Lydia's open arms. Maddie started the music again and within 30 seconds, Joy barked out.

"No, we're supposed to move around one another there. Why don't you just let me do it?"

Lydia had dropped her arms from the hold she and Joy were in, and placed her hands on her hips, then took an exaggerated step away from her partner. "I'm doing the step that Maddie taught us but you're not letting me lead it."

"Well, you're not doing that thing that Maddie does." Joy received a scowl from Lydia. "The thing she does when her body twists. That's what I have to follow. Otherwise, I don't know what you want me to do."

"Well, I'm trying but it's like I have to do opposite things with my body at the same time and it's really frustrating."

Maddie couldn't hold back a laugh. "You're right, Lydia, it's not easy at first but it will get better. It's because of the disassociation between your upper and lower body. It's part of what gives Argentine Tango dancers that ability to look like they're gliding across the dance floor."

Joy crossed her arms in front of her body and sulked. "I know how hard it is. In case you haven't noticed, I've been dancing here too."

Lydia turned away from her partner. "I know that."

This was Lydia and Joy's fifth class and Maddie felt more a marriage counselor than a dance teacher. Maddie needed to stop the new argument she could hear coming.

"Both roles in tango are challenging. It's harder at the beginning for the lead role so there's an uneven learning curve. The roles are different and you're not helping yourselves by trying to learn both of them at once." Maddie could feel her student's boiling points reaching a critical level, particularly Lydia, as a pained expression passed over her face and she guessed that the elegant woman was successful in whatever she did off the dance floor and was used to getting things right on the first try.

"I know five lessons seem like a lot, but remember, it's just the beginning. You have to give yourself a break." Lydia shook her head in disagreement.

"I just want it to make sense. If can understand it, then I can go home and practice it until it's perfect."

"My suggestion is that you give yourself some time off from the pressure of learning and let yourselves fall in love with it."

Both women spoke at once. "But we do love it." They turned and nodded at one another before Joy continued. "We both love it. Ever since we saw the show *Glamourtango*. That's what made us come to you."

"I've seen it too. It's an inspiring show. I just want you to take a step back and focus on the movement that's happening inside your bodies rather than what you think it's supposed to look like."

Looks of consternation passed between Joy and Lydia.

"I want you to fall in love with the music without moving, without expecting anything from yourselves." Maddie handed a CD to Lydia. "Here's another compilation. It has a variety of music on it from di Sarli that you'll recognize from our classes, to Piazzola, which you probably won't be able to dance to. Just listen."

Lydia reached out and took the CD before Joy could. "Thank you, Maddie. We'll do that." It sounded to Maddie like Lydia was receiving a financial report and assessing the whole procedure of dancing as an ordeal to get through.

"It's not a homework assignment as much as it is an invitation to get to know the music."

Joy looked embarrassed beside her partner. "Sorry about that, Maddie." She squeezed Lydia's waist affectionately. "Let's do as the teacher's instructed, and go get a drink and relax."

Maddie watched them leave together, Joy's hand still on Lydia's waist, then walked to the table where her bag sat and looked at her mobile. It was four thirty. She would love to have a drink too but she still had several hours before she'd be finished. As she left the classroom, she could hear the sound of an energetic cha-cha-cha from the room next door and a voice that carried over the music.

"Oh yes! Thrust-thrust-thrust! Now deep, go-go-go! And again, bing-bing-bing!"

Maddie stopped at the door and listened to several more rhythmically thematic vocal inventions until she felt someone come up behind her. Laura had silently crept up to within an inch of Maddie's back. She turned quickly and instinctively lengthened the distance between herself and the studio secretary.

"Anything good going on?" Laura stood with a box in one hand and an ashtray in the other, her mouth pursed and eyebrows raised. Since the studio had been implicated in a murder investigation the previous month, it seemed to Maddie that she was the chosen accomplice to the secretary's desire to become involved in further nefarious activities. More and more often she had found Laura retreating from closed doors, her ears perked and her eyes eager.

"Now, I'm no prude, you know that." Laura balanced the ashtray on top of the UPS box and patted her unruly hair ineffectively with her free hand as they both continued to listen to the sounds of an accented soprano ring out from behind the door.

"And yes! Go-go-go. Don't stop! Push-push-push!"

"As I was saying, no prude, but really? What are people going to think?"

Maddie had heard all this before, *ad infinitum*. Their boss, Peter St. Claire, had had to hire a new Latin dance teacher after the abrupt departure of Ricky Russo the month before and the ones he'd found were Nikki Chua and her partner Grant. Nikki had created quite a stir in the month that she had been at the St. Claire Dance Studio and, Laura's comments aside, Maddie saw that the stir she created was good for the studio, both because she was a popular teacher and because her enthusiasm was infectious.

"Laura, I don't think anyone's complaining."

"Oh, what was that?"

From inside the classroom, the two women heard a yelp, followed by a thump. The door opened a few inches and Nikki's partner, Grant Armstrong, a slight man with a constant bemused expression, floated out of the room, closing the door behind him.

Maddie smiled guiltily as he closed the door. "Hi, Grant. Sorry; I hope we didn't disturb the class."

Grant looked over his shoulder before answering, but didn't stop his progress down the hall.

"No, it's fine."

In the month since the new Latin couple had been at the studio, Maddie had yet to hear Grant string more than four words together.

Halfway down the hall, Grant arrived at the janitor's closet and opened the door. Maddie looked at Laura and suspected that they both were thinking similar thoughts. Grant hadn't been at the studio when Maddie had found a dead body in that closet, and the cavalier manner in which he opened the door and pulled the broom out without pause led Maddie to believe that if he'd known anything about it, he wouldn't let it bother him. Maddie didn't like to admit that she still avoided eye contact with the closet when forced to walk past it.

As Grant slid by Maddie and Laura and opened the classroom door, he tipped his head as if tipping a hat.

"If you'll excuse me."

Maddie almost felt like she should curtsy in return. Grant and his proper British reticence would seem to be a foil to Nikki's Philippine-born, Honolulu-raised spitfire personality. How they danced together boggled the mind. But they did and somehow it worked.

In the office, Laura put the box on her desk and emptied the ashtray into the wastebasket, wrinkling her nose as she did.

"Oh, hats! I blame all the shenanigans of last month for this dirty habit." While Laura had carried an unopened pack of cigarettes with her every day for three years to remind herself that she was stronger than the urge to smoke, the murderous events of the autumn had sent her back into the habit. She had kicked it for three years and she now vacillated between righteousness and condemnation on an hourly basis.

"Though, of course, no one could possibly blame me, right?" Laura didn't even glance at Maddie as she retrieved a pair of scissors from a drawer overflowing with hair products used to tame her unruly mane and sliced the taped box open. Maddie had been asked the same question at least 700 times in the last month and she always answered with the same mumbled affirmative.

Maddie looked around the office at the ever-increasing accumulation of bright buttons she'd witnessed over the past several days.

"What are these?"

"They're Luttons. All the craze."

Maddie read an inspirational button perched on the edge of the computer screen saying "For Peace Press Here," then looked at the file cabinet.

"Inspiration on the filing cabinet?"

"Have you seen my filing? I did that to show Peter I was working on it. Here, why don't you take this one?"

Laura handed her a button and motioned towards the photo hanging above her desk showing Laura and her husband in a formal studio shot. "I have all I need."

Maddie took the proffered button and read "For Love Press Here." She felt herself color as she imagined Laura thinking about her and Joe Clancy. Not that anything had happened between her and the detective.

Just when Maddie and Joe were supposed to be getting to know one another again, Joe's beloved grandmother had taken a fall and broken her hip. She'd had been sent to the hospital and while there had contracted pneumonia and, thinking her death was imminent, Joe and his sister Maureen had gone to her bedside in Ireland. Maddie had been frustrated when he first announced his plans but had grown to appreciate the forced space it had created. Returning to her hometown after a fifteen-year absence and having to deal with two murders, an attempt on her life and the possibility of starting a relationship with her high school boyfriend, she realized that the imposed separation could be well spent finding some balance.

Laura looked at her knowingly. She sucked in an enormous amount of air and huffed it out in three equal bursts before speaking. "Maddie, if you're not going to tell me then I'll just have to ask. So just exactly what is happening in the romance department?"

From the keen look on Laura's face, Maddie knew she wanted a story, but Maddie put the Lutton in her bag and smiled in what she hoped was an elusive way. Laura waited several seconds in vain, then shook her head with an annoyed huff.

"Are you sure you're all right? Maybe tonight is just going to be too much for you. They say women who've been through emotional upheaval, such as murder," Laura paused at the word but not having elicited the intended response and faced with Maddie's growing scowl, continued, "Well, they say that they are unable to commit to intimate relationships. Is that the problem?"

With perfect timing, Peter St. Claire walked into the office and saved Maddie from further conversation with the gossipy secretary. Peter's infant daughter, Lauren Sophia, immediately took all the attention in the room, as Laura scurried over to her and started cooing. Maddie sat heavily in a chair and watched Peter bask in the adorableness of his new daughter. Kristy, Peter's wife, followed a minute later, looking annoyed as she dropped a baby bag onto Laura's desk. She then looked around the room with a weak smile until her eyes fell on Maddie and the already faint smile dropped from her face as if she'd seen an unpleasant stain on her blouse.

Peter apparently didn't notice his wife's displeasure. "Hello, people!" His voice boomed out as he absently protected the sound from reaching his daughter by shielding her tiny ears. "How is life in the world of my dance studio?"

For the first month of Lauren Sophia's life, Peter had taken time off from the studio but seemed unable to get through a day without popping into the studio with his daughter in tow for what he called "social time." He carried her in a contraption adhered to his chest and he looked like he enjoyed every minute of it. Maddie had been taking several of Peter's classes and was frankly, getting worn out.

"Maddie, what time does the Shadylawn gig start? Kristy is getting a massage until six so I can't get there until 6:15, earliest." As Peter mentioned his wife's name, she perked up and a smile returned to her face. Maddie still felt uneasy in her presence. She had only met Kristy on a few occasions but never got a warm reception. She smiled tentatively at her.

"Hi, Kristy, you're looking great. How's everything going?"

Kristy did look great, aside from the sour look on her face. She glowed and her black hair hung to her waist in a shiny cascade. She may have put on some extra pounds, but they suited her.

Kristy's face scanned the room. "Hi, everyone." Then, unexpectedly, she beamed at Maddie. "Thanks, Maddie. I feel good, particularly because I'm off for some pampering while the best dad in the world is taking over." Kristy squeezed her husband around his back and then nuzzled her daughter. She turned back to Maddie. "Peter says you've taken a lot of his classes this past month. Thanks for that."

Maddie felt herself turning pink and lowered her face, suddenly thinking that she'd been uncharitable to Kristy. Maybe she'd just imagined that Kristy didn't like her. She looked up to see the rest of the room looking at her.

"Oh, it's fine. I'm glad you guys could be together so much with Lauren Sophia." Maddie suddenly felt tongue-tied and she wasn't sure why. "You know, it's really not a problem if you can't come tonight, Peter."

"You've helped more than I should have asked, and I want to repay the favor. You know that lot up at the retirement village are a feisty bunch. Don't let their ages fool you."

Maddie laughed. "Trust me, I know. If the rest of the group is anything like my Tuesday morning class, I'm going to be earning my money. The class doesn't start until 6:45, so take your time."

Peter and Kristy turned to leave, and Maddie couldn't help but catch the disapproving glance Kristy threw at her. She was out the door, but Maddie knew that she hadn't imagined the animosity that Kristy felt towards her. Laura followed the couple out the door, considering another cigarette judging by the way she snatched the ashtray. Maddie wasn't alone in the office for more than a minute before Frank, the custodian, walked in.

"Yes, Maddie, the weekend is supposed to be mild, considering." Frank had picked up a habit in the past month of starting conversations as if the participants had already been talking for several minutes, then promptly ending it.

"Hi, Frank. Um, great. I'll be looking for an apartment and I'd rather not do that in a snowstorm."

"Now, you know what this town needs? A good real estate agent, that's what it needs. Seems like just when you find a good one, they up and disappear."

Maddie looked at Frank to see if he was serious but saw nothing more than casual interest on his face. Most of the staff had come to realize that Frank seemed to be loosing part of his memory, and they were all worried for him. Maddie had no love of real estate agents, that was for sure, but she didn't want to continue this conversation.

Frank sat himself down with a sigh and a scratch to his belly. "Maybe you'd make a good real estate agent, Maddie. Ever think about it?"

Maddie choked on the water she'd just swallowed and ended up spitting it out and down her shirt. Frank looked up in surprise. She didn't think it was possible but suspected that Frank had forgotten that she was a dance teacher. Laura reentered the room with Cathwrynn wafting in behind her, a magenta cape cascading over the redhead's tresses and down her back, a hat that looked like it was made of leaves perched on top of her curls. She hovered in the doorway for a moment as if assessing the energy of the room, then drifted to where Frank sat and positioned herself next to him.

"Speaking of murder," Laura pulled a pack of gum out of her bag and after taking one, offered it around the room. Laura was doubtless aware that no one was talking about murder, but was also clearly determined to set the conversation to her liking. "I would have thought that the murders would have kept people away from here but it seems it's anything but. Look at how many people have signed up for December's classes."

She tapped her computer screen to life and pointed at the spreadsheet displayed. Maddie took the offered gum and casually looked at the screen, nodding encouragingly. Neither Cathwrynn nor Frank seemed to have been listening to Laura but were in some sort of non-verbal communication with one another. Though the strange pair was not looking at one another, Maddie watched as each nodded in what looked like a response to something the other had said. Laura gave a couple of aggravated huffs before turning on Maddie.

"Oh, and Maddie, I forgot. There's a message for you. I couldn't quite make it out. It was a man but he sounded, well, I don't like to say, but he sounded downright drunk." Laura very clearly wanted to say that he sounded drunk as she indicated towards the clock on the wall. It was just before five o'clock and her disapproval was evident as she passed a piece of paper to Maddie. The note was in Laura's Catholic school handwriting, yet it didn't make much sense.

> Maddie,
> A gentleman called and asked me to tell you that he is ready for you to pick him up. He said that you need to bring him his (sorry, I couldn't make out what he said) and that if you are there

long enough he will make you pie. (I
think that's what he said anyway.) I
asked for his name but he hung up.

Laura watched Maddie as she read the note. "I don't
think it was the detective . . . ." Laura let the end of her
truncated sentence rise to the ceiling. Maddie ignored
the implied request.

"I don't know who this could be. He said that he was
ready for me to pick him up? The only man I know in
the area is my father." Maddie pulled her mobile out of
her bag. She didn't think it was her father but she had to
make sure. She walked into the hall as she hit the speed
dial. She could hear Frank's voice as she left.

"In my day we just called up and asked if your
refrigerator was running."

"Dad, hi. Everything all right? You didn't call the
studio for me, did you?" Maddie felt, rather than saw,
Laura sidle up to the door in an effort to hear the
conversation.

"Great, no reason. Just got a strange message but it's
not a problem. I'm going downtown just now and I'll
pop into the library to see Mom while I'm there."

Maddie hung up, used the restroom and then
returned to the office. When she got there, she found
the door blocked by Frank, his portly body shaking in
laughter and Cathwrynn's tinkling laughter layered on
top of it.

"Oh, Frank, you are the essence of youth. I would
like to bottle that up."

Frank promptly stopped laughing and a look of sheer
terror crossed his face. "Bottle...what?" A further panic
crossed his face as he sat down heavily in the chair next
to Laura's desk.

"I think I'll just sit for a minute, if you don't mind."
He then started quietly humming.

Laura glanced at Maddie then at Cathwrynn until the phone rang, sending Laura into a hand-waving frenzy in Frank's direction, for what reason Maddie could only guess. She didn't know what she could do to help and she already had several errands to run before her class at Shadylawn.

"I'm going downtown, then on to the retirement village. Have a good night, everyone."

As Maddie moved down the hall she could hear Frank exclaim, "Now if only I could remember." Cathwrynn sat next to him, and was stroking his arm when Maddie turned to look a last time. She let the door close behind her and walked into the beginnings of the first winter storm of the season. So much for a mild weekend.

Chapter Two

Pembroke was blanketed in a light coating of snow that really looked no more than icing sugar but it still made Maddie nervous to drive on it. She made a mental note to remind herself to ask her father if she should change her tires. Did they even make snow tires anymore? Maybe all tires were all-terrain. The last time she'd driven in snow was when she was seventeen and she had gracelessly slid into a stop sign. She smiled as she remembered that Joe was in the car with her then and had insisted that she'd done everything right, turning the wheel into the direction of the slide just like they'd taught in driver's ed, but as she remembered it, she'd done nothing more than grip the wheel for dear life and hoped that she'd live through it. He'd told her that she'd acted instinctually and that her instincts were good. *I should remind him of that,* she thought as she drew to a slow stop at an orange light. She ignored the driver honking his horn behind her. *Arrive alive, buddy,* she muttered to herself.

She continued on to the library slowly, passing several groups of children, optimistically dragging sleighs toward the hill above the municipal buildings. The library was the height of civic design in 1963 when it was built to replace the archaic building on Main Street. It was a depressing illustration of the wholesale covering of the town in red brick but the roof was covered in a coating of snow that made it resemble a spice cake, and that made Maddie smile. While the library was not pretty, it still contained a certain magic for her. This was the building she must have spent as much time in growing up as she had in her own house. She still felt overwhelming feelings of acceptance and calmness when she looked at the building and laughed as she remembered the hours she'd spent lying in the sunken story-telling room, followed by the graduation to the big kids room and then the stealth maneuvers into the adult section to sneak *Flowers in the Attic* into a quiet corner. Smiling, she carefully steered into a parking spot in the surprisingly full lot, picturing her then thirteen-year-old self with a stuffed bra and lipstick trying to pass by the circulation librarian to get to the clandestine books. As she turned off the ignition, her mobile beeped to draw attention to a message:

> Just arrived home. Storms meant detour through Boston. Looking forward to seeing you. In a meeting now until late. Dinner tomorrow? 7 p.m. at L'oca al Forno? Have eaten more potatoes in the last week than I can shake a stick at. J

Butterflies cavorted in her belly as she texted back that dinner would be great. She asked how Joe's grandmother was and was told that she was hanging on but probably wouldn't for much longer. He'd tell her all about it when he saw her on Saturday.

Maddie locked her car and as she crossed the parking lot, a skip in her step courtesy of the unexpected communication from Joe, heard her name called as if from the end of a long tube. She turned to find an elderly man in a faded blue parka buttoned all the way up to his chin who—once he'd caught Maddie's attention—transferred his attention to the sky. His bare hands stretched in front of his chest as if he were trying to catch the falling snow, the expression on his face making clear that the snowflakes puzzled him. Maddie had never seen him before and looked around the parking lot to see whether there was anyone else nearby. As her gaze focused on him again, he spoke.

"Maddie, why is it snowing so early?"

"Sorry, sir; can I help you?"

From the slow speech of the man, Maddie surmised he might have a psychological issue; he was certainly old enough to be suffering from some sort of dementia. Keeping her eyes on the man, she scanned the whole parking lot again. She couldn't figure out where she knew the man from, but he'd called her by name. Was he an old teacher of hers? In high school, a middle-aged man had taught geometry. He would actually check to make sure that each student had at least three pencils when they walked into the class, all sharpened before they sat down. The class quickly worked out that if each of the twenty students in the class had to sharpen each of the three pencils required of them, the line at the sharpener could delay the class by twenty minutes. Maddie's parents blamed that teacher for the fact that she'd lost interest in math and never found it again.

Looking at the man in front of her, Maddie couldn't see her sophomore year teacher in his wizened features. She couldn't even remember his name, only that he'd left Pembroke High that year after some whispering about needing to take a break.

"Maddie, the leaves need to be raked before the snow comes down."

She'd grown too cold to stand out there any longer and was increasingly uncomfortable that she didn't know who the man was. Maybe he was an ancient neighbor from her family's old house? The house she grew up in was up the hill on Sycamore, an easy five-minute walk to the library. Each house in this old part of town was surrounded by an acre of yard, allowing for plenty of leaves needing raking in the eighteen years she'd lived there.

"Can I help you into the library? It's warmer in there."

The man didn't answer but when Maddie touched his arm slightly, he didn't resist and Maddie was able to lead him inside. She opened the first door to the vestibule and out of the chilly air. When she opened the second door into the library proper, she was welcomed by a gust of hard-working heat and her body relaxed. Maddie had always hated the cold and only more so after fifteen years in temperatures that rarely dipped below 65 degrees even in the dead of winter.

Once inside the library, the man seemed to become more sure of himself. He looked at Maddie and shook his head slightly, then shot off in the direction of the men's room. Glad to be free of that obligation, Maddie turned to the right and headed toward the reference desk where she knew she'd find her mother.

Hillary had worked at Pembroke College for twenty years running the International Student Office but had retired from the college three years earlier. Unable to sit idly, she started working three afternoons a week at the library. It was actually Hillary who'd turned Maddie onto the job at the St. Claire Dance Studio.

Several months after ongoing phone calls discussing the saga of her stint as a reality television choreographer for the televised dance contest *Dance for Your Life*, followed by the continuing saga of her break-up with Craig, and that followed by the university calmly telling her that they thought maybe she should take a break from her Ph.D. research, Hillary had told Maddie that she'd just met the owner of a dance studio. The query that had brought Peter into the library was quickly forgotten when he'd found out that Hillary was the mother of the choreographer of *that* performance.

When he was told that Maddie was thinking about coming back east and would be looking for a job, all the pieces fell into place. After a telephone introduction, things went fast. Before Maddie knew it, she'd driven the almost 2500 miles from L.A. to northern New Jersey and for the last two months, Peter St. Claire had been her boss. A couple of murders during that time aside, things had been going pretty well.

"Hi, Mom."

"Sweetie. Is everything okay?" Hillary took the reading glasses that had been perched on her nose and let them drop on the chain to her chest. A momentary wary look crossed her face, one that Maddie had become accustomed to during the past month. Her parents hadn't been in town during the murder, and her mother continued to regret that she hadn't been able to do more to help Maddie during that time.

"Everything's fine, just cold." Maddie unnecessarily rubbed her hands together. There was plenty of heat in the library, a notion she couldn't quite accept with the energy crises everyone talked about daily but the hand rubbing came about more because she still felt a little awkward with her parents. They'd taken brilliant care of her when they returned early from their holiday to South Africa, but Maddie couldn't rid herself of the notion that by coming back to her home town and living with her parents, she'd been relegated to nothing more than a thirty-three-year-old failure.

"I'm teaching a class at Shadylawn and then I have the rest of the weekend off." Hillary was still seated and looking at Maddie. "And Joe's just gotten back. We're having dinner tomorrow night." Hillary raised her eyebrows but she didn't utter a word. The Fitzpatricks' relationship with Joe had been complicated for a long time, and Maddie appreciated the fact that her parents were going to let her decide what was going to happen between herself and Joe Clancy without interfering.

"Well, you certainly have been working hard so I'm glad you have some time off. How are Peter and his family doing?"

"Great by the looks of it. He and Kristy popped in this afternoon. She looks fantastic, very happy." Maddie thought about how she wanted to describe Kristy's attitude toward her. "Kristy was outwardly friendly, but I always get the impression she doesn't like me."

Another librarian walked up to Hillary and interrupted.

"Sorry, just wanted to say, have a great trip. I'm so jealous I could spit. Just bring me back some Whippets, the raspberry ones if you can get them."

"I'll add that to the list." Hillary took a piece of paper tucked between the pages of her daily planner. "Carla has already demanded Dare cookies and Crunchie bars, and Mark wants something called Sucre le Crème."

"Oh, me too, please. I forgot about them."

Hillary laughed. "Barbara, this is my daughter, Maddie. She's teaching tango if you and Lee want to take the plunge."

"Hi. Of course! I recognize you. Though the day I get my husband to a tango class is the day he agrees that it was a good idea when the Dodgers left Brooklyn. Gotta run! Thanks for bringing back the goods and be safe."

Maddie's parents had been offered an unexpected week-long trip on the Canadian rails from Winnipeg to Churchill via Hudson Bay and they couldn't refuse. When Hillary'd booked the time off, all the Canadian ex-pats at the Pembroke library had come out of the woodwork. Hillary had compiled a list of treats to tote back for the candy-craving Canuks. Hillary took a sip of coffee that had been sitting next to her and grimaced. "Well, what did you expect, Maddie?"

Maddie looked at her mother thinking she'd missed a part of the conversation. "What do you mean? What did I expect of what?"

"Just that. How did you expect Kristy to react to you?"

"Mom, I have no idea what you're talking about."

Before Hillary could answer, the phone rang. Hillary swung her head around but could see that the other reference librarian was busy with another patron.

Maddie could feel her face growing warm. She looked away as her mother answered the phone, mainly because she was embarrassed. She had an inkling of what her mother was going to say and she didn't want to hear it. When her mother hung the phone up, her eyes leveled on Maddie's. She seemed to see something in her daughter's expression and made a decision as she lifted a newspaper and presented it to Maddie.

"By the way, I saw this." Maddie let out her breath thinking she was lucky to have gotten out of that conversation. However, she knew it was a momentary reprieve.

Hillary handed Maddie the local weekly, the *Pembroke Telegraph*, folded into half its size to show the real estate section. Maddie looked down and noted a couple of multi-million dollar homes, typical for Pembroke and its Manhattan-commuter population. One listing showed a house asking 7.3 million. Maddie looked at her mother and pointed to the listing.

"Thanks, Mom. This one looks like just the right place for me to start over."

Hillary looked briefly, then snorted. "Not that one." Just then, the phone rang again. Hillary sighed. "Last day and it's always non-stop. Hang on just a second. Hello, Pembroke Library reference desk."

Maddie turned back to the paper, smiling to herself. Getting her own apartment was top of her priority list. She scanned the page, looking for the place her mother had found. She giggled as she read some of the classifieds, loving the quaint charm the local paper still managed to exude in such close proximity to New York City. A half page was taken up with the headline *Rotten Trees Fall in Back Yard* and another showed a photograph of a man and woman dressed in angel and devil costumes that read *Nursing Home Welcomes New Staff from Out of Town*.

"Sorry, darling. Did you see it?"

"What?" Maddie let her eyes drop to the paper in front of her again.

"Look at the bottom of the page."

Maddie looked and found an ad for a one-bedroom apartment with a full bathroom and a small back yard. It was on Rosemead, not the center of town, in fact almost out of town, but it was only $1000 a month and worth a look.

"Thanks, Mom. Do I get the impression that you and Dad are trying to get rid of me?"

A look of anxiety crossed Hillary's face as she peered at her daughter. "No, Maddie, you know that your father and I..." Maddie didn't let her mother continue. The look on her face told her that she still worried about the mental state of her daughter.

"Mom, I was kidding. I know I'm welcome but I also know that I need to look for a place. I feel like if I get too complacent, you may never get rid of me."

Hillary jumped slightly, pulling the sides of her mouth together and Maddie guessed her mother was debating whether she should let the conversation fizzle out. Maddie had grown used to the poignant pauses between her parents' conversations when she came within earshot. She knew they struggled between wanting to take care of their younger daughter and wanting her to stand on her own feet. Not least because they hadn't had either of their offspring living with them for fifteen years and Maddie suspected that they liked their independent lives as much as she liked hers. Maddie smiled as she spoke over the telephone ringing again.

"Thanks, Mom. I'll check this one out." Hillary nodded and answered the phone with her customary greeting. As Maddie was turning to leave, she noticed a photograph of her pinned to a bulletin board behind the counter. She stopped and waited for her mother to get off the phone.

"Oh, sweet aren't they? During the cherry tree festival we thought we'd bring in photos of flowers. I always loved that one of you." Hillary coughed into a tissue. "I hope you don't mind it being up there."

Maddie looked at the photo again. It was one taken of her while she was living in California. Craig had shot it with some new camera he'd bought, something expensive and the very best for its day, she was sure. It would probably be considered a dinosaur today and Craig would no doubt have replaced it three or four times over in the past decade. The photo was from one of their first holidays together. They'd gone to Butchart Gardens in British Columbia, and Craig had taken the photo of Maddie poised in the middle of a field of tulips that must have stretched back five acres. The blossoms were overpowering and were the main focus of the photo but Maddie did have a look of a young woman in love and it was charming. Maddie had her own copy in some box too but she wasn't likely to bring it out any time soon.

"It's fine. I always liked it too." Hillary and Maddie exchanged a look as Hillary reached out and squeezed her daughter's arm.

After picking up a couple of books, Maddie said good-bye to her mother and left the library. Outside, it had grown dark and she zipped her coat against the wind and pulled her hat from her bag and slipped it on. The hat was her mother's and she only brought it with her when her mother had threatened to bring it down to the studio herself if she didn't take it. Several months back in New Jersey and she should have re-accustomed herself to the weather she'd grown up with but she belligerently ignored it, hoping the dropping temperatures would prove themselves to be a bad joke.

Taking up the whole of the disabled parking area, a mini-van stood with its door wide open accepting a slow procession of elderly people, most using walkers or canes. Maddie did a double take when she read *Shadylawn Retirement Village* on the side panel of the van. A tiny woman with a scarf wrapped several times around her neck so that it bulged out almost as wide as her shoulders swatted away the efforts of a man three times her size as he tried to help her into the van. Finally she relented and let the orderly take her arm, coaxing her with a hearty voice.

"That's it, Georgia; you just stop bein' so stubborn and let me help you. I hear you got some dancing to do tonight. Can't have you fallin' all over on the ice, can we?"

Maddie didn't hear a response from Georgia because from behind her, a voice rose above the wind. She turned and found two men bearing down on her. Her heart dropped as she recognized the old man she'd encountered on her way in. The voice she heard belonged to another man equally as ancient and, judging by the color of his face and increasing pitch of his expletives, irate verging on enraged.

"You blasted fool! You keep causing trouble; I'm going to make you sorry!" The man talking was nearly the same size as the man Maddie had previously encountered, and with both men wrapped up in their scarves and hats, Maddie could hardly tell the difference between them. The man she'd escorted into the library now wore a turquoise and orange beanie with an emblem of a dolphin on its front, pulled down so far it nearly obliterated his face. He pushed it aside with a feeble movement of his gloved hand and then had to duck to avoid his pursuer as he rushed into Maddie's path.

"Maddie, take me home now!" At the outburst, the other man stopped and squinted over at her. Then his eyes widened.

At first, Maddie thought it was recognition she read in his expression but the look transformed into something more like fear. His mouth had opened into a wide *o* giving Maddie a glimpse of yellowed teeth. Then he clamped his mouth shut and turned back to the other man.

"You just shut up, old man! Don't you go bothering a person. You're going to be taken away and put away for good!"

The man in the turquoise hat continued to gaze at Maddie, but now the other man had his hand on his arm in what looked like a powerfully strong grip. The man in the turquoise hat finally stopped his forward motion and swiveled back on his assaulter.

"You just wait! I'll shown you; then you'll be sorry!"

"You're full of it! I'm telling you I'm not leaving you alone, not ever! You stay out of my stuff! And you stay away from people you have no right to talk to. I'm watching you!"

The man she'd led into the library made a weak fist then flailed it in the second man's face. And while it caused the second man to flinch, he didn't let go as he propelled the man away from Maddie and toward the waiting van.

Maddie couldn't take her eyes off the two men as they passed in front of her, neither one paying attention to her any longer. The orderly from the van had finished helping Georgia and turned to the two men approaching the door.

"Now what are you two old Joes bickering about?" He tossed a glance over at Maddie and said, "You'd think they were a couple of old married diddies by the way they're always at one another. Ain't that right, Floyd?" The man in the turquoise hat grunted as he pushed the orderly's outstretched hand to the side.

"Now, Floyd, don't you go being rude to me, ya hear? And you, Owen, what's with the moaning today? Remember you just had your birthday. You turned eighty-seven, not seven." From inside the van, a woman's voice briskly shut the discussion up.

"All right, Sean! We don't have all day!" A nurse poked her face out of the van, her nose coming into view seconds before the rest of her face.

"Get them in; we're late as it is!"

Sean gave Maddie a wink. "Yes, Nurse Spring!" Then in a slightly lower voice added, "Whatever you say, Nurse Spring."

Owen allowed the orderly to help him into the van, seeming to have given up the fight that had been in him minutes earlier. Then the orderly closed the door and turned to Maddie.

"Sorry about that, ma'am. Sometimes that's the way it is though. It's like once we reach a certain point, we start going back to being a kid again, don't it?" The orderly didn't wait for a response. "Don't matter what age you are; there's just some point in the middle of your life, you ain't going forward no longer; you're going back."

He gave a quick salute to Maddie as she mumbled something about it being all right and that it wasn't a problem, wishing the whole time that she hadn't seen any of it. Once in her car again, she watched the van pull away. Two faces were pressed up against the window staring at her until the van turned the corner. Maddie shivered. All of a sudden, she was not looking forward to teaching the class at the Shadylawn Retirement Village that evening.

Chapter Three

The Shadylawn Retirement Village lay at the edge of town, beyond Loantaka Park but before the vast tracks of pharmaceutical companies began snaking their way towards Manhattan. The retirement village was an estate in itself and reflected the high-income area it resided in. It had mature trees, tennis courts, indoor and outdoor swimming pools, an arboretum and plenty of winding walkways with strategically placed benches hidden amongst the manicured gardens, all set within its high-walled borders. A uniformed employee in a guard booth glanced up from his computer screen as Maddie drove in the gate, then directed her to the main building as if he'd been expecting her.

The Argentine Tango class was being held in the Grand Ballroom and Maddie didn't know why she was surprised to find that the ballroom was just that—grand. Anticipating the equivalent of an elementary school gymnasium, Maddie caught herself gasping when she entered a room straight out of an F. Scott Fitzgerald novel. The ceiling was at least forty feet tall and in its center hung a crystal chandelier that blazoned brightly. The walls were covered in yards of gold fabric. Tables that may have earlier littered the floor were now pushed to the edges of the room. Several people looked questioningly at her and she checked her watch. She always made sure she was early for a new class but, obviously, the people at Shadylawn made a point of being even earlier. There were at least twenty people already in the room talking in small groups and three couples were already on the dance floor dancing to a fox-trot. Maddie scanned the room, located the sound system and worked her way over to it with the intention of changing the music to an Argentine Tango to set the mood. As the fox-trot ended, she lowered the volume, attached her iPod to the sound system and then raised the volume again. Carlos Gardel started playing and there was a hush around the room, followed by several *oohs* and *aahs*. She greeted the tentative *hellos* from several people near her and said that class would start in ten minutes. As she sat down to change her shoes, wondering when Peter was going to show up, she heard a discreet cough to her left. Looking up she found herself looking into the piercing blue eyes of a young man who looked remarkably like a young Denzel Washington. The eye color had to come from contact lenses, Maddie deduced. His outfit, a light blue, short-sleeved shirt declared he was an orderly, and his orange and green striped jeans, that he was from a circus school. Maddie squeaked, then blushed at the sound. The man—Or was he a boy? Maddie could only guess his age to be somewhere between 20 and 25—smirked but took a step away.

"Just wondering if you were the teacher or what."

Maddie must have looked as flustered as she felt, absorbing his intense good looks because he nodded sagely.

"I work here. Name's Billy." Billy lifted an eyebrow and looked past Maddie's shoulder as if he was already bored with the conversation. Then it seemed he'd spotted something he didn't like or didn't understand across the room and a frown formed at the corners of his mouth.

Maddie snapped out of her momentary idiocy. "Hi! Yes, I'm Maddie Fitzpatrick." He didn't respond and she watched as he turned and looked behind his back. "The teacher."

Billy's face snapped back to hers. "Thought you'd be, you know, darker. Like Spanish or something."

"Yes, well, we're not all Spanish. Or South American as the case may be." Maddie wanted to end the conversation immediately. "You could help me. I'd like a pitcher of water with two glasses. Lemon if you have it." Maddie had bottles of water in her bag but she'd formed an instant dislike for this young man.

Billy shrugged his shoulders and turned to go. "Sure, whatever I can do to make your stay more enjoyable here."

Maddie watched as Billy sauntered away, stopping in front of two orderlies assisting residents in wheelchairs into positions at the tables around the room. She noticed the macho gesticulations Billy was making towards the taller of the two orderlies, another astonishingly good-looking man, but in a completely different way—more a Pierce Brosnan look-a-like. The conversation gained momentum and Maddie wondered if the two of them were going to come to blows. However, as heated as their bodies looked, Maddie didn't hear any of the conversation and abruptly, the taller orderly backed off and attended to one of the patients. The potential altercation over, Billy ambled out of the room just as Peter slipped in. As he drew near to her, his eyes roved around the room in much the same way Maddie's had when she came in.

"This is some place, isn't it? Guess retirement in Pembroke isn't all that bad."

Peter lowered his head to hers and whispered, "I know. I'm kicking myself for not having done this a lot earlier. There's a hell of a lot of money here." He drew away from her quickly, apparently not wanting to appear to be in clandestine conversation.

The couples dancing when Maddie arrived had now taken seats, possibly discouraged by the song *Orillera* that had replaced Carlos Gardel. Maddie frowned. She hadn't intended on having a fast-paced *Milonga* on her playlist for the retirees and chastised herself for slipping. Peter quickly put his shoes on as the room filled. Maddie hadn't realized that so many people would come out for the class and while the sheer numbers flowing into the room were alarming, it was a couple at the threshold of the ballroom that caused Maddie to gawk. The couple seemed to be the only ones who'd decided to dress up for the occasion: he in top hat and tails and she in a peacock blue ball gown. Maddie marveled at the dress as it would have suited the ballroom competition circuit. From the stance that the two held in the doorframe, Maddie guessed that that was exactly where they'd come from.

The reaction in the room was split. One half seemed to be enraptured by the vision of this couple—their eyes upturned, breaths caught, as the couple passed, she with her hand resting daintily on his raised arm, a radiant, yet fake smile plastered on her face. The other half of their audience didn't seem impressed. Many of them were covertly snickering as feathers floated off the woman's peacock dress. Maddie overheard a remark describing exactly what the speaker would do if she got a hold of those feathers.

In the wake of the competitive duo, Maddie watched with a sinking heart as the two old men she had encountered in the library earlier in the day came in through a side door, apparently still bickering. She quickly turned towards Peter and tried to get his attention, however he was occupied with soothing the concerns of several single ladies who didn't have dance partners. Looking back towards the door, she could see that the two men from the library—Floyd and Owen?—

were entangled though she couldn't discern which man was responsible for propelling the unlikely male couple forward and which for keeping it at bay.

Maddie straightened her shoulders and pulled out her iPod intending to turn down the music so that she could start the class but felt a tap on her shoulder. She turned to it and was pleasantly surprised to find Dottie and Sam, two of her Argentine Tango students from the studio, smiling broadly at her.

"Dottie, Sam! It's great to see you both!" She meant it so the light hugs she gave each of her two students were real. Maddie tried to keep her eye on Floyd and Owen now working their way haphazardly across the room, so she only caught part of what Sam and Dottie were nattering on about.

"Oh, we've been talking you up a storm. Don't think there's a commission in there somewhere, do you?" Sam looked at her eagerly while Dottie swatted his comment away.

"Don't pay any attention to him." Then, turning to Sam, "You keep talking nonsense and you'll have to find yourself a new partner."

As Dottie continued on about all the people she'd personally convinced to come tonight, Maddie saw a quick movement to her side and couldn't help but turn. She let out an involuntary groan when she realized that Floyd had managed to extricate himself from Owen and was now heading straight toward her.

Both Dottie and Sam turned to look in the direction where Maddie was staring.

"What is it, Maddie?" Dottie asked.

"Do you know that man coming across the room?"

Maddie indicated towards Floyd, now barreling across the near-empty dance floor, a frantic look on his face as he nearly collided with the elaborately dressed ballroom couple in the center. Both Dottie and Sam turned to look, then Sam swiveled his head slowly back to Maddie and spoke under his breath, "Don't worry. I'll protect you, Maddie."

Maddie didn't think she needed actual protection, but she couldn't hold back a laugh when Sam briskly marched over to intercept Floyd on his way over. She turned back to Dottie.

"What's that all about?"

"Oh, that's Floyd, poor man. He's been living here for over five years, I think. Lately he's been going downhill. Can't remember anything and just as argumentative as a coot in a cage."

Maddie watched as Sam intercepted Floyd's flight, standing squarely in front of the man who looked clearly intent on getting to Maddie. Floyd's eyes were glued to hers as he raised his arms and spoke to Sam, first with an annoyed shake of his fists, followed by his arms crumpling into his face so that it looked like he might burst into tears. While Maddie was glad not to have a run-in with the man again, she didn't want to watch his distress either. What she hadn't anticipated was the other man coming from her blind side.

"Maddie?" Her name was asked as a question, barely a whisper so that Maddie wasn't sure he'd really said it. Dottie raised her voice and turned to speak to the man.

"Owen, we don't see much of you these days. Good to see you here and dancing."

Owen took a step back, gulped as if he only just realized he was in a ballroom, then brought his hands together at his chest. Taking a step closer to Maddie again, he inhaled loudly and spoke.

"Don't let him bother you! Has no business in my stuff. Has no business here! He should be in a mental hospital and stop causing trouble!"

"Um, thank you, Owen? Isn't it?" Owen beamed at Maddie in response and remained standing in front of her.

"Are you taking the class tonight?"

"You've always been a sexy dancer. I love watching you," he replied.

Maddie took a deep breath and glanced at Dottie who was still at her side but whose attention had been pulled away to the conversation that Sam was still having with Floyd. It wasn't what Owen had said that was bothering Maddie so much as the leer on his face that was growing by the second.

Owen looked evasively toward the door. "So, when did you get back?"

Maddie stood frozen, her mouth open for a moment. "Back from where?"

Owen looked at Maddie in a manner that she could only describe as lascivious. "I liked what I saw," he said. Maddie watched a self-satisfied grin take over his face. Disgusted, she turned away then, in a moment of insight, whipped back to face him.

"Excuse me, Owen. I don't know what you mean by that, but I need to start class and if you'd like to join it, you need to find a partner."

She then turned away from him and walked to the center of the room, her heart pounding with a sense of satisfaction she rarely felt. She heard Dottie from behind her and saw that she had clasped Owen on the arm and pushed him toward a woman sitting by herself against the wall.

"Owen. I think you need a dance partner and I have just the person for you." Dottie turned to Maddie and winked as she ushered a perplexed Owen across the dance floor to the other side. Maddie was relieved until she saw the vile look on Owen's face as he allowed Dottie to lead him away.

Maddie motioned to Peter from the center of the room and lowered the music on her iPod. Anticipating her need, Peter clapped his hands together. Maddie stood in the center of the dance floor.

"Thank you, ladies and gentlemen! I'd like to ask you to form a circle around the room to start our Argentine Tango class. My name is Maddie Fitzpatrick and I teach Argentine Tango at the St. Claire Dance Studio. Assisting me today is Peter St. Claire, the owner of the studio." Several of the elderly people started clapping and as Maddie blushed, Peter smiled graciously at them.

As everyone gathered in a circle around the perimeter of the room, Peter joined Maddie in the center. Maddie noticed the woman in the peacock ball gown and her partner stood slightly inside the circle, separating themselves from the rest of the group. Now that she was closer to the couple, Maddie could see the only incongruous aspect of their pristine, if not outlandish outfits, were the woman's obviously chewed fingernails.

The couple seemed to be at the end of an argument as the man took her hand more gracefully than Maddie would have expected from the timber of his voice.

"All right, Berta. Enough." However, his warning worked and his partner again took his arm and stood quietly at his side. While Maddie hadn't heard the comment from Berta that had elicited the anger from her partner, she could see that Berta was not pleased to be reprimanded in public.

Nervous titters simmered as the new students formed a circle around Maddie and Peter.

"Thank you for coming tonight. We have great music for you and an exciting dance to explore for the next four weeks. This is the first of four classes which will culminate on December 21st with a *Milonga*, or tango party."

Before she could continue, the man in the tuxedo took a step forward and spoke.

"Excuse me. We are Rolf and Berta Rapp." The man spoke with a slight accent. *German*, Maddie thought. "At what level will this class be taught? We are, of course, already competent dancers in every style. Most particularly the tango."

Maddie heard Peter suck his breath in, then he spoke in a voice that Maddie had never heard from him. "This class is a beginner class. Should you feel that it's not appropriate for you and your partner, please feel free to stay and watch. You may want to join after the class when we will be playing music for everyone to dance to."

Berta placed an elegant hand on her hip. "Yes, but which steps will be taught tonight?"

Maddie didn't want Peter running interference for her. "Thank you for asking, Berta. I am going to talk briefly about the differences between Argentine Tango and Ballroom Tango." Maddie opened her gaze to the whole room.

"Unlike Ballroom Tango, Argentine Tango does not focus on steps." An annoyed cough accompanied several condescending looks between Rolf and Berta."

"So you won't even be doing an 8-count basic or La Cruzada?"

"No, as I was saying, we don't focus on steps but rather on a connection between the dancers. And so, with that in mind, please everyone, if you have not already done so, choose a partner and then turn to face them."

Maddie watched Peter's face tighten as Berta and Rolf stood defiantly in the center of the circle with them. Peter was one of the most diplomatic people she knew, but these two twits were pressing his buttons. Rolf and Berta had not turned to face one another so Maddie plastered her benevolent teacher's smile on her face.

"Berta, while I understand if you choose to sit this class out, it would be a great help to me if you and Rolf would dance with some of the less experienced dancers." Looks of disdain passed between Rolf and Berta but they didn't leave the dance floor. Several elaborate sighs could be heard around the room and Maddie surmised that the residents of the Shadylawn Retirement Village had experienced Rolf and Berta's performance before.

Maddie proceeded to explain how line of dance worked, though it seemed most of the dancers that evening didn't need to be told. Unlike younger generations, the residents of Shadylawn had grown up dancing and had an implicit understanding of a dance floor. And by the looks of the well-used ballroom at the Shadylawn Retirement Village, these retirees looked like they took every opportunity to dance.

"Okay, as I started to say earlier, Argentine Tango is similar to Ballroom Tango, but they are not the same. One of the most visible differences is in the position of you and your dance partner. In Ballroom Tango, the dancers connect at the hips, while creating space in their uppers bodies."

Berta let out an elaborate gasp and Maddie felt compelled to look at the woman. "Maybe Rolf and Berta will show us the elegant hold of the Ballroom Tango."

Maddie sometimes hated the fact that she was a peacemaker at heart but in times like this she recognized her skill. The scowl on Berta's face vanished and a smile plastered in its place, transforming the elderly woman into a consummate performer. Rolf raised his arm up to receive his partner with barely a glimmer of emotion in his face. After the two danced once around the room, Maddie put a stop to their exhibitionist behavior by clapping until most of the room had joined her.

"Thank you, Berta and Rolf. And now, I will show you the hold of the Argentine Tango. Peter drew closer to her as she continued explaining and demonstrated the movements as she spoke.

"Rather than our hips being close to one another, our upper bodies are. We form what looks like an A-frame." Some of the more game residents began experimenting with the hold.

"One of the most important aspects of this hold is the position of your weight." A couple of giggles and several mutterings about having a bit too much weight caused Maddie to add, "While you dance, your weight is centered in the balls of your feet. And for a visual example of this, I'd like to ask Dottie and Sam, and Rose and Ben, to demonstrate for the class." She motioned to the two couples who enthusiastically left the circle to join Maddie and Peter to stand in the center. Maddie started the music again with a click of her iPod.

"See how the space between their chests is smaller than the space between their hips?" Maddie scanned the room. A couple of the residents looked blankly at the dancers but most of them were smiling and nodding.

"Notice how they remain in this position as they walk into each other's space. The first exercise we are going to do will help get you used to dancing in this position."

As the remaining single people scurried about the room looking for dance partners, the door opened and Billy came through the door followed by the orderly he'd been arguing with earlier. Billy negligently held the pitcher of water and two glasses Maddie had requested. While Billy strolled straight through the center of the dance floor, the other orderly stopped just inside the door looked questioningly around the room. After depositing the water on a table, Billy interrupted the class.

"Hey! Just thinking I can help you out here. I know how to dance."

Billy provided a couple of subtle gyrations and looked around to see if anyone was watching. Maddie groaned inwardly but then noticed that some of the women near her, the ones without partners, were looking at Billy with smiles on their faces. One of them fanned herself whimsically and called over to him.

"Oh, Billy, come and be my partner first, otherwise I'll never get these vixen off you." Several women laughed and Billy continued his slithering over to the group of women. When he got to them, he cheekily wrapped his arms around two of them and turned to wink at Maddie. She turned away and saw that the Pierce Brosnan look-alike fellow had also joined the class but was respectfully standing next to a portly woman in an old-fashioned dress.

Maddie was able to move through the beginning of the class quickly because it was working surprisingly well; the students, save for Berta and Rolf, were enthusiastically tackling the new movements. She could see Dottie and Sam, as well as Rose and Bert giving encouraging words to other dancers.

Billy had claimed he could dance and he hadn't lied. Each woman he partnered with perked up as he led them around the dance floor and continued to smile even after the dance was over. *A charmer*, Maddie thought. He reminded her of someone but she lost the thought as she noticed the old man—Floyd—from the library sitting on the sidelines and couldn't help reflect that he looked like a classic wallflower—head drooped, arms listless in his lap. Maddie knew that as a teacher she should encourage him to dance, but when she drew closer to him and heard a congested snore, she sighed with relief. As she turned away, a nurse with dark hair pulled into a loose bun, pale skin and beet red lips which gave the impression that Disney's Snow White had just sprung from the screen, walked up to him and placed two glasses of juice on a table.

"Floyd, what are you doing sitting down? Don't you want to join in the dancing?" This nurse was young, probably around Maddie's age and, adding to her improbable cartoonish looks, spoke like she was an opera singer warming up her voice. The beginning of her sentence started low and rose until the end, the whole thing capped of with a little squeal. She beamed at Floyd as he slowly raised his eyes to hers. Maddie walked by the nurse and her charge and continued to eavesdrop.

"No, I don't dance," he replied.

"Oh, sure you do, Floyd. I saw you just the other day dancing around in the hallway. You thought no one was looking, didn't you? I saw you though, so you can't lie to me."

Floyd looked distressed again and he started shaking his head. "Get away from me, you bitch! You're all liars. You're all thieves!"

The smile on the young, sing-song nurse faded but she didn't give up on him.

"Now, we've talked about language, Floyd. You know I don't like it when you talk to me like that. How about you get up and try some dancing?"

Floyd did get up then and for a moment looked as if he was going to come out onto the dance floor, but before Maddie was three steps away, he screamed.

"Maddie, you've come to take me home! You have, haven't you?"

The nurse with the big nose from the library parking lot appeared instantly and took hold of him.

"That's fine, Nurse O'Neill," she said. "I'll take Floyd back to his room."

"No really, Nurse Spring, I think Floyd will be fine. He was just telling me how much he was looking forward to dancing," replied Nurse O'Neill.

Nurse Spring yanked the arm that Nurse O'Neill was trying to lead and growled, "Nurse O'Neill, let go of this man's arm!" Then to Floyd, she added, "Mr. Donaldson, you're not behaving and I'm going to have to put you to bed."

"I want to dance! I want to dance with Maddie!"

Nurse O'Neill bravely took Floyd's hand and, ignoring Nurse Spring, led him further onto the dance floor. "Will you dance with me, Floyd?" she asked. Floyd kept his rheumy eyes on Maddie for a moment, then looked at Nurse O'Neill and another look of panic crossed his face. "Don't you worry, Floyd," she said, "I'll be with you every step of the way."

"Yes. Yes, I would like to dance," Floyd replied.

Nurse O'Neill smiled triumphantly at Nurse Spring.

"See, I told you he wanted to dance, Nurse Spring. I'll dance with you first, Floyd. Then we'll get you dancing with some of these other ladies."

Maddie watched as Nurse O'Neill held onto Floyd's arms and shuffled him next to Billy and his new partner. She was deep in thought when Peter scooted up to her side.

"Maddie, you look worried. The class is going great. All I hear in between dances is how much fun they're having and that they can't wait for next week."

"Thanks, Peter. It's not that." She had become distracted by Billy's theatrics with his new partner. She

Peter's attention slightly toward the orderly. "I hate that gross machismo act of his. It's worse than mediocre dancers thinking they have exceptional talent."

Peter looked surreptitiously to his side. "I don't know. Coming from a man's perspective, I think he's just young and cocky. I mean, he's good looking. The whole world's his oyster."

"Are you saying I should be more charitable?"

Peter flipped his hand in the air. "I would never stoop to such a cheesy Christmas sentiment. Not past September anyway."

Maddie smiled. Peter had a way of making her see the error of her ways without making her feel like a complete jerk. Silently congratulating herself on a successful class, Maddie turned the music down again to get the attention of the class and suddenly had the breath knocked out of her as someone barreled into her side. At the same time, a blood-curdling scream pierced the room, sending fifty retirees into a frenzy that ended only when a voice sounding like something coming out of hell silenced the room.

"Hah! The bastard's finally dead!"

Chapter Four

Gasps from around the room soon overcame the silence. To her horror, Maddie found that her assailant was Owen. Together they lay in a heap on the floor, his hands grappling for a hold of her body like a leathery octopus. To add insult to injury, Billy was at her side immediately extricating Owen's limbs from hers. Preoccupied with getting both Owen's and Billy's hands off her, Maddie didn't immediately register that an entirely different commotion on the other side of the room had reached critical point. Shrieks from multiple directions led the way for another piercing scream that destroyed any remaining calm in the room.

By the time Maddie had regained some composure, several orderlies had descended on Owen and led him out of the room. Peter seemed to have disappeared as Maddie pulled herself away from Billy's enthusiastic ministrations, murmuring an attempt at a *thank you* as she craned her neck to see what was happening within a group swarming on the other side of the room. The horrible words someone had spoken appeared forgotten as a path was made for the shrieker who turned out to be Dottie. She had her hand to her throat and a wild look in her eyes and Maddie's stomach dropped, the image of another death from just the month before crashing into her psyche. When Dottie dropped her hands from her neck and instead wrapped them around her thin body and allowed Sam to lead her away from the commotion, Maddie sighed in relief.

As people moved away at the orders of a voice from within the huddle, Maddie saw that all attention was now on Floyd who lay on his side and was convulsing so hard that his head lifted in the air and when it hit the ground, it hit so hard his dentures flew out of his mouth. Lending a gruesome patina to the event was a pool of blood on the floor which seemed to have come from his mouth. Nurse O'Neill was crouched next to him and had ripped his shirt open. While Maddie stood there, the nurse jabbed something into his chest before anyone could blink and slowly the convulsing slowed down. However, more blood could be seen coming out of his mouth and now his ears as well. Several anxious moans exploded around Maddie as people turned away from the catastrophe on the ground. Maddie, however, found she couldn't turn away from the sight and even as Peter reappeared and tried to drag her away, she stood rooted above Nurse O'Neill and Floyd and watched as the nurse jabbed something else into the man now lying quietly on the ballroom floor. From behind her, Maddie heard a new commotion and turned to find a gaggle of nurses and orderlies flying through the now open ballroom doors, rolling a gurney and unsympathetically pushing residents aside as they did so. Nurse O'Neill had lowered her head to Floyd's chest and the Pierce Brosnan lookalike orderly practically had to pry her off Floyd to be able to get to him.

"I got him. I saved him." Emotion bubbled over in Nurse O'Neill's face and she broke out in sobs. Within a minute, Floyd was on the gurney, a doctor and Nurse Spring hovering over it as the gurney was raised and began the trip across the room. As the group moved across the floor, the doctor motioned to Nurse O'Neill to follow. She quickly wiped her eyes of tears and caught up to the doctor, then proceeded to walk out next to him, heads bent in conversation, leaving Nurse

Spring to follow in their wake, her hands clenched and her face pinched in fury. Several staff members had arrived to help those residents who wanted to leave and needed help to do so, and a cleaning crew immediately set to mopping up the blood on the wooden dance floor.

It all happened so quickly that Maddie was left breathless. Peter asked if she was all right with a raise of his eyebrow and she nodded as she poured herself a glass of water. It was a little too similar to the recent night at the studio when another student had had a similar attack, but it looked like in this case everything was going to be okay.

Surprisingly, a majority of the residents didn't seem that upset by Floyd's sudden collapse and convulsions or the blood which had been cleaned up with astonishing speed. Though Dottie remained seated with a look of extreme sadness on her face, her body collapsing onto Sam's frail frame, some of the other residents were treating the commotion as if it were part of the entertainment and were looking at Maddie as if waiting for the class to start again. Maddie looked at Peter and shrugged.

"I guess that happens a lot around here."

Maddie announced to the students that there would be two more dances to bring the class to a close and started the music up. As she moved around the room, she came to Billy in the corner as he was trying to get a black and pink lace ensconced woman's attention with poorly performed pirouettes, his voice rising over the music with syrupy expressions that made Maddie's skin crawl.

"Hey, gorgeous! Have I missed the chance to dance with you? Have I lost you forever?"

A girlish giggle was heard as the woman with closely cropped jet-black hair, now turning pink in front of the young orderly, swatted affectionately on his arm.

"You didn't miss anything but a bunch of old people shuffling about just trying not to make fools of themselves. And don't you start getting smart with me. I'm old enough to be your...well, you're much older sister anyway."

Maddie rolled her eyes. She hoped nobody saw her petty reaction, but she couldn't help herself. She had to scoot out of the couple's way as they swept past her, and she noticed the look on the woman's face—a wry smile caught at the corners of her mouth. Maddie saw that she didn't have to save this lady from Billy's charms; the woman saw through him but was enjoying it all the same.

The whole evening felt long and Maddie was glad when it was over and she could look forward to falling into bed. She was particularly grateful that Peter helped her through the protracted good-byes when she knew he'd rather shove off to be with his family. They walked out of the ballroom together and, as they passed the nurse' station, couldn't help but overhear the irate voice of Nurse Spring.

"You will not give him any further special privileges, Nurse O'Neill! He knows how to behave appropriately when he wants to and you're not doing him any kindness by letting him get away with being impossible to live with."

"I don't agree, Nurse Spring. He's obviously suffering from dementia and he's not getting any better. I consider it part of my job as his nurse to make his last days, if not happy, at least comfortable."

"You have no idea what you're talking about! You have little experience with patients of dementia and very little regard for the administrative responsibilities we've been entrusted with in order to ensure that all our charges have a good quality of life. I hand it to you that you were able to help him in this situation." There was a pause as Nurse Spring inhaled so deeply her chest pushed against the buttons of her blouse. "Possibly you saved his life but that was lucky and I do not want to witness you deviating from standard procedure from this day forward."

The door opened and Nurse O'Neill, clearly emotional, came into the hall, bumping into Maddie as she did. The door slammed behind her.

"That woman is a witch. She has no compassion whatsoever." Nurse O'Neill glanced behind her at the closed door, then back at Maddie and Peter. "To have the nerve to say that I *may* have saved his life. She wasn't there to help him, was she?"

Nurse O'Neill yanked her coat around her back. "Thank you so much for the class tonight. The residents enjoyed it enormously. You could see the sparkle in their eyes, couldn't you?"

Maddie could and she told Nurse O'Neill so.

"I saw what you did for Floyd. That was amazing too."

Nurse O'Neill's eyes narrowed for just a second then she waved her hand. "That's what I'm trained for. I wouldn't be much of a nurse if I couldn't save a life, would I?" The door behind the trio began to open again and without having to discuss it, they all sped away in an effort to avoid running into Nurse Spring. Maddie and Peter said good-bye to Nurse O'Neill then exited out the front door, eager to escape the volatile energy at the Shadylawn Retirement Village.

"Wow, that was a little more than I expected." Peter fished in his pocket for his keys while Maddie found hers in her handbag. "But the class was great, Maddie. Thanks. Now go home and relax."

"I plan to. Thanks for helping, Peter." She said good-bye and headed for her car.

Maddie held her hands in front of her car's heater vents, willing them to warm up. As the car idled, she saw a side door of the facility open and Nurse O'Neill came out, followed by the good-looking doctor that Maddie had seen in the ballroom, his hand on the small of the nurse's back as she descended the stairs. At the bottom of the steps, he wrapped his arm around her shoulders and the two continued around the building and out of sight. Maddie sighed. It looked like Nurse O'Neill had acquired some fringe benefits while working at the Shadylawn Retirement Village. Maybe they made up for having a boss like Nurse Spring. Maddie was left looking at the snow as it fell in the glare of an overhead parking lot light as she put the car into gear and drove home.

Chapter Five

Maddie was deep in a dream when an annoying sound insistently pulled her out of it. It took half a minute for her to fully wake and recognize that the irritating noise was not a band playing in the sultry bar from her dream, but her mobile phone. She had picked Marvin Gaye's classic, *Let's Get It On*, as Joe's ring tone, though she hadn't told him yet.

"Hello...Joe?"

"Maddie..." Joe cleared his throat abruptly. "Maddie, do you know a man named Malcolm Donaldson?"

Maddie sat up in the dark, struck by the fact that Joe hadn't even said hello. She turned on the light—it occurring to her that she might be dreaming—and looked at the screen of her phone to make sure she wasn't.

"No, no. I don't think so. The name doesn't sound familiar."

"So if you don't know this man, why would he have a photograph of you in his possession?"

"I'll say it again, Joe. No. Why don't you ask him?"

"Because he's dead."

"Okay, wait, Joe. Start again. Where are you?"

"I'm at the Shadylawn Retirement Village." Just hearing those words sent Maddie's heart into a staccato rhythm. Floyd.

"What was the name again?"

"Malcolm Floyd Donaldson. He was known as Floyd. A resident at the Shadylawn Retirement Village, eight-eight years old."

"Um, yes, I guess I do know him. Sort of."

"What do you mean, sort of?"

"Well, I can't really say that I know him."

"What can you say?" The timber of Joe's voice wasn't one she wanted to hear.

"What I can say is that I met him yesterday, or today. I don't even know what time it is."

"It's one a.m., Saturday. Please explain what you mean, Maddie." Whether he heard Maddie's frustration or not, Joe's voice had softened a bit.

"I met him yesterday at the Shadylawn Retirement Village. Well, actually, I saw him first at the library."

"Okay, Maddie, start again. Tell me how it happened and in the order it happened."

"Joe, you're talking to me like I know something and that I'm purposefully not telling you."

There was silence on the other end of the phone.

"I don't know why you're so bothered," she said. "I mean, he was almost ninety years old." Not getting any response from Joe, and feeling keenly unmoored as she had weeks earlier while Joe ran an investigation into the deaths at the studio, Maddie told him about coming across Floyd at the library and then again in her dance class.

"And when did you give him a photo?"

"What? I didn't. That's preposterous, Joe. I didn't even know the man. I didn't even know his last name."

"And yet he had a photo of you?"

"Are you sure it's me? What am I doing in the photo?"

"It's you, Maddie. You're in a red dress. Your hair is up. It looks like you're..." Joe paused. "It looks like you're about to go out for the night."

Maddie was racking her brains, trying to remember a time when she'd been photographed in a red dress and came up with nothing. The only red dress she owned was likely still in a box in a closet at her parent's house.

"It can't be me. Are you sure?"

Maddie could hear the rich sigh from the other end. "Yes, I'm sure. It's old, probably taken while you lived in California, but it's you."

"Joe, I have no idea. I certainly didn't give it to him. Look, he had some sort of attack in my class last night, but a nurse was able to revive him." Maddie had a whimsical thought. "Joe, did you call because you missed me?" Maddie waited, hoping Joe would respond with an equally flirtatious remark. He didn't.

"Joe, why the fuss? He was in a retirement village. He was old."

"It's more complicated than that, but I need to see you tomorrow." Maddie could tell the conversation was over and not much was said after that. They agreed on a time for Maddie to come to the police station and then they both said good-night.

Maddie closed her mobile and seconds later she heard a soft rap on her door, her mother's voice followed it.

"Maddie, is everything all right?" The door opened slightly and Maddie could see her mother in her nightgown, her reading glasses resting at the end of her nose.

Maddie couldn't speak for a minute and she shivered under her duvet. Before he hung up, Joe had asked her not to speak about it to anyone and she'd agreed, even though she had no idea what it was he was asking her not to talk about. She looked at her mother. Hillary wasn't anyone and as Maddie felt a tear slip down her cheek, she knew she was going to say something. Noticing the tear, her mother came immediately to her side.

"Maddie, what is it, darling?"

Maddie wiped the tear away. She didn't want to get emotional about this but she couldn't rid herself of a deep sense of having messed something up with Joe again. She accepted that the tears were actually shed over the fact that, once again, Joe had treated her as if there was nothing between them. Nothing. But Floyd Donaldson's dying had nothing to do with her and that knowledge made her angry.

"That was Joe."

Hillary looked at her daughter and for a minute Maddie thought she was going to criticize Joe for calling so late, a replay of a thousand mother/teenage daughter conversations. But Hillary waited.

"He told me there was a death at Shadylawn tonight. Someone I'd just met. A man named Floyd."

"Oh, Maddie, I'm sorry. That's not easy." Hillary raised an eyebrow. "But why was Joe calling about that?"

"Because this Floyd somehow had a photograph of me with him when he died." Before Hillary could say anything, Maddie continued, "A photo of me that I did not give him."

Hillary reached her hand forward and gave Maddie's arm a squeeze. Then she straightened her back and looked Maddie in the eye. "Maddie, do not get involved in this."

"I'm not, Mom. I can't imagine how this Floyd got my photo, but Joe's convinced it's me and that's the only reason he called." Maddie's voice cracked a little at that. "I have no idea why it's important. Maybe Joe is just exhausted from all his traveling and tomorrow we'll both laugh about it." Maddie tried to look confident to convince both herself and her mother that her interpretation of events could be true. Then she had a thought. "Mom, maybe it's that photo you had up at the reference desk. That would explain it."

"Maddie, I didn't give that photo to anyone."

"No, of course you wouldn't. But what if he stole it?"

"Stole it?" Hillary looked dubious. "It's possible, of course, but highly unlikely."

"Maybe, but it's the only explanation I can think of right now. Nothing else makes any sense."

"Maddie, I mean it. There's no reason you have to get involved in this."

"I have to go to the police station in the morning."

"Fine, but that's it. You tell Joe what you know."

"Which is nothing."

"Exactly. Then you leave. Now try to get some sleep." Hillary eyed her daughter thoughtfully. "Are you going to be all right with us gone for the week? Maybe Sylvie could come back down for a couple of days."

The thought of her sister coming down from Vermont after she'd just been there with her family for Thanksgiving, only to make sure Maddie wasn't going to get involved in another police investigation, was absurd. Maddie wasn't going to get involved in a police investigation.

"I'll be fine, Mom."

"Okay then. Get some sleep."

Maddie turned the light off, but she couldn't sleep right away. The thought of her mother turning back into the mother she knew when she was eighteen years old, when Joe was calling for a completely different reason sat uncomfortably next to the fact that another death could come between her and any possibility of a relationship with Joe.

Joe closed his cell phone, tapping it against his hand as he did. He had a bad feeling about this situation and it wasn't simply because he'd spent the previous 24 hours on several cramped flights from Ireland to New Jersey. A storm had diverted them to Boston and he'd had to spend the last leg of his journey on an Amtrak Express next to a surly teenager playing a handheld computer game without earphones and behind a man with unkind gastrointestinal issues. An hour into the trip south, he decided that standing in the vestibule was a more restful choice.

His legs hurt and his head hurt but all he could wonder was how the hell did a photograph of Maddie Fitzpatrick get into the hands Floyd Donaldson. What bothered him the most was that he didn't know if he could believe that Maddie didn't know anything about the photograph. She must have brought it with her to her class last night. But why?

Joe reached for a bottle of Tums and mused as he chomped on four tablets. Why Maddie? Of all the women in Pembroke, hell, of all the women in the world, why did that old man Floyd have that particular photo of Maddie Fitzpatrick in his hands when he died? Joe hoped that he could prove it was a coincidence because if he couldn't, it meant that Maddie was lying to him.

Chapter Six

Maddie hadn't set foot in the police station for three weeks, not since the time that she and Joe had met for lunch after he'd closed the investigation into the studio deaths and before he'd left for Ireland. Driving up to the station on Saturday morning, she remembered why. Even outside the building, her heart started racing and she paused on the steps, visualizing the dance studio filled with students and staff around her to calm the anxiety she still felt. Several deep breaths later, she stood in front of the automatic doors and waited for them to open to her. The smell of floor wax and sweat permeated the room, reminding her more of a gym than a police station.

As she crossed the threshold of the station, she entered immediately into the lobby and utter chaos. The front desk was crowded with people, all vying to get themselves heard by the two officers behind the counter. Maddie could hear several of them arguing about illegal holes in back yards, trespassing laws and mitigation. Maddie presumed them all to be neighbors, each one blaming another and threatening lawsuits.

"Sir, are you sure these holes haven't been made by an animal? A dog for instance."

The largest man erupted. "These damn holes are not being made by any animal known to man! I've already had an officer out there and there's no explanation for it. It was a human who dug them. They're deep. Six feet deep!" He said the last sentence pointing a finger at the man next to him, saliva flying out of his mouth. The recipient of the spit stepped back, his head shaking and hands in the air.

"Why in the hell would I dig a hole in your garden, George? I have two holes in mine. Who's to say you didn't dig *them*? And it's my dog that's dead!" This man turned back to the officer, his voice more sad than angry. "His throat was slit. My kid's dog's throat was slit. Who the hell does something like that?"

Another wave of anxiety forced her to sit down and take several belabored breaths before heading upstairs to Joe's office, but finally Maddie was able to walk by the confusion at the counter. One of the officers paused and Maddie recognized him as Officer Dinhop from the studio investigation the previous month. He looked concerned but Maddie saw he had enough on his plate and didn't want him worrying about her. She lifted a hand in greeting and pointed upstairs. He nodded in understanding as she ignored the stairwell door and pushed the button to call the elevator.

The hallway on the 2nd floor was unearthly quiet compared to the bustle from below. Maddie had anticipated Maureen, Joe's sister and secretary, to be sitting at her desk in the outer office. However, it was empty and Maddie paused when she realized that Maureen wouldn't be working on a Saturday morning, if she was even back from Ireland. Her stomach tightened when she heard a sound from behind Joe's closed door. She'd been counting on Maureen to be there to dissipate the often strangled tension between Joe and herself. She didn't have time to reconsider her options when the door to his office flew open.

Maddie squeaked, then laughed at herself, blushing and looking down at her feet. Joe looked gorgeous. The shadows under his eyes told her he was tired, and his clothes could use an iron but he still made her heart beat a little faster. His black hair had grown longer in the three weeks since she'd seen him and he hadn't bothered to cut it. She'd always liked it when it grew a little longer over his ears. He hadn't shaved either and she felt a flutter in her stomach as she thought about running her hand over the stubble on his cheek.

"Maddie, hi! Thanks for coming in." Maddie was happy to see Joe smile. It was a sad smile and it faded quickly but it had been there and it was a smile that she had known since she was sixteen.

"It's not a problem," Maddie lied. "It's hectic downstairs, a lot quieter up here." Maddie looked around the room and shifted her weight until Joe walked over to her.

"Come here." He opened his arms and took her into a delicate hug, as if he thought he might break her. Maddie wrapped her arms around his solid middle and hugged him back. When she pulled away, he bent down bringing his face close to hers. Maddie held her breath as he lowered his lips. The kiss was as light as a feather and sent an electric shock through her. His eyes popped open as they separated.

"Wow, we're going to have to get going with this thing, aren't we?"

Maddie nodded but knew enough about Joe to know she had to count her blessings while she had them. The hug and the kiss might be a prelude of things to come but before that could happen, she knew she'd have to get through his interrogation.

Joe separated himself from Maddie and motioned her to sit. After reiterating the story of how she'd first seen Floyd outside the library and how she'd watched the whole altercation with the van from the Shadylawn Retirement Village, she revisited the night of the Argentine Tango class and how Floyd had sat on the sidelines until a nurse had convinced him to dance.

"Then he collapsed. He had a fit of some sort. His legs and arms grew rigid while his body flailed about. It was awful. There was blood coming from his mouth and even his ears, I think."

Joe nodded as if digesting the information.

"And you spoke to Floyd?"

"Not really. He kept saying odd things but I didn't get into a conversation with him."

"But it seemed like he knew you? Did he use your name?"

"Yes, but I'd introduced myself to the whole class. He was there. So I guess that's why he knew it." Joe shook his head.

"I meant earlier, at the library."

Maddie felt queasy as she remembered Owen and Floyd in the parking lot of the library.

She must have looked alarmed because Joe perked up. "What is it, Maddie?"

"You're right. Floyd definitely used my name there. He kept saying it, but it wasn't like he recognized me. Does that make sense? Now that I think of it, it was actually Owen who was acting more strange."

"Tell me."

"It's hard to explain. While Floyd did use my name, he didn't really seem surprised that I didn't know him. It was like he was just saying words. But Owen, the other guy, he seemed to recognize me and it really made him angry that Floyd was bothering me."

"And didn't you think that was odd?"

"Yes, but then I went inside and I was talking to my mother. He was there and I suppose I just thought that maybe my mother had spoken to him about me. It didn't seem suspicious at the time. Joe, I hate to sound like a broken record, but why is all this important? Is there a reason his death should be anything more than an old man dying?" Maddie bit her lower lip, a habit she'd had since she was a teenager that came out when she was stressed. Joe knew this too.

"And another thing," she added, "my mother had a photo of me up at the reference desk. I'll bet that's the photo you're talking about. Which, by the way, why won't you just show it to me?"

"Just one minute," Joe said, cutting her off. "I can't answer all your questions now, Maddie."

"For future reference, you're not answering any of them."

Joe smiled. "Just trust me and tell me everything you know. Is there anything else out of the ordinary that has happened during the last couple of weeks?"

"Well, this could have absolutely nothing to do with it."

"A man is dead. I want anything you think of, even if you think it may be crazy."

Maddie marveled at the fact that Joe was asking for her opinion. The fact that he valued her opinion was a step in the right direction.

"Yesterday, a man called the studio asking for me. Laura took a message but it didn't make much sense."

"Describe it."

"He said something about picking him up and then about how he would make me pie."

Joe regarded Maddie with an expression that could be called painful humor. "Pie?"

"Look, I said it didn't make sense. Laura never got a name. I just assumed it was some kind of crank call."

"Could it have been Floyd?"

"I suppose so, but why? Before yesterday, I'd never even heard of the man. It seems a bit strange that all of a sudden he's trying to get in touch."

Joe gazed out the window. "Yes, strange because you said you hadn't met him before yesterday and then you ran into him in the library before seeing him again later that night at the retirement village. Stranger because he had this photograph of you clutched in his hand when he was found."

"Well, I certainly didn't give him one. Like I said, maybe he stole it from my mother."

Joe looked surprised for a moment, then the slight smile faded and he shook his head. "It's not the kind of photo your mother would put on display at the public library."

Maddie didn't want to fall into that petulant game again. "Can I just see this infamous photograph?"

Joe lifted a clear plastic bag out of the file on his desk and handed it to Maddie. Up until that moment, Maddie had entertained the thought that maybe the photograph was an elaborate charade on Joe's part to get her down to the police station. One look at it, however, and her stomach tightened. Joe was right. It wasn't the kind of photo her mother would have displayed.

As Joe had said, the photo showed her in a red cocktail dress with her hair up, a feather to match the dress peeking out around her ear. Maybe because it was late at night when Joe had described the photo to her on the phone, she'd been unable to recall where or when it could have been taken. But looking at it now, she was instantly drawn back to the event almost ten years ago. She and Craig were still in the honeymoon stage of their relationship. That night, Craig had taken her to a burlesque show and they had gorged themselves on lobster and champagne. The dress, which in the photo looked halfway decent, was actually a cheap polyester number that Craig had bought especially to rip off her. And he did, that night. Her nipples were clearly visible through the cheap fabric, her breasts as uncovered as they were covered, the round of her cheeks visible at the hem of the dress. Maddie could feel the color rise up her neck, imagining that Joe could read the story behind the photo. He watched her intently and she knew that the next words out of his mouth were going to be a request to tell him where and when the photo was taken. She was right. She gave him the bare bones.

"It was taken in California. The person who took it was my ex-boyfriend, Craig." Maddie had imagined that mentioning the words *ex-boyfriend* and *Craig*, so monumental in her mind, would elicit a response from Joe, but he merely nodded his head, indicating that she continue while he wrote something in his file.

"I don't know what else to say about it. It was a night we were going out to this really lovely place in LA. You had to book months in advance." Maddie felt the more left unsaid about the place, the better.

Joe took the plastic bag back from Maddie. "You look stunning."

Maddie colored. She did look good, but what was being left unsaid was that the photograph was just shy of being pornographic. "Thank you."

"Do you have a copy of this photo?"

"No."

"Who did?"

"Only Craig as far as I know. I can't imagine him making one for anyone else. It was just a photo before a date. I can't see who else would be interested in it."

"Back nine or ten years ago, maybe, but what about now? What about after you choreographed for the reality dance show?" Joe raised his eyebrows, searching for the name.

"*Dance for Your Life*." Maddie muttered the name, not wanting to waste her breath.

"He could have given a print to someone who saw the show and wanted a little souvenir. I imagine he could make some money."

Maddie interrupted him. "No, Joe. That's not it. Apart from the fact that Craig is what you'd call independently wealthy, that wasn't his style. He wouldn't have done anything so crass."

"Then it was stolen."

"No. I just don't get it. I mean, it's not anything I'd send home to Mom but it's not as if it's revealing anything people will get up in arms about. I wouldn't care if it got published so it's not like anyone would get any money out of me."

Joe was looking at the photo again and appeared not to have heard Maddie. "Are you positive you didn't bring this photograph with you to the dance class last night?"

Maddie didn't need to think about it and blurted out. "Absolutely, Joe. I haven't even seen that photo in years. I have no idea how it got there."

"And yet it did. I'm going to need Craig's number."

"What? Craig? Oh, come on, Joe. I mean, this can't possibly have anything to do with Floyd's death." But as she said it, another thought occurred to her. Was Joe pushing the situation with the photograph because he was worried about Maddie getting back together with Craig? Was he jealous? Maddie let her comment fade as she reconsidered. There was absolutely no reason that a photo of her, however it got into Floyd's possession, had anything to do with his death. So the only reason Joe would be going to such lengths to find out where the photo came from would be because he was curious about the photo and about her relationship with Craig. Maddie suddenly felt quite optimistic.

"Fine. I can get it for you." Maddie knew Craig's number of course, but she said that she'd have to go back to her parent's house to get it. There was no way she was going to have Joe cold call Craig.

"So, about tonight. Any chance we can meet up again? I mean it's not like this has anything to do with me, right?"

Joe shook his head. "I can't, Maddie. Not until this is sorted out."

Maddie's heart sank. The fact was, Floyd having her photo was really weird but the thought of Joe Clancy calling Craig Cavendish made her feel absolutely nauseous. She left Joe's office agreeing to text him the number when she got home. One thing she was sure of was that she wanted to talk to Craig before Joe did.

Joe walked her out to the elevator and as they waited, he reached out and pulled her to him. "Listen, I don't want you to worry, but be careful."

"What do you mean? This doesn't have anything to do with me. I'm getting worried every time you do that, Joe. What is it you're not telling me?"

"Maddie, I can't. But I also know that we made a deal to get to know one another again and we haven't been able to do that with me in Ireland. I'd really like to, so I don't want anything to happen to you before we get that chance."

Maddie stared up into his green eyes, loving the way he said *Ireland.* Joe's mother was right off the boat and had a thick West Country brogue. Both Joe and Maureen spoke with American accents but there were words every now and then that he said with an Irish accent that made her heart skip. Joe pushed the elevator button for her.

"Okay then. I guess we'll talk soon."

"Yes, I promise, as soon as I can." Joe didn't take his eyes off Maddie's. "And text me that number, Maddie."

As the elevator door opened he added, "And please, be careful."

She waved her hand at the elevator and opened the door to the stairwell. "I'll be careful." *Whatever that means*, she thought as she headed back downstairs.

Chapter Seven

When Maddie returned to her parents' house, it was empty. *Good*, she thought. She didn't want them to overhear the conversation she was about to have. It wasn't like she was going to call Craig and tell him what to say. It's just that she felt it was the right thing to do to call her ex-boyfriend to tell him that a guy, who happens to be a police officer and also happens to be a guy she might start dating again, is about to call him because some octogenarian had died three thousand miles from where he lives. The fact that the detective was going to ask him about a photo he took of her before they went to a raunchy show nine years earlier— a show followed by raunchy sex backstage with drag queens in the next room—was an aspect of the conversation she would ignore for the moment.

She felt foolish as she dialed the number and began to sweat as she listened to the phone ring. On the fourth ring it occurred to her that Craig probably wasn't even awake yet. It was only 10:30 in New Jersey, making it 7:30 in California. As she made the decision to hang up, the phone stopped ringing.

"Hello?"

Craig's voice, she'd know it anywhere. Still youthful even though the speaker was thirty-six years old. It still held that optimism that the owner was going to find something fantastic to do that day and that the entire world was his playground. It was part of what had attracted her to him ten years ago. Maddie cleared her throat.

"Craig, hi. It's Maddie."

"Maddie! Are you okay? Is everything all right? Where are you?"

There was genuine concern in Craig's voice and Maddie smiled, thinking that if Craig could do anything to keep Maddie from being hurt, she knew he would. She'd managed to convince herself that the fact that he'd broken her heart when he'd ended their relationship in order to *explore* his sexuality was an inconsistency in his character which was otherwise caring and gentle, if maybe a little immature. However, the fact that he'd been able to turn off emotionally when he finally got around to telling her that he'd been cheating on her with Paul for a year prior was still painful and she was still angry.

"I'm fine. Everything's fine, well sort of. Anyway, I'm in New Jersey." Maddie looked at the clock on the wall as if she'd just realized the time. "Sorry about calling so early."

"It's all right. I was just getting out of the shower. I'm testing out a new board today. It's amazing. It's actually carbon fiber. It acts like a spring that allows the shell to flex but prevents hyperflexion."

Maddie sat silent on the other end of the phone, a wave of gratitude washing over her. She used to get bored stupid listening to Craig go on about all his boy toy acquisitions. If it wasn't a new paddle-board, it was a hovercraft, or a para-glider or a vintage Camaro. She was glad she didn't have to pretend to be excited anymore.

"That sounds great, Craig."

There was silence on the other side of the phone. And when Craig spoke again, there was less enthusiasm in his voice. Maddie told herself she didn't care. She didn't have to be the attentive girlfriend anymore because she wasn't.

"Yes, well, you said that things were sort of okay. What's up?"

"I know what I'm about to ask is going to sound strange."

Craig coughed from the other side of the line. Maddie couldn't imagine what he thought she was going to ask of him.

"Do you remember a photo you took of me about nine years ago. It was the night we went to that burlesque place. I was wearing a red dress."

"Yes, Maddie, I remember. Why?" His voice was clipped. More so than she thought it should be.

"Well, is there any reason that anyone else would have that photo?"

"What do you mean? Who?"

"Just anyone."

"No. I remember the picture but I haven't seen it in years. That was the dress that..."

"Yes, that was the one." Maddie debated what she should tell Craig.

"Listen, there's just some weird stuff going on around here."

"Like what?" Craig's voice was guarded, like when she used to ask him if he was busy because she could really use some help in the garden.

"Well, a man died."

"Maddie, who?"

Craig sounded surprised but not overly. Maddie had to remember that Craig knew nothing about the murders that had occurred the previous month. For a couple of seconds she grew dizzy. How could a man who was once so important to her for so long not know that someone had tried to kill her?

"He was at this retirement home here in Pembroke. He was old but for some reason, the police are looking into it."

There was silence for a full ten seconds before Craig's subdued voice came back over the line.

"When did this happen?"

"Last night. I taught an Argentine Tango class in the evening and it happened some time after that."

"What was the man's name?" Craig sounded concerned.

"Floyd Donaldson Why? Craig, what's wrong?" No, Craig didn't just sound concerned. He sounded frightened.

"Floyd? Are you sure?"

"Of course, I'm sure. The reason I'm asking about the photo is because—and I know this is going to sound crazy—but Floyd had that photo of me in his hand when he died."

"Are you sure it was a photo of you?"

"Yes, Craig. I'm sure. I saw it with my own eyes. That's the other reason I'm calling. There's a guy, a detective who's going to be calling you."

"Calling me? Why? What the hell is this about, Maddie?"

"The photograph is what it's about, Craig." Maddie didn't keep her irritation out of her response. "I never had a copy of it and if I had, I certainly wouldn't have been showing it around. It's not the kind of photograph you send home to your parents to tell them what a great time you're having. So how did it happen to get in the hands of a dead guy in my hometown?"

"I sent a copy to my uncle."

"What?" Maddie couldn't say anything else. She felt as if her stomach had been punched and she'd been left gasping for air.

"It was years ago. I sent it to my uncle. He was old and I thought it would be a little joke. You know, give the old guy something to look at. And he'd asked about you so I wanted him to see what you looked like too."

"Craig, what are you talking about? Was Floyd your uncle?"

"No, that's the thing. My uncle's name is Owen Cavendish."

"Owen." Maddie said the name as her stomach dropped again. "Your Uncle is Owen?"

"Um, yes. He's actually my great uncle and I hardly remember him. He lived out East. A lawyer got in touch with me about three years ago when his wife died. It was left to me to get him into a nursing home."

"In Pembroke?"

"Yes."

"And you never told me?"

"No."

Maddie couldn't control the waver of her voice. "You never told me that you put your great uncle into a retirement home in my home town? What the hell is that about?" Maddie sat with her mouth wide open, then closed it when she realized that Craig couldn't see her incredulous gape.

"Look, Maddie, I didn't know the area. I looked on a map and saw that he lived near to where you said you grew up. Then it just so happened that there was this place in Pembroke, *Shadylawn* or something like that, and I remembered you talking about your hometown. It was convenient."

Maddie thought for a moment before speaking again. After digesting the absurdity of Craig sending his uncle to a retirement home in Pembroke, she focused on what was really bothering her. What she'd first imagined Craig sending his doddering great uncle a racy picture of his girl friend because he was in love with her and thought she was gorgeous turned into the realization that he'd sent the photo when he was probably already out of love with her. Hell, he'd probably been looking for a boyfriend by then. Maddie didn't want to talk to Craig any more.

"I still can't believe you didn't tell me. That's just weird. Look, this detective is going to call you. His name is Joe Clancy." Maddie knew she didn't need to worry about Craig recognizing Joe's name. She'd never mentioned Joe, the first man she'd married, to him.

"Do you think I'm going to have to come out there?"

What a weird thought, Maddie mused. In the whole time they'd been together, Maddie had never invited him to visit New Jersey, and he'd never asked her why she never had. Maddie was still lost in thought when Craig continued tentatively.

"I should probably come out anyway. I haven't seen Uncle Owen in at least twenty years. I suppose that's how this Floyd guy got the picture. But I don't get why the police are looking into it."

"Hmm. Me neither. Anyway, I guess call if you're going to come out."

"I will, Maddie."

While Maddie hadn't done anything more strenuous after seeing Joe Saturday morning than take a bubble bath, the weekend hadn't been restful. Sunday morning she received a call from Joe asking how she was and telling her that he'd spoken to Craig and that her ex-boyfriend would be flying into Newark Airport on Monday. She then received a text from Craig telling her the same thing. Maddie didn't even ask Joe if Craig had said anything about having spoken to her earlier on Saturday; she'd forgotten to ask Craig not to say anything.

By Sunday night, she felt emotionally drained and annoyed. Annoyed because she hadn't even begun to look at apartments and if she didn't start soon she'd be too late to sign a lease for January 1st. She'd gotten it into her head that she wanted to start the year out on a pro-active note and getting her own place was going to be the start of it.

Monday morning, she had a two-hour class. She wouldn't have normally scheduled a class that long; an hour was usually the longest novice students could hold concentration and energy, but the couple had insisted. Joelle and Liam's wedding was one month away and they had decided, after seeing *Tangohouse* perform, that they wanted to recreate an Argentine Tango they'd seen in it for their wedding dance. Maddie had diplomatically tried to tell them that a lot of the moves they'd seen performed on stage were going to be too complicated to learn in the time that they had available to them, at which point, Joelle took that to mean that they should double and triple up on classes. Maddie gave up trying to explain that sometimes the time in between the classes was when students learned the most about dancing. Even so, Joelle, undaunted, booked two, two-hour sessions a week for the whole month. This was their third class and Maddie was depressed. Neither student showed more than a passing aptitude for Argentine Tango and yet they, specifically Joelle, insisted that Maddie choreograph them a dance that had as many *boleos, ganchos and caricias* as she could stuff into it. For Maddie, it was a laborious, headache-producing endeavor.

"That's not the way they did it on *Tangohouse*. They did this." Joelle grabbed Liam by the arm to support her and all but toppled over as she proceeded to demonstrate the intricately choreographed show for Maddie. Maddie thought that Joelle was trying to execute a *boleo,* a step where the follow whips her free leg over her standing leg. Joelle seemed to be trying to add a wrap around Liam's leg to the end of the step but it was hard to tell. Out of breath but with a smile on her face, Joelle continued, "I went online and learned how to do those."

Maddie wondered whether she really needed every student she could get and couldn't help a churlish response. "What were they?"

When Joelle mispronounced *boleo* with a broken voice and Liam's shoulders sank, Maddie relented. "Okay, how about I teach you how to do them properly?" They both brightened somewhat. "I have to tell you though, that they're difficult and that you're not going to look like they did on stage."

"That's okay. As long as we don't make complete fools of ourselves and we feel good doing it." It was the first time Liam had spoken about the proposed choreography and Maddie could see that he'd been railroaded into it. She glanced at Joelle who nodded vigorously.

"Okay, but if this is going to work, you're going to have to trust me." Maddie held her hand up in front of Joelle's face before she could say another word. "You have to trust that I know a lot about Argentine Tango and that I want you to look good at your wedding. You have to trust me when I tell you that I can teach you some steps that will make you look fantastic and that they will impress the hell out of everyone watching more than all the high kicks in the world will."

Liam grabbed Joelle's hand and spoke quickly. "Yes, Maddie, that's exactly what we want." To give her credit, Maddie watched as Joelle let a smile slip out and nodded towards her.

"All right then, let's start with your music. I want to see a connection and I want to see you dance nothing more than walking turns for the whole of the song."

By three o'clock that afternoon, Maddie felt like it should have been Friday and was in a foul mood when she walked into the office to grab her bag. She was astutely aware that Craig had probably landed by then and that neither Craig nor Joe had called her. Laura sat at her desk gazing into the distance, her eyes seemingly fixed on the coat rack.

"I haven't seen you all day." Maddie cringed after she'd spoken. She sounded petty and Laura didn't deserve that. Laura, however, remained impassive.

"Oh, that's right," Laura huffed, then coughed a couple of times for dramatic effect. "I had a doctor's appointment. My husband made me. He said that a month is long enough to be a smoker again and he wants me hypnotized."

"Do doctors hypnotize people?"

"Seems so these days. Problem is it's not going to work."

"Why not?"

"Because the doc says that I have to really want to quit and, well, I don't." Laura took out the pack of cigarettes from her top drawer and looked at it.

"Terrible, isn't it? I love smoking. That's the problem with smokers. I feel like a teenager again. I don't want to come to work. I just want to stay home and smoke all day."

Laura looked at Maddie defiantly as she took out a cigarette and put the rest of the packet back in the drawer.

"Wow."

"I can understand why my husband wants me to quit but I'll tell you, I'm not happy about it. I feel like I just need a couple more weeks of it. Then maybe I'll get it out of my system."

Laura walked out of the office as Cathwrynn came into the room. As Maddie navigated her bag out of her cubbyhole, Cathwrynn gazed around the room.

"I think perhaps, Laura should move her office outside."

Maddie grinned. "She does spend more time on the front steps these days than inside, doesn't she?"

Maddie turned around and caught a whiff of the scent that permeated everything Cathwrynn wore. It was different from the scent she'd worn when Maddie first started at the St. Claire Dance Studio. In the aftermath of the two murders in the building, Cathwrynn had explained the intricacies of her new blend to Maddie.

"It's a balance of peace, perseverance, perception and longevity." Maddie must have looked skeptical. "That really means neroli, lavender, frankincense and vanilla. I added a bit of rose for cleansing." Cathwrynn then took both Maddie's hands in hers. "Believe it, Madeleine. It works."

The next day, Cathwrynn had come in with a vial of the mixture for each staff member. She'd waited expectantly until each of them had applied some of it to their necks and wrists. Surprisingly, Maddie had been feeling calmer since then.

"What are these?"

Maddie had picked up one of three bottles of pills sitting on the filing cabinet and read the names on them. They were prescriptions made out to Frank.

"Oh, Frank's medication." Cathwrynn lowered her eyes and looked as if she were praying. "Only he won't take them."

"And he just left them here?"

Cathwrynn's slight rise of her shoulders appeared to be the only answer Maddie was going to get from her.

Laura barreled back into the office in a trail of cigarette smoke and Maddie silently prayed that she would get hypnotized. "I don't know why he doesn't just open up those capsules. He could put them in soup. But then he doesn't cook, does he? Gets it all made for him. Heaven knows that's going to cost a fortune but then he has the money, doesn't he? I mean, what else is he going to spend it on?"

Maddie had no idea what Laura was talking about and as she finished her diatribe on Frank, Maddie backed out of the office. She had over an hour before her next class and all of a sudden she felt claustrophobic in the dance studio. She was in a bad mood and knew she should get herself away from sane people. In the hall, she found Claire and Philip rolling toward the office wearing in-line skates.

"What do you think? A roller-Lindy class?" Philip twirled on his blades, his dreads flying around his head like helicopter blades.

Claire came to an abrupt stop next to Maddie. "It's so cool. Watch this! It's a duck and dive, then a judo flip." She spun around toward Phillip. "Hey, do you think we could add a slingshot?"

It looked as if Phillip and Claire were about to attempt the series of aerial moves Claire had just spewed out.

"Whoa!" cried Maddie. "Hang on a second! What about the lifts? What happens if you whack him in the face with your blades?"

"Not going to happen. Come on, Phil. Let's ask Peter." The two skated on, jabbering about what a great idea it was. Maddie opened the front door to a blast of cold air and, from behind her, heard Laura screech.

"Not in this office you won't! Now out with the two of you on those damn contraptions!"

The last sounds Maddie heard as the door closed behind her were a thud, glass breaking and Cathwrynn's nervous giggle.

As Maddie crossed the parking lot to her car, her cell phone beeped, letting her know a text had come through. Pulling it out and seeing the screen, she sighed as she read a message from Joe informing her that Craig had arrived and would she come down to the Shadylawn Retirement Village *if she was available*? She didn't know whether she was more annoyed with Craig for not letting her know that he'd landed or Joe for issuing an impersonal request like that. She stopped for a coffee at Vito's before she took her time showing up at the Shadylawn Retirement Village.

Chapter Eight

Gaining entrance to the retirement village was a more complicated affair than it had been Friday night. Maddie's license and registration were checked before she was waved through and into the parking lot and guided to a parking space by a uniformed police officer. She then noticed that the officer had a camera and thought that he may have even taken a photo of her. When she looked up at his face though, he didn't appear to be interested in her but was engrossed in the image on the camera's screen. Maddie had no idea why Floyd Donaldson's death was causing such a stir, but she suspected Joe hadn't told her the whole story, which was just making her more irritable than she already was. Locking her car, she guessed that the silver BMW convertible she'd parked next to was a rental and that it was rented to Craig. How he thought he'd have use of a convertible in this weather, she had no idea.

It had been four months since she'd last seen the charismatic bastard, and seven months since she'd been blissfully unaware that the charismatic bastard had no intention of marrying her, at least not until he'd figured out a couple of things about himself—namely whether he was gay or not.

Maddie had gotten over most of the anger, had forgiven Craig, for the most part, and had even forgiven herself for being so blindingly naïve at the same time she'd been arrogantly sure she was going to marry him. The anger she felt was not that Craig had put a stop to her teenage fantasies, but that he was so categorically anal about the whole thing. That he was trying to be honest was acceptable. That he was critical in the face of Maddie's tears and disappointment, leaving her to face her emotional crisis on her own, was harder for Maddie to forget.

So when Maddie saw Craig again, she anticipated that she'd feel anxious, probably sad, maybe angry. What she didn't expect was to have forgotten how incredibly sexy he was. Craig was seriously the hottest man Maddie had ever dated, and if anything, had somehow grown more alluring since she'd moved from the West Coast.

Unable to take her eyes off his razor sharp jaw line and the swollen lips above them, she wished that she'd made a plan to meet up with him somewhere other than the retirement village. She was now painfully aware of both Craig's and Joe's eyes on her and managed to formulate an abbreviated greeting but was unable to move since she couldn't decide which man she should acknowledge first. Craig looked momentarily perplexed, then a grin spread across his face, causing his lips to break into something animalistic and intoxicating. The man she'd lived with for ten years then sprinted across the room and lifted Maddie off the floor in a full throttle hug.

Joe's eyes widened at the same time his cell phone rang and he took the opportunity to turn away from the reunion. Not before Maddie registered a look of sadness though. Disengaging herself from Craig, she took a deep breath.

"You still wear Paco Rabanne." Craig hadn't taken a step away from Maddie, forcing her to do so.

"Yeah, some things never change." His eyes clouded over and Maddie could see him battle with what he was going to say next. "Maddie, you look great. And I'm sorry."

"Craig, you don't have to keep saying that." Maddie was uncomfortably aware that Joe had ended his phone conversation and had turned back to them. She took a further step away from Craig. "So, I guess you two have met?"

Without any preamble, Joe put the infamous photograph onto the table in the middle of the room, forcing Maddie and Craig to walk over to it. Though Maddie knew she was about to look at the same photo that Joe had showed her on Saturday, here at the retirement village with Joe and Craig on either side of her, the photo had taken on further sullied overtones. Once Maddie had conjured fun memories from it, but in the last forty-eight hours, it had brought nothing but anxiety and shame. Maddie shuddered.

"Mr. Cavendish, can you explain why Floyd Donaldson was clutching this photo at the time of his death?"

Maddie could hear the disdain in Joe's voice and saw Craig bristle accordingly.

"No, not at all. I can only assume that the dead man took the photograph from my uncle and that has nothing to do with me. Or my uncle."

Joe's eyebrows lifted clear to his hairline, which Maddie noticed in the clear winter light from the window, was going an extremely attractive silver. She had the urge to reach out and pull it and as neither man was paying attention to her, seeing as how they were locked in a battle of horns with one another, she giggle at the thought of actually doing it. The giggle interrupted their challenge, and they both swiveled on her but didn't say anything. She quickly looked out the window and the snow falling and wondered if it could get any worse. Maddie liked to think that Joe was doing all this out of some misguided chivalry which, while it made her feel good, she couldn't quite believe was true. Something was up.

"I think that I should see my uncle," said Craig.

"You can, shortly. Owen Cavendish has given us a similar story. He claims that he didn't give the deceased, Floyd Donaldson, the photograph but that Mr. Donaldson was often found in your uncle's room and that other items had gone missing prior to this event."

"Well, that's that then. Why does my uncle have to be involved in this? The dead man sounds like a crook and my uncle was just one of his fixations."

"The situation that I am concerned about..." Joe's eyes darted to Maddie and back to Craig before he could stop himself, "is that the photograph shows a woman who lives here in town and that the woman was involved in a murder investigation one month ago." As this piece of information dropped, Craig's mouth dropped open too. He turned to Maddie.

"What? Maddie, you didn't tell me. Are you all right?"

"Well, yes. Obviously."

"But why didn't you call me?"

So many answers flew around in Maddie's head that she thought she might spew them all out, all over the room. Words like, *cheating* and *break-up* and *gay* and *marriage* splatting themselves all over the walls. Joe cleared his throat.

"We can get back to that in a minute. Maddie was also involved in a highly publicized television event that could bring unwanted attention." Maddie grinned thinking that Joe was laying it on a little thick but she also thought that Craig deserved it.

Craig relaxed the tension he must have been feeling by alternately lifting his shoulders and cracking his neck, first to the left, then to the right.

"Look, I probably shouldn't have sent Owen that photo. I can see that now." Craig glanced at Maddie then back to Joe and shrugged his shoulders. Maddie felt a wave of heat rise to her face and felt an inexplicable desire to punch him. "But it was—I don't know—six years ago or something. I had actually forgotten about it."

Joe seemed to take the comments in and flip them over in his head.

"I've interviewed several residents and employees of the Shadylawn Retirement Village and they all come up with similar stories. Floyd Donaldson and Owen Cavendish fought constantly. They were often heard being verbally abusive to one another and on at least two occasions, physically abusive."

"I wouldn't know anything about that. Apart from overseeing the monthly bill for this place, I haven't had any contact with my uncle in years."

Maddie thought of the old man and felt sorry for him. What kind of creep leaves a relative in a retirement village and then conveniently forgets about them, assuming money will take care of the neglect? Looking at Joe's pained expression, Maddie didn't think he was any more impressed with Craig's behavior than she was. And she was further outraged with herself because she couldn't rid herself of that feeling that she should defend Craig. Torn between saying something to lighten the mood and just keeping quiet, she made a decision. Whatever was happening, she didn't want anything to do with it.

"What is this about, Joe?" she asked. "Is there any reason I need to be here?"

Joe's finger fell to the photo again. "This photo, Maddie. That's why you need to be here."

"So you're telling me that if Floyd had been clutching a photo of Jessica Simpson, you would have called her to come down for questioning at the Shadylawn Retirement Village?"

A glimmer of humor crossed Joe's face and Craig laughed from across the room where he now leaned indifferently against the radiator.

"You're probably right; I wouldn't have asked Ms. Simpson to come down to Pembroke. But Ms. Simpson wasn't present the night Floyd Donaldson died. Because while you insist that he almost died in the dance class, he didn't. He wasn't dead until a knife was thrust through his chest, instantly piercing his heart and killing him. And clutched in his right hand, was this photograph of you!"

Chapter Nine

"Why didn't you tell me that?" Maddie heard the pitch of her voice rise to the level of hysteria but couldn't control it.

Joe turned to Craig who Maddie could see was looking somewhere at the floor, shaking his head as if Joe was making a big deal out of nothing. Both men seemed to have forgotten Maddie.

"Are you the executor of your uncle's estate?" Joe had taken another file out of his briefcase.

Craig lost the sheepish expression and nodded.

"Then I need to tell you that your uncle is under investigation for the murder of Floyd Donaldson."

Maddie's mouth dropped open but Craig stormed across the room before she could comment.

"That's preposterous! My uncle is almost ninety years old. Surely a doctor could tell you that he wouldn't have been capable of killing a man."

Maddie felt dizzy and sat in one of the chairs pulled up to the table as she breathed in and counted to ten. *Floyd's death had turned into a murder investigation?* The heated discussion continued between Joe and Craig and Maddie couldn't understand why Joe hadn't said anything about a knife to her earlier. Maddie put her head between her knees.

"That may be the case, but until proven otherwise, he's being considered a suspect."

"I thought we were innocent until proven guilty in this country. Or are things different out here in the East?"

Joe's eyes narrowed. "I said he is suspected, not that he had been convicted."

The two men shut up for a minute and must have both looked at Maddie at the same time, because they both started to speak but stopped instantaneously when Maddie lifted her head. She considered both men, alternating between them as to which one she wanted to scream at more. She let out a long breath and looked at Joe who was doing his best to ignore her by picking through a file, then spun her head around to face Craig instead. She'd wondered why Craig was behaving as if this information wasn't a bombshell when she realized it was because the news wasn't a bombshell to him.

"You knew he was murdered, didn't you?"

Craig shrugged." Well, yeah. Why else would I be out here?"

"Why didn't you tell me?"

"I thought you knew. Shouldn't the police give that kind of information out?"

It was true. The person Maddie was angry at was Joe. The annoyance she was still directing at Craig was just a residual injustice she felt from their breakup.

She flipped back to face Joe. "I can't believe you didn't tell me!"

"Maddie, you said yourself that you didn't see Floyd after the class. It really doesn't have to involve you."

"Then why am I here?"

Joe looked perplexed and lowered his eyes briefly. When he looked up, his eyes had cleared. "It's my job to protect everyone in this town, Maddie." As he spoke, his cell phone rang again and he turned away as he answered it. Craig took it as his cue to speak to Maddie.

"Look, I need to speak with my uncle and then I have to book into a hotel. Some place called the Pembroke Manor."

Maddie sat down again, her hands aching as she tried to knead the anxiety out of them. It figured that Craig would book into the most expensive hotel in the area. Maddie watched as Joe left the room, his phone to his ear.

"So what was all that about?" Craig asked. Maddie didn't answer. "Jeez, I thought he was going to come out with *information's on a need to know basis, ma'am.*" Craig had taken on a faux gangster voice to lighten the mood, but Maddie remained silent, unable to understand how Joe could have kept this information from her.

"So he seems quite adamant that you be protected. Am I reading the situation correctly and that you two are dating?"

"Um, something like that."

"So are you or are you not?"

"Look, Craig, don't start getting all demanding on me. No, we're not. Yet. But we kind of are."

"Don't you think that was something you should have told me?"

"Uh, pretty much like you should have told me that you were gay?"

"That's not fair, Maddie. I've been working on myself for years. It took a long time...."

"All right, I really don't want to start this conversation, Craig. Aren't you at all concerned that your uncle is under investigation?"

"Of course. But this is all ludicrous." Craig tilted his head to the side as if an idea had just struck him there. "So, no, actually, I'm not all that worried." Craig's eyes grazed the ceiling as he shifted from foot to foot. Maddie had known him a long time and she knew when he was lying but she didn't have the energy, or time, to consider Craig's ulterior motives.

"Well aren't you concerned that there's a murderer running around here?" Craig looked baffled. "Your uncle? He's old. What happens if the murderer comes back? What did he want? Aren't you at all disturbed by all this?"

Craig looked surprised like he either hadn't thought about it before or wondered why Maddie was so upset by the prospect of a homicidal lunatic lurking about the retirement village.

"Yeah, of course. I'll make sure Owen's safe."

Maddie saw Joe in the hallway and tried to get his attention. She couldn't rid herself of the impression that he had withheld the fact of Floyd's murder so that he could tell her in front of Craig. Glancing at her watch, she realized she'd be late if she didn't leave in ten minutes and she wanted to talk to Joe alone.

"I have to get back to work."

"Can we meet tonight? Dinner. You name the place."

Maddie didn't want to but also knew a conversation was going to have to take place some time. She might as well get it over with. And from the look on Joe's face when he left, she didn't think she would be getting a date out of him.

"Sure. Six o'clock at the Grass and Toad. It's on Main Street. Hard to miss."

"Great. And Maddie? I'll explain more tonight but could you do me a favor?" Craig looked in the direction Joe had gone and lowered his voice. "This is all bull. I mean, you know that, right?" Maddie remained silent. She had a feeling Craig was going to ask her to do something that Joe wouldn't approve of and her loyalties were so split they hurt.

"Look, Owen is old; there's no way he could have done this. You know some of these people. Who else here could have done it?"

"What are you asking me?"

"Just think about it. Who else could have done it? Then we can talk about it tonight." Maddie winced. She was right. Joe wouldn't like that. She didn't feel like it was an appropriate request but, as usual, she didn't know what to say that wouldn't sound irritable. And if there was anything that closed Craig off, it was when Maddie was irritated at something he had done and told him so.

"Sure. See you at six."

Maddie walked out to the hall and stood behind Joe to make sure he didn't slip away. She felt like the girl who really liked the guy and just didn't get it through her thick head that he just wasn't that interested in her but she didn't leave. Drawing closer to his back, she could hear the end of his conversation.

"Turns out it was Billy Holiday." The officer standing next to Joe looked up with a smile on his face. "No joke; that's his legal name. He was the orderly on duty last night and the last person to admit to seeing Floyd alive. He says he went in at 11:35 and Floyd was breathing; a bit labored, but still breathing." Joe noticed Maddie and spoke to the officer quietly before turning back to Maddie. "And make sure there's a constant guard on Owen Cavendish. I'm in a meeting in the ballroom. Get me if you hear anything."

Maddie interrupted. "Billy? You mean that young orderly. He was really annoying during my class."

Joe lifted his hands up, exasperated or bemused— Maddie couldn't tell. He let them drop and waited for Maddie to continue.

"There's something wrong with him. I think he just wanted to hit on me but I wasn't interested and he's slimy. I wouldn't take his testimony as being truthful." Joe shook his head.

"Maddie, being slimy isn't a crime. And unfortunately, hitting on you or on any other woman in the room, for that matter, isn't a crime either. My advice is to keep those thoughts to yourself."

"I know but I have a gut instinct about him. You should look more into his past before you decide he's innocent."

"Maddie, I know that the situation last month was tough but you're just going to have to trust that I'm doing my job."

"I know, Joe, but to assume that Owen has something to do with it and not even consider Billy is— well—it's a bit presumptuous, isn't it?"

A sad look passed over Joe's face, making him appear as tired as he probably was. Maddie regretted her words immediately.

"I think it's more presumptuous to think that a man is guilty of a crime simply because he didn't court you the way that you would have wanted." Joe didn't move but kept an even stare on Maddie.

Maddie felt dumbstruck. "Joe, I..."

Joe ran a hand through his hair. "I know you didn't mean it like that. Neither did I. I have to go now. Will you please go home and stay safe. I'll call when I can. Although Joe had already turned to leave, she nodded at his retreating form. When he was safely out the door, she turned around and headed to the front door. As she reached it, her mobile rang. It was the studio.

"Hello, Laura?" Maddie spoke into the phone as she checked the time, worried she was late. No, she still had ten minutes.

"Maddie, your class cancelled. She went into labor."

"Oh, how great." Maddie smiled, both because she was happy for the young couple who'd only just started classes because Maria wanted her baby to dance tango while still in the womb but also because she just had a brilliant idea and now she had the time to act on it.

While Maddie could keep quiet about her thoughts on Billy, her opinion of him wasn't going to change that quickly. She didn't like him and she knew he was up to something. And Craig had asked her to think about other people who might have been able to kill Floyd. It wasn't her fault Joe wouldn't listen. Trying to figure out if Billy Holiday had something to do with why Floyd Donaldson had died wasn't going to hurt anyone. She was just going to ask a few questions and for that she hoped she could find Sam and Dottie. Maddie ducked back into the hall and followed signs that led the main lobby.

"Is there something I can do for you?" Maddie jumped. *Damn*, she thought. Nurse Spring was not the nurse she wanted to run into.

"Oh, yes. Actually, I was hoping to speak to Sam and Dottie." Nurse Spring's glare intensified. "They're students of mine." Nurse Spring remained motionless, blocking Maddie's path. "At the dance studio."

The nurse seemed to speak without opening her mouth. "I'm sure it's possible to see them. We're not a prison, after all. However, I think they are in a meeting. Most of the residents are with the director of the community who is trying to limit anxiety." Maddie heard the sarcasm in Nurse Spring's voice.

"Don't you think that it's appropriate that the residents worry about the attack?"

"Of course, we should be vigilant. Don't put words in my mouth!" Maddie took a step back from the irate nurse as she continued to rant.

"There's no proof that any of the other residents are in danger." Nurse Spring took a breath and turned away from Maddie as if weary of the conversation. "What is your connection and why are you so interested?" Before

Maddie could say a word, Nurse Spring snapped her head back to gaze at Maddie with disdain.

"You're the one in the photograph, aren't you? I almost wouldn't have recognized you. You've cleaned up your act."

Maddie could feel the blush rising up her neck and she unconsciously pushed her hair behind her ears. "It was a costume," she stammered as Nurse Spring smirked and clasped her hands in front of her stomach as if she were about to start singing *Do-Re-Me*.

"The unfortunate altercation was a spat between Owen and Floyd and allowing the residents to become hysterical is not going to help the situation. I imagine your presence here is not going to help either."

"Do you really think Owen Cavendish killed Floyd?"

"What I think is neither here nor there and you'd best remember that."

"But you just said that it was an unfortunate altercation between the two men."

"What I said or didn't say has nothing to do with you and I would advise you to stay out of it!" The nurse primly tilted her head to the left. "I imagine the police detective would say the same thing to you." Nurse Spring gloated as if she was privy to inside information.

Maddie did shut up but only because Nurse Spring didn't make any sense. *There was a woman with issues,* Maddie thought as she gave up on the idea of talking to Sam and Dottie. But as she turned to leave, the young nurse from the previous evening rushed by her and into the office.

"Nurse Spring, Mr. Rapp is having difficulties! He asked for you specifically." Nurse O'Neill uttered the last sentence as if she couldn't believe anyone would willingly ask for Nurse Spring's assistance.

"Difficulties? What does that mean, Nurse O'Neill? Be more specific. Nurse O'Neill, if you had wanted a job as a cruise director then I would like to point out that your nursing qualification was a waste of time." With that, Nurse Spring turned stiffly, leaving Nurse O'Neill fuming. The second Nurse Spring turned the corner, Nurse O'Neill exploded.

"That bitch has no compassion, whatsoever! Poor Mr. Rapp, the man is so proud. To be losing his faculties so quickly is just killing him. And his wife, Berta...they are so lovely." Nurse O'Neill's fury petered out to be taken over by an overwhelming sorrow. She glanced at Maddie while she wrung her hands in a manner Maddie thought belonged on a much older woman.

"I'm sorry, that was unprofessional of me. I just can't stand it. I don't know how much longer I'll be able to work under her! Luckily, they have some really wonderful staff members working here too."

Suddenly, Maddie knew where she'd seen Nurse O'Neill before.

"Didn't I just see an article in the paper about you? A welcome to the town?" The image of the couple in the angel and devil costumes suddenly came into focus as Maddie realized it was a photo of Nurse O'Neill and the young doctor.

Nurse O'Neill returned the smile. "Wasn't that sweet? I started here three months ago." Nurse O'Neill seemed to think of something. "Oh, I don't want you to think that I don't like it here. I love it! I just find working with Nurse Spring, um...challenging."

"Of course, I didn't think anything of it. She is a bit stern."

Nurse O'Neill laughed. "Stern? Yes. Anyway, I really like it here. I'm from upstate New York— Potsdam, which is practically in Canada and really cold.

The weather here is mild in comparison. And there are additional benefits."

As if on cue, the good-looking doctor Maddie had seen Friday night approached the two women. "Susan, can I interrupt you? Nurse Spring will need some assistance. Rolf needs sedating and his wife could use some support."

Nurse O'Neill gave a knowing smile to the doctor. "Yes, of course, Doctor Marlowe." Turning back to Maddie as she followed him out the door, she continued. "I hope you come back on Friday. I mean it. The residents loved the class so much. Argentine Tango is such a beautiful dance."

"Of course," Maddie answered so that Nurse O'Neill could hear her. Under her breath she added, "A little murder's never put me off."

Chapter Ten

Maddie had some time before her dinner date at the Grass and Toad, a date she regretted making exponentially as the hour grew closer. At home, her parents had pulled two small suitcases out of the attic and were now trying valiantly to pack them with at least twice as much as could fit in each one.

"Is this self-punishment?"

Martin shook his head. "We have exactly sixty-six pounds of luggage allowed to each of us and that's exactly how much we're going to take."

Hillary looked up from her bent over position on the suitcase. "Of course, 100 pounds of that is being taken up by your father's photography equipment, relegating a week's worth of clothing into one suitcase." Hillary glanced affectionately at Martin. "He's lucky I'm a one pair of slacks and one skirt kind of girl."

Without looking up, Martin added smugly, "We're also, I'd like to point out, positively effecting global consumerism by not buying or transporting more than is absolutely necessary."

"Except all this camera equipment."

"That's necessary. I clearly said only what is necessary."

Maddie's parents were acting a little too much like a sit-com these days and Maddie had the feeling it was for her benefit. She debated not telling them about what she'd just learned at the retirement village, but knew they'd find out sooner or later and she'd hear it if it didn't come from her.

"So, Mom, Dad, I have something to tell you."

Both Hillary and Martin popped out of the suitcases, their eyes alert and resting intently on Maddie.

"Um, well where to start."

"At the beginning."

"Okay, that man who died at Shadylawn, turns out he was murdered. It also turns out that he had a photograph of me when he was murdered and that the photo came from Craig who sent it to his uncle who also lives at the retirement village and who's being investigated for the murder. But don't worry. Everything's fine and I hope you have a great trip."

While Martin looked pensive, Hillary looked aghast.

"We're not going! Unpack, Martin."

"No, Mom. Don't be silly. I'm fine. It has nothing to do with me. I only told you so that if you heard about it you wouldn't worry. It's all under control." Her father still hadn't said anything, but his eyebrows were dancing across his forehead, a sure sign that he was categorizing the threat. Hillary nudged him and he finally spoke.

"Joe's leading the investigation?" Maddie nodded in the affirmative. "And Craig?" Hearing her Dad say Craig's name was odd and Maddie answered slowly.

"He's here too. He arrived today to see his uncle Owen."

A brisk nod to Maddie and Martin turned to Hillary. "Maddie will be fine."

"What? Because two of her ex beaus are here in town to protect her? The man was murdered, Martin!" Hillary turned back to Maddie. "How was he murdered? Why? How did this happen again?"

"Mom, I don't think it had anything to do with last month." Maddie corrected herself with a shake of her head. "I mean I'm certain it doesn't have anything to do with last month's murders. I don't know why he was murdered and I'm not getting any further involved in this. You guys go and have a great time." In that moment, Maddie realized that she was speaking the truth. She wasn't going to get further involved. She wasn't going to think about who else at the retirement village could have stuck a knife in Floyd as a favor to Craig. She didn't owe him anything. She was going to teach her classes and look for an apartment and get on with her life.

Martin had started futzing with the suitcase again. "And no, I don't think Maddie will be all right because her ex-boyfriends are here, together." Martin looked up with a sly grin lighting up his round face. "I'm saying it because I know Maddie will be fine."

"Thanks, Dad. Speaking of Craig, I'm meeting him at six."

Hillary still hadn't resumed packing and she looked undecided as she tapped the fingers of her right hand onto her left. With a slight nod, she seemed to make up her mind.

"All right. Have a good time, dear. We'll see you in the morning. The taxi's coming at eight."

Maddie pulled into the parking lot of the Grass and Toad at precisely six p.m. and saw Craig's rented BMW already parked by the door. Inside the pub, the windows steamed against the cold and Maddie took her coat and hat off in the vestibule. The heat from the two fireplaces, roaring on either side of the dining room welcomed her and she crossed to one of them as she waited for Craig to leave the bar and join her. She'd seen him as she entered and returned his wave so she expected him imminently. When she found herself still standing by the fire after five minutes, she walked into the bar area. She watched as Craig laughed with the bartender, a young man Maddie had seen serving several times. This was the first time she'd seen him so animated and, looking at the pair talking, she realized for the first time that he was gay too. Feeling her world tilting a little, and recognizing that Craig was probably not going to hurry over to her, she walked up to the bar to join them.

"All warmed up then?" Maddie nodded, going along with the pretense that she'd been standing by the fire because she was cold and not because she'd expected he would come to her.

"Hi, Ben." The greeting more a question, hoping she'd gotten the name right.

"Hey, Maddie. Good to see you. Magic Hat?"

"Yeah, thanks."

Ben reached behind him to grab the beer, placing another one in front of Craig too.

"Craig here tells me that you choreographed that dance on that crazy television show. Pretty spectacular!"

Maddie turned to Craig and wondered if he could be any more tactless. Taking the cue from Maddie's fixed stare, he picked up his beer and made a move to a table. Maddie could have sworn he winked at Ben as they left. At the table he leveled a frown at her.

"You don't have to say it, so please don't."

"What? That it was remarkably indiscreet of you to share the most embarrassing, back-stabbing, soul-destroying, painful moment of my life with a bartender in my home town."

Craig shrugged. "Look, Maddie, I assumed he knew. I mean, doesn't everyone?"

"No, as a matter of fact, I have somehow escaped notoriety. I don't know how I got lucky, but I did. Until just now. Now it will be all over town by the end of the week."

"Oh, jeez, Maddie, people aren't going to care. In fact, I bet it will get you more students."

Maddie swallowed some beer, the fight in her already dissipating. Turns out she didn't really mind all that much. She had to admit that what made her uncomfortable was having to watch Craig flirt with someone else. What surprised her about her reaction, was that it didn't bother her that it was a man. Somehow it all made sense. More sense than the end of their relationship anyway. Craig sensed her change in temperament.

"Look, I'm sorry. I guess I just wanted to impress him."

Maddie grimaced. "Yeah, he's cute. Anyway, how's your uncle?"

"Good, as far as can be expected. He's nervous with the police officer camped just outside his door. Keeps going on about how he wants me to get him a gun and then he starts ranting about me taking him out of here. He wants me to take him back to California." From the look on Craig's face, Maddie could tell that was never going to happen.

"Isn't that a bit drastic?"

"That's just it, I don't know. I haven't seen him in twenty years, I don't know what normal is for him. I just remember Uncle Owen as being fun. When my father was always working, it was Uncle Owen who would show up out of the blue and have time for me. I mean it; he was really, really great. All this talk of him killing some other old man is garbage. There's no way." Maddie took a sip of her beer. Craig was getting uncharacteristically riled up and his obvious emotion made her uncomfortable.

"Maddie, you believe me, don't you?"

"What do you mean?"

"You believe that Uncle Owen's a good guy, that he couldn't have done it."

"Craig, I have no idea. I don't think Joe seriously thinks it's Owen but he has to look at everything, doesn't he?"

"Really? You think that your police officer was just trying to ruffle me up? Maybe he's jealous?"

Craig playfully took Maddie's hand and lightly grazed his fingers across her arm in a way she knew, that he knew, she liked.

Maddie pulled her hand away and the look that crossed Craig's face told her that she'd hurt his feelings.

"He's not my police officer and I really have no idea. I wouldn't get all worked up about it though. Have you called your parents?"

Craig looked surprised. "No, why?"

"Uh, well, because they might want to know."

Craig drained his beer. "No. They haven't seen him any more than I have. I meant it when I said I'm the executor of his estate. They gave up all familial responsibility years ago. They're not interested."

Craig laid the last statement out like he didn't care and Maddie had to look hard to see if there was any pain still left. She'd only met Craig's parents twice in the ten years they were together and she wasn't impressed with either visit. His parents were rich, vain and as far as she could tell, negligent of their only son. Craig had lived at boarding schools from the time he was thirteen.

She accepted a menu from the waitress and asked for a glass of water.

"That's not all you're drinking tonight I hope. I plan on ordering the nicest bottle of wine they have."

Of course you are. Probably two before the night is through, Maddie thought. But who was she kidding? She was going to enjoy every minute of it.

"Anyway, they're in the Caribbean so it's not like I'm going to call them up and ask. They make a point of telling people not to contact them when they're in retreat mode."

"It could matter. If Owen is under investigation, Joe is going to be asking you a lot more questions, and your parents too."

She sat quietly listening to the beginning of the DJ's oldie lineup. She didn't have to look at the menu. She would get clams casino like she always did, and follow it with a mushroom burger. They ordered food and a bottle of wine, Craig picking out the most expensive on the list as he said he would.

"Maddie, I know I asked you before if you'd think about anyone at the old folk's home who could have killed Floyd, but I thought of something that would help me even more."

Maddie finished the last of her beer in three gulps in an effort to squash the uneasiness she felt. She guessed that since she didn't say anything, Craig took it as a sign to continue.

"I could use your help. You know Joe. Couldn't you find out what's going on behind the scenes? I know Owen didn't do anything. I mean, he might be a cranky old geezer, but that's not against the law, is it?"

"So now you want me to talk to Joe? What is it you think he's going to tell me?"

Craig stretched his arms wide to his sides. "Anything. Who knows, in a moment of intimacy, you could get him to tell you anything."

Maddie actually snorted. "Hah, Craig, you have obviously been misled in your understanding of Joe's and my relationship."

"I know you were married."

That stopped Maddie cold. She could hear her own heartbeat as loudly as she could hear Ben over at the bar asking another patron what they wanted to drink. She still couldn't speak when Craig leaned forward, a cruel glint in his eye that Maddie had never seen before.

"So let's not pretend that we both didn't keep secrets from one another, okay?"

Maddie considered asking how Craig knew but dropped the question before it got to her mouth. She didn't know how she would feel if she found out that Joe had told him in the last twelve hours and she didn't want to sort through those emotions in front of Craig.

"I find it hard to believe you're trying to blackmail me."

"I'm not. I'm just saying it like it is." Craig leaned back, his characteristic charm rising to the surface again. "Come on, Maddie. You have access to the other residents. You can talk to them more easily than I can. You have access to Joe. You can find something out. Anything. Something." Craig actually looked like he was going to cry—a sight Maddie never thought she'd see outside a Harry Potter film. He didn't shed a tear though, just leveled his blue eyes on her.

"I haven't done the right thing, I know that. But I want to do the right thing this time. And the right thing is to make sure Uncle Owen doesn't get nailed for something he didn't do. Please help."

The pitiful part of it all was that Maddie knew she was going to help. "I can try. But all I can do is talk to Sam and Dottie. Maybe a couple of my other students. And I don't know what I'll get out of Joe but I'll try. That's all. Okay?"

Maddie silently chastised herself. *So much for not getting involved.* But she also made a vow. There would be no daring escapades in the dark of night and no lying to Joe, if she even had a conversation with him before the investigation was over.

The waitress had come with the wine and after she had given Craig a detailed description of the bottle and Craig had tasted it, she poured two glasses for them, never taking her eyes off Craig. Maddie had to ask for the glass of water again and when the waitress came back she carried a jug, plonking it near Maddie with a sarcastic smile. Maddie smiled back with a sugary one of her own. She was used to getting this kind of reaction from women when she was with Craig. *Little did she know,* Maddie smiled ingenuously at the waitress again.

Craig had stuck his nose in his glass, wrinkled it and then proceeded to shake his head in a manner that made him look like a horse. He then sighed heavily. "A nimble bouquet, with a hint of foggy nights looking for cabs in the rain and a suggestion of that bit of stubble I always miss on my chin."

Maddie laughed. She and Craig had taken a wine tasting course with friends and had come away with an appreciation for wine but, surprisingly enough on Craig's part, had left the pretensions behind. Maddie swirled then sniffed and tasted her own glass. After swallowing, she exhaled.

"I'm not sure I can agree with you. I taste the delicate fluff from the dryer filter and just a breath of an early morning paper thudding onto the front porch."

Craig took another sip. "Hmmm. Maybe you're right."

Maddie took a generous sip of wine but before she could think of anything to say, Craig jumped out of his seat.

"Oh, yeah! I love this song! Hang on a sec."

Maddie watched as Craig bounced up to the DJ. His animated gestures made Maddie chuckle. It was just like Craig to get so excited about something that pleased him that his eagerness for the subject would infect anyone he came across. Maddie laughed again as she remembered the pair of gravity boots she'd bought after listening to Craig talk about them for a solid hour. She still had them in a box lying at the bottom of a closet.

Maddie watched as the DJ looked warily at Craig, but soon he had a smile plastered on his face and was nodding enthusiastically along with Craig. By the time Craig returned to the table, Maddie had finished her glass of wine and was apprehensive. But as Craig leapt back to his seat, she understood that he had dropped the conversation about Owen and Floyd and was on to having a good time that evening.

"He's cool. He lived in L.A. for a couple of years and he knows the Icy Hot Club and the Red Skunk Band."

Craig looked like he'd just discovered that the Icy Hot Club were going to appear live at the Grass and Toad any minute. Maddie tried to suck back a retort. She loved the band and had bruised her feet many a night dancing to them but never with Craig. Knowing that he'd never gotten around to doing the one thing that she'd wanted them to do as a couple, was maybe, Maddie's biggest regret. The thought that he'd taken up swing dancing without her continued to make her want to break the hideously expensive wine bottle over his head.

She'd learned that Craig had taken up swing dancing from a mutual friend. The story went that Craig started dancing with Paul, a guy he met at a gay bar and started seeing while Maddie was still blissfully unaware that her life was about the make a radical U-turn without her at the wheel. Turns out Paul was also trying to figure out who he was and convinced Craig that they should do all the things they were afraid of. In Paul's case, that was dancing. Maddie surmised that it wasn't that hard to convince Craig. But she didn't want to think about that again. She didn't even want to be in the restaurant but before she could make up an excuse, the familiar tune of the Icy Hot Club's rendition of Russian Lullaby came over the sound system. She couldn't help but smile as Craig let out a hoot and he and the DJ gave each other the thumbs up. Then he stood up and held a hand out to Maddie. "May I have this dance?"

"What, you? You want to dance with me?"

Craig went into the explanation of his entrance into the dance world, unaware that Maddie already knew most of the story.

"Yep. After you left, I decided that maybe you had a point or two. Like about the fact that we didn't do very many things together. And specifically that you loved partner dancing and that I never bothered to learn."

"So, you're saying that after you broke up with me, you learned to partner dance?"

"Yeah, it's been great. I started with Paul." Craig coughed into his hand, a gesture Maddie found quaintly endearing. *Was he actually feeling awkward about having to speak about his boyfriend?*

"Look, I don't want to lie. You were working on your Ph.D. and the whole television thing was getting underway. I was a jerk. I should have said something before I started going out."

Maddie digested that information as she enjoyed more of the wine. She had an image of Craig going out for a gallon of milk rather than looking for a man to have sex with.

"What dance did you choose?"

"We started with swing dancing. It was really aerobic and Paul is fit." Maddie could see the color rising up his neck from under his collar. She should have looked away so that she didn't have to watch his embarrassment but she was fascinated by the fact that he was finally embarrassed about cheating on her the last year they were together. Craig raised his hand toward the waitress and asked for another glass for water. She was there in an instant with the glass and a smile and a whole lot of idle chatter. Even Craig looked like he'd reached his limit with her. When she finally left after asking if there was *anything* else she could do for him, he continued.

"Swing dancing didn't last long. I think I could have gotten into it but Paul's interest fizzled out. Anyway, then we got into country western dancing after that. Much more our speed and really, a bigger gay scene." Craig stood and once again offered his hand to Maddie.

Not sure if she wasn't accepting something more than a dance, Maddie allowed herself to be led to the small dance floor, the surreal tint to the evening not escaping her. As Craig led her through several songs, very well, she had to concede, she thought that knowing her luck, this would be the moment Joe walked into the bar.

After several dances, they ate and drank and talked and by the end of it she was pleasantly drunk. The only uncomfortable part came when Maddie tried to pay her part of the bill.

"Maddie, please. I owe you at least this much."

"No, Craig, you don't." Maddie's voice caught in her throat when she realized that she meant it. She wasn't the same person that she'd been in California and neither was Craig. She sighed as she thought that maybe she was finally letting go of the fantasy life with Craig after all and that it felt all right. In the end, Craig paid but Maddie insisted on contributing the tip.

The cold night air cleared Maddie's head and as Craig walked her to her car she thought that the night had been more enjoyable than she'd anticipated; less filled with recriminations. Outside her car, Craig grabbed at her gloved hand.

"Maddie, you won't forget what you promised."

Maddie fought to clear the remaining fog from her alcohol-soaked brain. *What had she promised?*

"You'll speak to the people at the old folk's home. You'll try to get information from Joe. I need to know what they're thinking."

Maddie pulled her hand from his grip. "Yes, I won't forget but remember, I said that I can try. I don't think Joe is going to give me much information."

Craig's forehead spread out again and he gave her that smile that charms everyone, men, women, children, waitresses, probably insects and fungus too.

"Thanks, Maddie." He pulled he into a hug which lasted a little too long for Maddie's comfort, then released her slowly, one finger sliding across her back at a time. "I've missed you." He then leaned in. His lips had just reached Maddie's when she came to her senses.

"Craig, no. Let's not go there. Thank you for tonight. I'll talk to you tomorrow."

Craig sprang away from Maddie.

"Okay then. I'm sure I'll see you. I'll be at Shadylawn most of the day."

Maddie got into her car and watched as Craig vaulted over the hood of the BMW and got in. While contemplating the Craig issue, she started at the sound of an engine, followed by squealing brakes that broke through the otherwise still night somewhere to the left of the parking lot. Maddie turned to see break lights illuminate a festive scene of reindeer and sleigh in sordid red as a car turned the corner. She was aware that the car looked a lot like Joe's but then dismissed the notion. She was just riled up. She watched as Craig reversed, then paused to wave to Maddie and give her the thumbs up from the driver's seat. She repeated his gesture and watched him drive away.

The fact that Craig was about to kiss her didn't bother her as much as the fact that she recognized that he didn't really care whether they kissed or not. He was just trying it on to see if it fit. It was just a game to him; a game that she no longer wanted to play.

She drove home completely sober and feeling like she was exactly where she needed to be. Well, maybe without another murder, but otherwise Pembroke was allowing her to get back on her feet. Now she just wanted Craig to go back to California and let her get on with her life. So she would help him if that would get him out of New Jersey faster.

Joe sped home, passing a traffic cop on his way. The officer looked up, instantly recognized Joe, and waved him on, ignoring the fact that the detective was driving ten miles over the speed limit in a school zone. Joe gripped the wheel and increased his speed. When he got home he changed into sweatpants and a t-shirt then threw himself into a rigorous hour-long workout.

Angry? No.

Jealous? Hell, maybe.

He had fought the word the entire way home and now, as he finished his one-hundredth crunch, he let the word explode in his head. Jealousy had reared its threatening head again and he hated that about himself. Fifteen years after high school graduation and he still felt like the angry adolescent he used to be.

After twenty minutes on the rowing machine and some of the demons had been subdued, he got in the shower. There, as his breathing steadied, he couldn't get the image of what he'd seen out of his head; Maddie and Craig Cavendish kissing outside the Grass and Toad.

He rinsed the shampoo out of his hair and found himself still rubbing his head five minutes later under the cooling water. He swatted the faucet closed. *Why did she have to be involved in this again?* The second murder in Pembroke in two months and there was Maddie Fitzpatrick right in the middle of it. Well, too close to the middle for Joe to ignore anyway. It wasn't just that he was interested in her. Hell, he was a lot more than interested but the fact that she'd come back to town and two people had been murdered at her dance studio and now, another murder in another dance class. That was just one murder too many.

Joe had an uneasy feeling and he didn't want it to grow larger so he went to the kitchen, opened the fridge and grabbed a cold beer. He then sat with his computer open in front of him and after re-touring the details of the case as it stood, he had to admit that it looked like Maddie Fitzpatrick was bad news.

Chapter Eleven

Only slightly hung-over from her evening with Craig, Maddie woke to eat breakfast with her parents before their taxi arrived. She sat at the kitchen table, a mug of coffee in one hand, the newspaper spread out in front of her. The lifestyle section anyway. Her father had commandeered the news and editorial sections. Just like old times. Maddie sighed. Some things didn't change and she was glad.

Her father put the paper down. Every time Maddie looked at her Dad she had to smile. He looked more and more like her grandfather every day, the grey hair now dominating the black that used to cover his head. Her father's eyes were alert though, as they raced across the pages spread out in front of him, then dropped to a pad of paper he kept at his side for notes, ideas and plans to take over the universe. She took a sip of coffee and sighed. She could see his eyes clearly since he'd had cataract surgery the year before and it had taken several weeks for her to get used to his face without the glasses that he'd worn since she was a child. He always chose the same pair of thick-rimmed, black specs, ordered from Sears every time he had to change prescriptions because he thought they looked like what a college professor would wear.

"Interesting fact; several members of the Lenape tribe have sued Westinghouse for infringement of patent on a combination solar furnace. Speaking of furnaces, you remember ours is a tad ornery."

Maddie must have looked a little bleary-eyed.

"Should I shut up right about now?"

Maddie looked at her dad as he stuck his head back into the newspaper, wondering if she'd hurt his feelings. When she saw the tweak of a smile as he peeped over the edge of the paper she knew she hadn't.

"No, Dad, not at all. I was hoping you could tell me about the history of our furnace. You know, maybe give me some of the old stories you grew up with, the ones that get passed down verbally, generation to generation."

As Maddie finished her request, her mother walked into the kitchen.

"Now, Maddie. Don't encourage him."

After agreeing that she'd call if she needed to and keep Joe informed if anything strange happened and eat well so that she didn't get sick, their taxi finally left. As Maddie turned to jump back into bed for a half hour, she caught the unconvincing look on her mother's face through the back window and returned it with a bright smile she hoped would alleviate some of her mother's anxiety at leaving. She poured another cup of coffee and took it back upstairs to think through her next moves.

While snuggled under her duvet, Maddie wondered if she'd actually be able to go through with Craig's request. In the heat of everything that had happened last night, it seemed perfectly reasonable that Craig should ask her to talk to her students about other likely suspects. It also didn't seem overly outrageous to talk to Joe about how the investigation was progressing. Now she recognized the absurdity of what Craig had asked her to do. There was no way Joe would tell her anything. As the only feasible conclusion came to her, namely that she'd have to tell Craig that it was impossible, her mobile beeped. Her stomach knotted as she read Craig's message.

I had such an awesome time last night! I'm going to see Uncle Owen now and then I'm going to check out this place Ben told me about. It's called The Den. You ever been? Wanna go? And thanks for talking to those old folks and to Joe. I REALLY appreciate it. Love, Craig.

She didn't type anything back but lay in bed for several minutes, her emotions in turmoil. Maybe she was the one being ridiculous and it really wasn't going to hurt anyone if she talked to a couple of people. She thought back to the day she first saw Owen and Floyd together at the library and remembered the orderly who'd helped them into the van. Draining the remainder of her coffee, she got out of bed knowing she was going to help Craig even if she felt like an idiot. She didn't have class until ten o'clock so she had time to stop by the retirement village and try to find the that driver. Her class later in the morning was with Sam and Dottie and the Shadylawn group which would give her an easy opportunity to talk to them.

The temperature had dropped during the night, leaving the air frigid, but the scene was picture perfect. There hadn't been enough snow to require either the services of the municipal snowplows nor the closing of schools, leaving the streets quiet, save for the odd parent and toddler out to explore the winter wonderland. Green swathes of garland topped with red and gold plaid bows adorned the lampposts to celebrate the season and Maddie felt a shiver of pleasure pass through her. After coming to the realization that California and Craig were over for her, Pembroke held an optimistic future out in front of her and, with caffeine surging through her veins, she felt ready to grab it. She just had to get through this interruption with Craig.

She drew up to the Shadylawn Retirement Village, but this time the gate was closed and the guard rooted in front of it. The day before the guard had taken her ID and license plate number. This time, he walked up to her window and no amount of cajoling from Maddie would keep him from his duty, which included searching the inside of the car. After he'd completed that task—one he didn't seem to mind doing in the biting cold air as Maddie shivered—he sauntered around the car, then looked down at a clipboard he'd produced from his guard booth and studiously flipped through the papers. Without moving his eyes from the paper, he shook his head.

"Name's not on the list. Have to call it in. Wait a sec."

Maddie's heart pounded. As casually as she could, she reached into her purse and pulled out her cell phone. Gaping at it in what she hoped looked like a surprised consternation, she let out a moan.

"Oh, hang on!"

The guard looked up.

"Um, I have to go. I'll have to come back later in the day. It's, um, a dance emergency."

The guard raised his eyebrows, his hand hovering over the receiver of a black, plastic phone attached to the guard booth wall.

"So, you don't want to go in?"

"Um, no, not right now." She indicated her cell phone, making a show of waving it around, indicating again that she'd received an important message.

He let his hand drop. "Right. Make sure you're on the list when you come back."

Maddie nodded, trying not to read a hidden significance in that statement. What if Joe had issued a description of her to the employees of the retirement village? She'd have to come up with another plan. Her initial jubilant mood garnered from the picturesque scene deflated and Maddie got back in her car. At least Sam and Dottie would be coming to the studio for their regular Tuesday class. She'd make a start with them.

The guard watched as she made a U-turn, then lifted his hand in a half wave as her cell phone beeped. She jumped when she saw it was Joe and looked wildly around her, certain he must be watching her. Pulling the car to the side of the road, she read that Joe wanted her to come by his office—again, *when she had the chance.* Maddie promised herself that she would never use that expression as she texted back that she would be there in ten minutes. The sense of foreboding she felt increased as she looked in her rear-view mirror to see the guard standing outside his booth, waving another car through the gate but looking straight back at Maddie. As she pulled away, she saw him reach for the phone in his booth again.

Maddie walked into Joe's office to find his sister and secretary, Maureen, at her desk. Maureen was engrossed in what was sitting on her desk and Maddie became fascinated as she watched Maureen lift a glass to her lips, gulp what looked to be the last of what was in it, swallow, grimace, then chase whatever the vile concoction was with water from a bottle. As she tilted her head back, she noticed Maddie standing in the doorway.

"Maddie!" she managed to squeak out before she took another mouthful of water. "How are you?" This time she sounded her normal self and she walked around the desk to give Maddie a quick hug. Without waiting for a response, she continued, indicating the glass she'd just put down.

"This gruesome concoction is my daily dose of green goddess. That's what I'm trying to call it anyway.

More like primordial sludge." She then pointed to a Tupperware full of a green powder. "It's full of everything Mommy and baby will need to be healthy. That is, when the little tyke decides that it's time for the show to start."

Maddie sat down. She knew Maureen and her husband Tim had been trying to start a family and, from the looks of it, a month into the endeavor, Maureen was still enthusiastic. And she looked fantastic too. The green goop seemed to be doing wonders for the translucency of her skin and the sheen of her red hair.

"Can never be too prepared." Maureen patted her flat stomach under a gypsy-styled blouse, already looking like she'd embraced maternity wear. "This kid is going to come out a superstar with all this gook I'm downing." She put the Tupperware into a drawer. "What can I do for you? Or, is this a social visit? Wink, wink, nudge, nudge."

Maddie forced a light laugh. "Nope, not social, unfortunately."

"Well, I guess it's about the goings on at Shadylawn. Seems murder follows you around, Maddie."

Maddie blanched. "That's not funny, Maureen. It doesn't involve me at all. I think Joe is just asking everyone who was there to come in and make a statement." Maureen raised her eyebrows, appeared to want to say something, then thought better of it. Maddie knew what she'd just said didn't make sense. She'd already told Joe what she knew and Maureen probably knew that.

"Relax, Maddie. I'm sorry. That was in bad taste on my part. Kind of like that green powder. I'm sure Joe will explain everything to you." Maureen spoke into the intercom phone, announcing Maddie, then hung up. "Go on in," she added. Maddie noticed a worried expression on Maureen's face but didn't have time to question it when Maureen turned back toward her computer. Maddie opened the door to Joe's office to find him standing next to his desk, bent over so that his hands touched the ground next to his feet. As she watched, he lifted himself back to a standing position in a perfect example of a Pilates roll-up. He breathed deeply once, then turned to Maddie and was back to business.

"Thanks for coming in. There's really only one thing I want to know. What's going on between you and Craig?"

Maddie swallowed, biting her lip unconsciously as she did. She moved her hair behind her ear several times trying to hide her discomfort.

"Nothing. We broke up eight months ago. He's gay."

Joe digested the information with a bland face. Maddie had the distinct impression he knew all that. She wondered just how many conversations Craig and Joe had had already and what had been discussed during them. She imagined the two of them sitting in a bar together, drinking beers. Then an outrageous image of Craig leaning over and kissing Joe exploded in her head. She jumped, startled.

"Stop it! I mean, stop looking at me like that." Maddie heard her voice growing louder. "What I mean is, why are you asking? You knew we'd gone out when I told you about the photo."

Joe ignored her question. "So you broke up with him because he was gay?"

"Not exactly."

"Why didn't you tell me?"

"Joe, I've hardly been able to have two words alone with you since you got back."

"So you weren't happy about the break-up?"

"Okay, Joe, I know where this is going." Maddie stood up. "No, I wasn't happy then, but everything is fine now. He's a friend. And no, I'm not pining away for my ex-gay-lover."

"So what was last night about?"

Maddie knew it. She *had* seen his car. "He's a friend. He needed support." Joe remained stoic. "I was with him for ten years, for God's sake! Sometimes you can't just write it off."

Joe winced and Maddie realized what she'd said. Joe sat down hard in his chair and moved some files around in front of him.

"Based on your previous behavior, I had assumed that would have been easy for you to do again," he said solemnly.

"That's completely unfair, Joe. How dare you? What do you think? That you behaved any better? That you were some knight in shining armor and it was me who did you wrong?"

Maddie's voice was louder than she realized, and she looked at the door between Maureen and Joe's offices. With effort, she lowered her voice.

"We were eighteen and we both did stupid things," she added. "Things I think we both regret now."

Maddie couldn't tell from Joe's barren expression what he was thinking. After an uncomfortable minute of silence during which she waited for him to respond, she stood up prepared to leave.

"I don't want to see you, Maddie."

"You can't be serious."

Joe had turned his gaze to look out the window, then turned back to Maddie, looked at the files on his desk and then back out the window.

"I'm serious. It's better if we don't see one another until I've finished this investigation." He turned his stare to Maddie. "And, Maddie, I don't want to see you anywhere near the Shadylawn Retirement Village."

Maddie forced herself to sit back down again as she pressed her hands into her thighs, afraid Joe would see them shaking.

"I'm teaching a class there every Friday night for the next three weeks!"

"Then I suggest you cancel it."

Maddie took a breath, more uncertain of what she was about to say than she'd ever been.

"If you're worried about my safety, then I suggest you get some extra police security down there because I *will* be teaching my class."

"You've heard me, Maddie. I don't want to see you there."

"And I've told you, I'm teaching my class!" She turned to leave the room as she spat out the final words, determined to have the last word. She wasn't at all sure that he wouldn't follow her out of his office, but breathed a sigh of relief when he didn't. She closed the door silently.

Maureen looked up as Maddie walked by her desk but closed her mouth when she saw Maddie's expression.

Chapter Twelve

The Shadylawn Retirement Village sent several vans down to the dance studio each week, packed with residents eager to fill time with the intricacies of the tango, fox-trot and rhumba. A couple of brave souls had even joined Philip and Claire's lindy hop class and had forced the young teachers to accept the fact that they didn't know everything there was to be learned.

Maddie had been teaching a class in Argentine Tango for two months and it had become one of her favorite classes. She loved the group of spirited octogenarians. Twelve dancers were in the room in various states of getting ready for the class when she arrived and Maddie sought out Sam and Dottie who were standing near the window while greeting the room at large.

"Hi, everyone! Glad to see you all here today."

And she was glad. When she'd left the retirement village the day before, she'd already sensed the unease amongst the retirees and she didn't relish the idea of losing students again. Not so soon after the last investigation.

Dottie squirmed as she tried to get words out of her mouth, ignoring Sam's persistent glare and tugs at her arm.

"Maddie, sorry to ask, but we thought that you might know that detective...um...who...um."

"I used to know him," Maddie replied. "Joe and I went to high school together. What is it you needed?"

This time Sam spoke up. "We know more than the police give us credit for. We know something that could solve this whole situation and stop wasting all our time."

"With all these things going on here. The deaths, we mean." Dottie looked significantly at Sam.

"She knows what you mean, Dottie," noted Sam.

Dottie tried to hide the sting she felt from that remark, but Maddie saw her wince and read both the confusion and the offense on Dottie's face.

Maddie didn't know what other *situation* they would help Joe out with, other than the deaths at Shadylawn, but it didn't stop her from conjuring an image of them trying to help him get a date with Maddie; a sort of retirement home dating service. The vision made Maddie laugh. Sam's insulting remark added to Maddie's apparent derision seemed to be too much for Dottie to handle. She stepped back, indignant.

"We might be old but we still know what we know. He might want to hear what we have to say."

"Oh, Dottie. I wasn't laughing at that. I...never mind. I'm sorry."

"Look," explained Sam, "First off, no one could stand being with either one of them for more than five minutes."

"You mean Floyd and Owen?" asked Maddie.

Sam turned away, apparently deep in thought. Dottie nodded and continued.

"*Nobody* had the patience for them, at least not in the past six months." Dottie included herself in that list judging from the look on her face. "Of course, nobody would wish a death like that on anyone, mind you! They might have been disagreeable, but you still don't want that happening."

Maddie wanted to tread carefully. "So, the police have talked to everyone at the retirement village?"

Both Sam and Dottie nodded.

"And people there think Owen killed Floyd?"

"Damnation, of course!" said Sam. "That's not what we're here to talk about."

Maddie had grown weary of Sam's obvious irritation. She looked first to Dottie to gauge her reaction to his outburst and knew from the embarrassed and wounded look on her face, that she wasn't going to say anything.

"Sam, I'm just trying to make sense of it all too."

"Just leave it..." Sam trailed off, then, as if he'd just discovered the murderer in a whodunit, he bellowed:

"All right then! What it is, is this. There was a fight that started it. Don't know how I could have forgotten about it, but I did." Sam scratched at his chin as if that helped him to retrieve the memory from deep within the recesses of his brain. "What was it they were getting all worked up about, you ask? Treasure! That's what!"

"Treasure? As in pirates?"

Dottie interrupted. "It was a guest speaker who started it all. He was one of those National Geographic type people who'd come around talking about hobbies. Anyway, his hobby was modern day treasure hunting. Well, I can't remember everything about that talk, but afterwards, by golly, did those two—Owen and Floyd––have it out. They were out in the hall screaming at one another! You'd have thought that one of them had killed someone!" Dottie gasped when she heard herself. "Of course, I don't really mean that."

As Maddie stood looking back and forth between Dottie's and Sam's expectant looks, a thought occurred to her.

"Doesn't Shadylawn back up onto the neighborhoods around Loantaka Park?" Dottie nodded and added, "We think they were digging for treasure."

Sam clearly liked this idea, "Maybe one of 'em even hid something out there."

Maddie nodded slowly, the memory coming clear. "I was at the police station over the weekend and there were people there who were talking about all these holes in their yards." Maddie gasped as she remembered the dog. "And someone's dog was murdered!"

"A murdered dog?" Dottie visibly paled. Sam shook his head.

"That Floyd, he hated dogs! I know that for a fact," Sam added.

Dottie butted in.

"Now how do you know that?"

"Well, I'll tell you if you just give me a chance." Clearly enjoying himself, Sam puffed up his chest. "Just so happens I heard Floyd talking the other day in the hallway. He didn't see me which was just as well because he was talking to himself. Going on about how he had to *get rid of the dog* and get his prize!"

"Well, if that's what you heard, you should go to that police detective and tell him," Maddie suggested. "It's a whole different story if the murder was premeditated."

"Why should I?" Sam crossed his arms in front of his chest.

Dottie pooh-pooh Sam with a wave of her impatient hand and turned back to Maddie, saying, "What if Owen is an animal lover and he killed Floyd because of the dog?" Dottie went on with her opinion with another flourish of her hand. "What I mean to say is that people can't just go around killing dogs, well, or people for that matter! The police are always asking you to tell them about anything strange going on."

"That's what I just said, woman!" cried Sam.

Sam and Dottie looked at one another. Whether they recognized that each one was as confused as the other, Maddie didn't know. The conversation wasn't going in the exact direction Maddie had hoped, but it was close. Dottie grabbed Maddie's arm.

"That's why we think they ought to look at all this. Before someone else dies. Maddie, you know that detective. He'll listen to you!"

This was the second time she'd heard those words and while that didn't make them any more true, Sam and Dottie were making it incredibly easy to ask her this favor.

"I could probably talk to Joe, but first I'd like to be able to get some feedback from some of the people who knew Floyd. I know Owen's nephew, Craig, and he just wants to make sure his uncle doesn't get all tangled up in something that doesn't have anything to do with him." Dottie eyed her suspiciously.

"I'm just saying that it's all got to be kept a little on the quiet side," whispered Maddie.

Dottie's face lit up. "Oh, I love a bit of 007 action!" Then she added quickly, "Not that I think Floyd deserved to go that way, of course."

Maddie nodded sagely.

"Of course not. He shouldn't have."

Sam, who'd been regarding Maddie silently, finally spoke concisely. "Maddie, you should come tomorrow night. You need to come after four o'clock because we have a Wednesday afternoon matinee. Tomorrow it's *The Man Who Knew Too Much*. Classic Hitchcock."

Dottie added, "Then we have yoga at 4:30, then dinner. You'll have to come after 6:30, Maddie. Is that all right?"

Maddie laughed, glad to have the mood lightened a little. These two retirees had more going in their lives than she did. "It's great! Fits in perfectly with my teaching schedule."

"Good. When we get back, we can book one of the smaller rooms for a little informal tango class, can't we, Sam?" Sam nodded, an idea moving slowly through his head. He then punched a fist into his open palm.

"And we can get to the bottom of this! They keep telling us that there's no danger but, by gum, Floyd had a knife sunk in his chest!"

Maddie had sucked her breath in at the thought of the knife thrust in Floyd's chest. She'd forgotten for a moment that he was a man who was now dead and not just a character in a book. When Maddie, thinking about that knife in Floyd's chest, didn't respond, Sam grabbed her other arm.

"It's true, Maddie. And what everyone is saying is that Owen Cavendish had something to do with it! So I don't know if we're going to find the information you *want* to find for that friend of yours."

When Maddie heard the emphasis Sam put on the word *want*, she realized that she hadn't thought about what she might actually find. Or what Craig would do with whatever she did uncover.

Sam continued to detail his observances. "Now Owen, he's not a strong man and I don't think he could have gotten that knife in that deep, but maybe he paid someone to do it."

Maddie watched as Sam and Dottie turned to rejoin the class. She needed to start the class but what Sam had said had got her thinking. The possibility that by her going out to Shadylawn again she might sever her relationship with Joe for good had vanished from her thoughts as an idea began to percolate.

Teaching the class right then was the last thing Maddie wanted to do, but the other class members had grown silent and were all peering expectantly at the now quiet trio of Sam, Dottie, and their teacher. Maddie quickly shoved her feet into her shoes with conviction and turned to warm the class up.

"All right, class! Let's continue from last week! We were working on *giros*, or turns. Can everyone take your partner? Remember that we're entering into this turn from the open side of the lead's embrace. Is everyone okay with this?" Looks of alarm crossed several faces.

"Okay, let's take a step back to reacquaint ourselves with the movement. Remember, every single one of you was doing this beautifully last week."

Maddie led the group through several songs and several changes of partners to bring them back to the turning step before finishing the class and leaving with a sigh of relief. After turning the sound system and lights off, she hesitated before pulling the door to the classroom shut behind her and debated whether she should stop by the office or just slink out the front door. She could see Cathwrynn's electric blue VW bug and Laura's sensible Ford Fiesta parked side by side through the window, so she anticipated the interrogation she would get if she stopped at the office but she also felt a certain obligation to her co-workers and, if she were to admit it, a desire to talk about the new developments. She took her time walking down the hallway, however, stopping to pick up a brochure that had fallen off the table, then unnecessarily reorganizing the pile that sat there as she figured out just how much she was going to tell her co-workers. As she wavered between staying and going, she heard Frank's voice crooning along with music from behind the closed door to Cathwrynn's class. Poking her head into the classroom next to it, she found the custodian swaying back and forth, a mop in his hand acting as his partner, to the rhythm of the ethereal music.

"Good stuff, Frank."

Frank casually turned to face Maddie, a whimsical smile on his face as he completed a full circle with the mop around his body.

"Just like they taught us in the canteen, Maddie. That young Gloria, she was something else." A shadow passed over Frank's expression but instantly fell away with another twirl of the mop. Maddie knew Gloria was his deceased wife's name.

"Did you and Gloria dance at your wedding?"

Frank stopped all movement with an indignant look. "What? Naw, that Gloria, she got away. Had to marry her sister."

Maddie wondered whether she'd gotten it wrong. She was sure she hadn't pulled the name Gloria out of thin air.

"Well, did you dance with your wife at your wedding?"

"Course, didn't you?"

Frozen, Maddie wondered how to answer that. The incredulous look on Frank's face told her that there was no ulterior motive on his part.

"Well, Maddie, if you're all done, I'll be off."

Maddie only noticed after he'd shuffled to the door that he'd left the bucket and that there was no water in it.

"Uh, Frank? Do you need the bucket?"

"Sure, thanks, Maddie. Got to get my food. Great system they have here. Those cute little nurses bring it. Now, what will they think of next?" Maddie nodded at the nonsensical stuff coming out of Frank's mouth as she watched him put the bucket back in the janitor's closet.

As Maddie half-expected, she found both women sitting silently in the office as if they'd been waiting for her, Laura typing away at her keyboard while

Cathwrynn sat as still and enigmatic as the Mona Lisa. Maddie wondered how she'd got to the office before her and as she watched Cathwrynn breathing placidly as if she hadn't left that seat in a millennium, she wondered what she did when she wasn't teaching because she seemed to materialize in the office every time Maddie came out of class.

Floyd's death was now common knowledge, but Maddie was pretty sure the crew here at the dance center didn't know it was murder. Maddie was greeted by Laura's elaborate huff before she barked.

"All right, you. Sit down and tell us what is going on here."

Cathwrynn motioned to the seat next to her. "I saved a spot for you."

Maddie looked around the otherwise empty room and pointed towards the three empty chairs, but Cathwrynn continued to smile inscrutably as she tapped the chair.

"No, really. The others are taken."

Maddie felt a wave of exhaustion and knew she didn't have the strength to combat Cathwrynn. She wasn't even sure she wanted to. If Cathwrynn continued her esoteric ranting at the studio, surely she would prove more interesting than Maddie. Then maybe Maddie's involvement with the current murder would be forgotten. However, as if cued by Cathwrynn's psychic energy, Nikki bounded into the room, her voice several decibels higher than the room could accommodate.

"Maddie, Maddie! What is it I've been hearing? Tell us everything!" Nikki managed to cover the space between the door and Maddie with three shakes of her hips, her pink streaked hair flying in after her, and landed on a chair next to Laura's desk, much to Cathwrynn's visible unease.

"Yes, do tell us everything!" Laura's voice resonated with annoyance and, judging by the way she attacked the stack of files and pushed them to fill the space between herself and Nikki, she wasn't impressed with Nikki's enthusiasm and apparent usurper of the role as head gossiper. Maddie felt the friction growing between the two extroverts and quickly tried to distract them.

"Well, you know there was a man, Floyd Donaldson, at Shadylawn Retirement Village. He died on Friday night."

Laura sighed heavily with impatient annoyance. "Yes, people die. He was old."

Equally annoyed because Maddie thought that Laura was verging on the getting old bit herself, she retorted, "Well, he was murdered!"

Nikki and Laura gasped simultaneously as Cathwrynn's head sank into her chest. Maddie briefly told them about the class and how the victim had collapsed and was only later found with a knife in his chest, but she left out the bit about Joe not mentioning that Floyd was murdered until Monday and that he'd waited until Craig was there to do it. Maddie also left out all the discomfort she'd felt from that experience.

Laura and Nikki vied to be heard first.

"What do you have to do with it?"

"Did you know him?"

All three women's eyes were now trained on Maddie.

"I'd met Floyd earlier on Friday, at the library, and then he showed up in the class I taught that night."

Laura heaved a great lungful of air and took out her cigarettes. "Well, isn't that a coincidence that you met him earlier in the day? What did he say to you?"

Cathwrynn had been silent up to that moment, barely blinking as she appeared to be calming herself with deep breaths and a slight hum. "There are no coincidences." Cathwrynn's tone was ominous and it infected Nikki who raised herself from her chair and sat on her hands.

"I think she's right, Maddie. I think this guy was following you."

It was uncomfortably close to what Maddie had been thinking herself though she didn't have a rational explanation for it.

"No, he was disorientated. I think he thought I was someone else. Maybe someone he used to know."

Laura put the cigarette in her mouth and lifted her hands to her hips.

"Okay, so he had nothing to do with it and you had nothing to do with it. Why are we talking about it then?"

Maddie savored the next remark, suddenly wanting to shock Laura into silence. "Well, he did have a photograph of me clutched in his hand when they found him."

Dutifully, Laura sank back into her chair. "What kind of photo?"

Maddie debated which pieces of the story she wanted to hang on to. "Oh, an old one. Floyd got it from another man at the retirement village—Owen Cavendish." All three women looked lost. "He's my ex-boyfriend's uncle."

Laura turned her face toward Nikki and prudishly commented, "Aha! Told you so."

Maddie ignored Laura's added smirk of triumph because she hadn't, in fact, told Nikki anything.

Nikki remained seated with her hands still under her thighs, lending the already petite woman the air of a ten-year-old.

"Maybe someone put it there! Like the person who sunk the knife in his chest."

Nikki's eye's sparkled as she spoke, making Maddie wonder at her extra-curricular activities but her comment made her reconsider a couple of things.

"I hadn't thought of that." That's all she said, but she kept on thinking while Nikki and Laura squabbled over whether Floyd was a stalker. If the photograph belonged to Owen and the killer put the photograph in Floyd's hand after he killed him then the obvious killer would be Owen, the owner of the photograph. Not the information Craig wanted to hear. However, if someone had taken the photo from Owen first, then murdered Floyd and placed the photo in his hand, well then, it could be anyone, including an employee like Billy. Maddie wasn't going to drop her misgivings about Billy yet.

Cathwrynn had been looking somewhere near the ceiling but lowered her eyes to meet Maddie's.

"And what about the beautiful one?" she whispered.

Maddie couldn't help but look over her shoulder to see if Cathwrynn was speaking to someone else.

"There's a beautiful one who hovers right next to you. So much distance in time but not in space," she intoned.

Maddie's mouth dropped open at what she would normally have considered Cathwrynn's obscure observations, but this time she knew exactly who Cathwrynn was talking about. Laura and Nikki had also ceased their bickering and gazed expectantly at Maddie.

"Um, yes, well there is one other slight complication."

The three women moved in closer.

"My ex-boyfriend, Craig. He's here."

Cathwrynn sighed. Laura huffed. Nikki just sat and waited for more.

"And his uncle is the prime suspect in the murder investigation."

"Classic." Nikki stood up and paced the room.

Laura, for once in her life, measured her words. "So, this boyfriend is, exactly what?"

"Ex-boyfriend," Maddie corrected her.

"Yes, him. What does the detective have to say about him?"

"Joe doesn't have anything to say because there's nothing to say." Maddie could feel the color rising up her neck. She wasn't going to mention her pseudo date with Craig last night and the way it ended. She particularly wasn't going to mention that she spent a restless night dreaming about how easy it would be to melt back into that life after she'd declared, to herself anyway, that Craig and California were over. Not that he wanted her back. She shook herself. She wasn't going to explore why she still felt like she had to stand at Craig's side during these events.

Cathwrynn nodded in agreement as if she'd heard Maddie's entire inner monologue, a gesture she then followed with a wave of her hands as if ushering someone into the office from the hallway. Within seconds, the silence in the room was interrupted by a rap on the partially opened door.

Oh, perfect, Maddie thought. *Cue the ex-boyfriend.*

Chapter Thirteen

When the manicured hand had pushed the door open fully, there was Craig in all his California-tanned, gym-honed, chisel-jawed glory, holding a box out in front of his stomach that looked suspiciously like it had come from Vito's. Maddie heard the collective sigh from the inhabitants of the office.

Nikki seemed to jump out of the spell first. "So you must be Craig. What did you bring for us?"

Craig looked to Maddie first, his eyebrows raised but Maddie remained uncommitted. He turned his smile back to Nikki.

"Pastries. I know Maddie has a sweet tooth."

Cathwrynn tilted her head to the side to receive an extra-terrestrial message and directed her voice up toward the ceiling, her eyes focused on something only she could see. "She's changed."

Laura looked like she hadn't made up her mind about Craig but was warming up to him. She quickly made room on the table next to her desk and patted the spot.

"How thoughtful! Here, put them down."

Craig didn't move fast enough for Nikki and she pulled him the rest of the way across the floor.

"I'll take them. So, how long are you staying?" She seemed to have forgotten that he was there because of his uncle and a murder investigation.

"Well, that depends." Another quick glance towards Maddie was knowingly categorized by Laura and Nikki. "I haven't seen my...uncle in a while. I may just have to stick around a while." He opened the box he'd brought and offered it around the room, starting with Laura.

"What dance do you teach?" he asked the secretary.

"Oh, no! *This* is my domain." Laura fluttered her hands around the room as if the responsibilities of the studio kept her too busy to dance, but she looked clearly pleased that Craig thought she was a dance teacher too. He moved the box around to Nikki and simply raised his eyebrows at her.

Nikki giggled. "What do *you* think?" She grabbed a cream-filled pastry and batted her eyelids.

"Latin all the way. Am I right?"

"Spot on."

Maddie marveled at how Craig could charm the pants off anyone, in any situation.

"So, as I was saying," he continued, "I may be here a while and I was thinking of taking some dance classes while I'm here."

Maddie's heart sank.

"It won't be long." These were the first words Cathwrynn had spoken directly to Craig since he'd arrived and, as usual, her words silenced the room.

Cathwrynn then granted Craig a dazzling smile and wafted out of the room, leaving Craig standing with a bemused look on his own face.

"Hey, didn't she want a donut?"

Maddie had to laugh. "No, probably not." Maddie shook her head when Craig offered her the box. "Can we talk in the other room?"

As they left, Maddie felt a tug at her sleeve. It was Nikki mouthing the word *nice*.

Once in an empty studio, she closed the door. "Look, Craig, if you want me to help, I need to be able to get into the Village. I tried this morning and security wouldn't let me in."

Craig shifted uneasily, a sight Maddie hadn't expected. "Well, sure. If you need to, I can probably get you in, Maddie."

She knew that he could, but why was he being evasive all of a sudden? Maybe his emotional plea last night had been more fueled by alcohol than she'd realized. She decided to ignore her doubt for the moment.

"Good. I've made a plan to teach a class tomorrow night, but I wanted to stop by there later this afternoon to see if I could talk to the orderlies who helped Floyd. Let them know that I'm on the list, and I'll see you at four o'clock."

"Great. So—you want to get a drink? You look like you need a break and little fresh air to get some color back into you. You look like a ghost, Maddie. That's what happens when you leave sunny California."

"A drink? No thanks, as it's only 11:30." Maddie bit back a further comment she wanted to make. Craig made it sound like she'd left California of her own accord.

"Besides, I can't. Contrary to popular belief, I have to work."

"Oh, come on, Maddie. Lighten up. Come and get a coffee then. That place Vito's is great. A whole Italian family works there."

"I know them. Their daughter, Rosie, was my best friend in high school."

Craig appeared to think that this was the best piece of news he'd heard all day, the way he skipped two steps ahead to open the door. "Tell me about you in high school. You never talked much about your childhood."

"Well, neither did you. That was one of the things I thought we liked about one another." Seeing that they weren't going anywhere, Craig had closed the door and picked up a brochure. He flipped through several pages until he reached the one with Maddie's credentials on it.

"Hmm." Maddie thought Craig was contemplating her accomplishments so she found she wasn't prepared for his next words, "I tried to talk to you, Maddie. You're startlingly evasive when you set your mind to it."

"What? Me?" Maddie looked at Craig with wide eyes and was dismayed to see the look she'd grown accustomed to in California. But standing in the St. Claire Dance Studio in northern New Jersey, she realized that she'd misinterpreted his expression. What she saw wasn't vagueness but vulnerability. Had Craig been trying to tell her something for years while they were together and she'd just been unable to hear it?

"Look, you said you wanted help and I'm trying to give it to you. Why, all of a sudden do I get the impression that you don't want me to talk to anyone at the retirement village? Have you changed your mind?"

"No, I do want your help. I just feel bad. I don't want you to do anything that will risk your job or your reputation."

Maddie burst out laughing. "Reputation? You've got to be kidding!"

"No, I'm not." Craig tried to look affronted but Maddie crossed her arms and didn't budge.

"Really?" he continued, "What you said last night when I told Ben—you know, the bartender?"

"Yeah, Craig, I know who Ben is."

"Well, when I told him about you and the television show, I realized that I had no right to do that and that you were probably going to suffer for it now."

Maddie shook her head. "Look, I'm sorry if I overreacted too. It's fine though, so don't worry. And I'm happy to talk to the people at Shadylawn. Like I said, I've already made an arrangement."

Craig dropped the brochure and did a little turn. "Great, thanks." He started down the hallway before turning around. "I think I'm going to take a Lindy Hop class while I'm here. I'll call for a schedule when I know what Uncle Owen's up to. Maybe I'll see if Ben wants to come too." After he'd left, Maddie finally let out her breath.

"Great. Just great."

Her afternoon classes over, Maddie left the building, pressing her cell phone to her ear as she did. She couldn't dislodge the idea that had been sparked while talking to her co-workers. And though she'd promised Joe that she wasn't going to get involved, she couldn't leave the niggling question behind. Maybe they had overlooked the obvious. Nobody was perfect. She called him, speaking to Maureen before she transferred the call to Joe's office.

"Joe, it's Maddie." She knew if she didn't just say it, he'd put an end to the conversation before she'd begun. "Listen, did it ever occur to you that someone could have put that photograph of me in Floyd's hand after he'd died? "

Maddie heard Joe sigh.

"There are three phone calls from Floyd's room to the dance studio," he said, ignoring her question. "Do you have any explanation for them?"

At her car, she got in and immediately turned on the heat. "Oh, Joe, don't be ridiculous!" Joe hummed, apparently considering her demand but didn't say anything.

"No, Joe! I don't have an explanation, but I can't get over the fact that you seem to think I had something to do with Floyd's death. And if you recall, I did tell you that I received a phone call at the studio, and that Laura wasn't able to get a name out of the guy. Well, I guess we know that it was Floyd now. And why won't you answer my question?"

"Okay, I'll answer it. Yes, I've considered that the photo could have been placed in his hand after his death. Surprisingly, they taught us those nifty tricks at the police academy. And as to why I think you have something to do with Floyd's death, well, it's because you do. He had your picture and he called your studio. So, if you'll do me a favor, please allow me to try to figure out what's going on while you do nothing more than continue to teach your dance classes."

"Oh, the patronizing tone is delicious, Joe. And by any chance, can I continue to live and work in Pembroke? Maybe if I get my daddy to follow behind me in his big car when I want to get a coffee, or will that be just a little too dangerous for little ol' me?"

Maddie knew she'd gone too far. She could practically feel the flash of anger course through Joe on the other end of the line. While Joe's darker side was always appealing, it was a little scary to be in its line of fire. Even on a phone. She reconsidered her words.

"Yes, Joe. I'll be careful and stay out of your way."

"Thank you. And I mean it when I say that if I find you on the Shadylawn Retirement premises, I will personally lock you in a cell."

Maddie gasped, then tried to lighten the mood. "That sounds a bit provocative, Joe."

"I'm not kidding. I want to make that clear."

Maddie ended the call, congratulating herself for successfully making sure he was in his office and would be for the near future. She hoped she had at least an hour before he might show up at the retirement village. It was four on the dot and she only hoped that in all of Craig's gallivanting around Pembroke, he had remembered to have her name put on the visitors' list. That was the exact moment she also realized that Joe would have access to such a list. She pulled over a block from the retirement village and debated the ramifications of Joe finding her there, settling finally on the greater chance being that even if Joe did find her there, he wouldn't actually put her in a cell.

She pulled her car up to the guard gate, finding a different guard this time. While he didn't wave her through immediately, he eventually did let her pass after a prolonged check of her I.D. and license plate number, then a search of both her car and body, followed by a phone call to make sure that this time she was expected. In the time it took to check her out, three other cars had pulled up behind her, and were waiting their turn. Maddie's stomach dropped when she thought that one of those cars might belong to Joe, but after dropping low in her seat and looking over her shoulder, she relaxed when she saw the same type of car Joe drove, but crammed with a young mother and four or five children.

Inside the main building, the atmosphere was subdued. While there were several groups of people milling about, there wasn't a sound above a whisper. At the reception desk, Maddie was asked to wait while they called Craig to escort her to Owen's room.

Maddie took a seat while surreptitiously looking around for a familiar face. She would have loved to have seen Nurse O'Neill but even a recognizable orderly would have been welcome. She regretted that thought as Billy sauntered around the corner and headed directly towards her.

"Hey, teach! We gonna *get* you again?"

"Excuse me?" Billy's emphasis on the word *get* didn't go unnoticed and Maddie cringed.

Billy raised one eyebrow then smirked. "We gonna get you as a teacher again? You comin' back?"

She looked behind Billy quickly, then drew herself up in the chair. "Yes, I'm teaching a class tomorrow, but right now I'm here to see someone."

"Oh, right. You okay after the other night? Hectic, all right." The improbable idea that Billy actually cared about Maddie's reaction to the evening made her pause.

"What did you think of Floyd and Owen? Do you think Owen could have done it?" she asked him.

"Oh, hell yeah. Those two mother..." Billy caught himself before the expletive exited his lips, but he mouthed the words before he went on. "Well, you know, it was going to happen anyway."

"What? That Floyd was going to be murdered?"

"Yeah and no. Maybe that's what happened. Wouldn't put it past him. But it didn't happen the way you think it did."

"How do you think it happened?"

"Well, I'll tell you, I think maybe it was like this. Floyd's old; he's not feeling well. He was going a bit mental, if you ask me. Then collapsing earlier. You know, I just think he died."

Maddie waited, expressionless.

"Then his friend Owen comes in, finds him dead, see? He decides he's going to have some fun. Shoves a knife in his chest, makes it out like he was murdered. That was so like them devils. They were like brothers, always shoving each other around, but they knew how to have fun. Yeah, that's what I think happened."

Maddie didn't respond immediately though Billy stood in front of her waiting, it seemed, for her to react. If there was any truth in the preposterous notion that Billy suggested, it still wouldn't bode well for Owen.

"Mr. Holiday, what are you doing?" came a new voice. "You've been told more than once that you are *not* to comment on the situation with Floyd Donaldson or Owen Cavendish to anyone! That was a request from the police, might I remind you."

Billy rolled his eyes as he turned to face Nurse Spring. "It's cool, Nurse Spring. It's the dance teacher. She's cool."

"Cool she may be, but please get back to what you are paid to do here. Mrs. Flynn needs the floor mopped in her room." Turning to Maddie, Nurse Spring folded her hands in front of her stomach. "You're back. I was under the impression that you were not teaching here again."

Maddie bristled at the idea that anyone had spoken to Nurse Spring about something that was clearly not her business.

"Then you are incorrect in your assumption. Not only am I continuing with the Friday night course, but I am teaching the class tomorrow night."

Looking bored, Nurse Spring said, "You're early."

"I have other business here today."

"Look, I don't have time for a game of cat and mouse," the nurse continued.

"I'm here to see Owen Cavendish. His nephew is a friend of mine." Not that that was Nurse Spring's business.

"Well, then I suggest you wait in the lounge. This area is frail care and, as I assume you can imagine, some of the residents are weak and not capable of dancing." She said *dancing* with such disdain that Maddie wanted to pull the nurse's hair out.

As Nurse Spring was clearly waiting for Maddie to leave, she stood up and pivoted quickly, and in doing so nearly ran into a man with his head engrossed in a file he was carrying open just inches away from his face. He lowered it when he heard Nurse Spring cough expectantly. Maddie saw that he was the same doctor she'd seen twice before and watched as he muttered something under his breath, clearly annoyed with something, before looking up. Appearing not have noticed Maddie, he spoke to the nurse.

"Nurse Spring. I see that Mr. Rapp has been transferred back to frail care. I understood that he wanted to remain in his suite with his wife."

Nurse Spring bristled. "Doctor Marlow, the decision to move Mr. Rapp back to his accommodation was an ill-thought out, emotional response to the man's situation. The decision was carried out, unorthodoxly, by Nurse O'Neill who has little concern for the true state of Mr. Rapp's health."

Feeling as if she were eavesdropping, Maddie edged her way down the hallway. Assuming that Nurse Spring was aware of the relationship between Nurse O'Neill and Doctor Marlowe, Maddie anticipated that this conversation was not going to end well. The disdainful nurse seemed to have forgotten that Maddie was even there as she continued:

"As I'm sure you agree, Mr. Rapp will be far better cared for here under my watch than with the frivolous antics of a newly qualified nurse."

"On the contrary, Nurse Spring. The *frivolous antics*, as you call them, of Nurse O'Neill, appear to be the only thing keeping him alive right now." At these words, Nurse Spring's hair seemed to stand up on end as her face flushed an unhealthy scarlet.

"Furthermore, experienced or not, I have witnessed Nurse O'Neill as a caring, knowledgeable and sympathetic professional. I advise that if you have anything further to say regarding Nurse O'Neill's qualified efforts, that you do so with management present in my office."

There was dead silence in the hallway as Doctor Marlow marched in the direction of the frail care area. Maddie felt, rather than saw, Nurse Spring's gaze fall on her and, like a deer caught in the headlights of an oncoming car, she couldn't move a muscle. Nurse Spring finally pulled herself to her full height.

"Are you waiting for another show, Ms. Fitzpatrick?"

Maddie walked away thinking that she'd never met such an unpleasant person in her life and felt sorry for the people in her care. As she entered the lounge, she found Craig on his cell phone. When he saw her, he made elaborate sounds as he ended the call."

"There you are! Collecting reconnaissance?"

"I don't think so. I don't know how much help I'm actually going to be."

Craig came directly to Maddie and enveloped her in yet another hug. She slowly put her arms around him too. "Oh, you already have been. I didn't know how emotional this was going to be. You've been my biggest support." He finally released Maddie, but didn't step away, forcing Maddie to take a step backwards to create space between them.

"Um, shall we go see Owen?"

Craig shifted his weight. "I'm sorry, Maddie. I hope you don't think your trip was wasted but Owen isn't feeling great. You know, it's been an emotional toll on him too. He asked the nurse for a sleeping pill and pretty much fell straight asleep."

"Of course. That's to be expected, isn't it?" Maddie said the words but she didn't look at Craig. Instead, she reached into her purse and fumbled about unnecessarily for her keys. "Well, I guess I'll go. It'll be nice to get home early today."

"Great, I'll walk you out."

As Craig needlessly led Maddie out the door, she couldn't shake the idea that he was both lying to her and trying to get her out of the building.

"That's okay. I have to use the restroom before I go. I'll talk to you later okay?"

"Sure thing. And Maddie?" Craig pulled her to a side room and lowered his voice. "You are going to talk to Detective Clancy again, aren't you?" Craig looked a little too eager and Maddie had another unexplainable, uneasy feeling in the pit of her stomach.

"Yes, I said I would and I will. I just have to figure out what to say."

"Say that you've known the family for years and that there's no way Owen could have done it. Joe will believe you."

"I don't know why you have such faith in that scenario, Craig. And I don't understand. If Owen didn't do anything, he has nothing to worry about."

An ugly look streaked across Craig's face before he was able to wipe it away.

"That's not the way it works. You know that, Maddie."

"No, I don't know that, Craig. I believe the police will find the murderer."

"Oh, really? Like in an Agatha Christie? Everything will turn out okay in the end. The hero and heroine will catch the bad guy and walk happily off into the sunset?"

Maddie didn't understand the venom coming out of Craig. She took a step back. "Yeah, I guess that's what I think."

Craig made a show of twisting his head to indicate the space around him. "Now that I've actually been here, I get where you got your Pollyanna attitude. You never really fit in in LA, did you?"

It was such a nasty thing to say and uncharacteristic of Craig, that Maddie stood mute, her stomach churning.

But almost immediately, Craig snapped out of a trance with a fevered shake. "Jeez, sorry, Maddie. I'm just tired and emotional. I just want to get Owen out of here."

"Oh? I didn't realize he was going to leave Shadylawn. Where will he go?"

"Back to California. It hit me that with no other family around, it's inconsiderate of me to leave him out here. I've already told Shadylawn that after the investigation is over, I'll be taking him back with me."

Maddie marveled at the about face in attitude. "That's a big change in plans."

"Yep, well, I've had a big wake up call. Anyway, I'm going to go back upstairs. Let's talk later, okay?" Craig disappeared into the elevator, leaving Maddie to decide whether she should defy both Joe and Nurse Spring and venture further into the frail care area to find Nurse O'Neill. Hearing the voice of Nurse Spring speaking harshly to yet another staff member, Maddie decided it was a better idea to cut her losses and get herself out of there. It would be difficult enough to make tomorrow night work and for that she had to devise a plan.

Chapter Fourteen

Wednesday dawned cold and cheerless. Any positive festive season feelings Maddie had harbored were gone as she thought about the day and evening ahead of her. She wished madly for her parents to return so that she could crawl back into bed and be a child again. That wasn't going to happen though and after strong coffee and a bowl of oatmeal, she trudged back to work.

Her classes flew by, which suited her. She'd agreed to meet with Sam and Dottie and could only imagine what Joe would do if he found her at the retirement village. The previous evening while eating a lasagna her mother had prepared before she'd left and watching four episodes of *Elementary*, a plan had been hatched and orchestrated. She'd called Craig and arranged for him to meet her at her house and smuggle her into Shadylawn in his car, hidden under a pile of blankets.

"That's a bit drastic, isn't it?" he asked, "I mean, do you really think that Joe is going to arrest you?"

"Not arrest, no. But I wouldn't put it past him to lock me up. He wants to keep me away from there."

"Well, that's kinda romantic. Is he jealous of us?"

"What do you mean *us*? There is no *us* anymore and he knows that." Maddie intentionally hurt Craig with her comment and she felt glad, though she would probably suffer pangs of guilt later.

After a couple of uncomfortable seconds, Craig cleared his throat. "Okay, anyway, if you think you have to hide to get in, I'll do it. It's the least I can do."

"Good. See you at my house at six. I'll text the address. And just come up the drive. I'll be watching for you."

"Whatever you say, MacGyver."

"Damn it. Damn it. Damn it!"

Maddie walked into the hallway at the studio to find Frank embroiled in a confrontation with a ladder and a broom, and she wasn't certain who was winning.

"Here, let me help." Maddie lifted the ladder away from Frank so that he could extricate the broom handle from between the bars. As she did so, he seemed to become flustered and dropped the broom altogether.

"Damn it! What's the problem with this? What's the problem with the world?"

"I think you just need three hands, Frank. Here, let me get that for you." Maddie reached out to pick up the broom, but Frank's next words stopped her.

"Gloria, what's happening to me?"

Maddie glanced around her. "Come sit in the office, Frank. Let me get you a glass of water."

Maddie helped Frank into the office, feeling like she was leading a ninety-year-old rather than a seventy-year-old. Laura lifted her head from her computer when they entered, and jumped up when she saw the look on Maddie's face.

"Now, Frank, did you forget your medicine?" asked Laura.

Frank shook his head, mouthing the word *no* but nothing came out. In that time, Laura had reached into a bag that Maddie assumed to be Frank's. Laura read the labels on several bottles.

"Frank, it says here that you should take one tablet, three times a day. Have you taken one this morning?" Laura asked.

Frank looked blankly at Laura, then Maddie. Then his eyes cleared.

"I took two. Those are the ones that I take two of. I know that."

"No, Frank, it says *one* here. See."

Laura pointed at the words on the bottle, but Frank wasn't looking. He'd put his head into his hands, so Maddie took the bottle from Laura's outstretched arm.

"She's right, Frank. It looks like you've taken too much. Maybe that's why you're confused." Maddie looked at Laura and was comforted to see that contrary to the habitual look of gossip-monger on Laura's face, right then she looked genuinely concerned.

After Maddie had closed up the classroom following her last class, she found Peter waiting for her. She hadn't seen him for any length of time since Friday night and she realized that in all that time, she hadn't even thought to call to find out how he was.

Peter held the door open for Maddie as she put her hat and gloves on, but he looked pre-occupied. Maddie was prepared to just leave it at that, but he started talking before she'd fished her keys out of her purse.

"First full day back and I feel like I've hammered my head to the wall. I actually taught a cross swivel in a foxtrot class," he sighed.

Peter tucked his arm into Maddie's as they walked to their cars. While Maddie was glad that Peter would be around the studio again, she couldn't help but rerun the conversation she'd almost had with her mother before she left for her holiday. She unlinked her arm from his before he deposited her at her car with a move to look for her keys. She felt like an idiot and was probably over-analyzing the situation, but then realized that Peter hadn't noticed anything. Without further conversation, he waved absent-mindedly and drove away.

Craig pulled his car up the drive of her parent's house at exactly six o'clock. Maddie had brought a pile of blankets and a sleeping bag from the house and pulled them on top of her as she sat on the floor of the passenger seat. Craig looked gleefully at Maddie as she brought her legs up to her chin to fit in with all the coverings.

"Sure you don't want to get in the trunk? It would be much more authentic, wouldn't it?"

"Shut up, Craig! I'm doing this for you, you know."

The short ride to the retirement village was interminable and when Craig stopped at the gate, Maddie thought the prolonged conversation he had with the guard was unnecessary. She let out the breath she'd been unintentionally holding when the guard let them through without asking to see inside the car. When Craig finally pulled around to the back of the building to park so that Maddie could extricate herself from her hiding spot, she was in a foul mood.

"Do you have to flirt with everyone you meet?"

Craig laughed. "I just like to make people happy. People are happy when you let them know you like them. You used to like it, Maddie."

"Yeah, when I thought I was the only one you were flirting with."

"Well, then, I guess it's a good thing you don't have to deal with that anymore."

"Got that right." Maddie slammed the door leaving Craig looking bemused. As she walked, she spoke over her shoulder.

"I'll meet you here in forty-five minutes. Don't be late!"

At reception, she was directed to one of the smaller rooms down the west hallway. When she arrived, she spotted Sam and Dottie in a heated discussion in the corner of the room. As she moved closer to the elderly couple, she saw that Sam had a newspaper he was unsuccessfully trying to hide behind his slim body.

"Just show her. She should know," argued Dottie.

"Show me what?" asked Maddie.

"It's nothing really, Maddie," argued Sam. "Doesn't mean anything. It's just the *Mordon County Enquirer*. Piddly local paper that only comes out once a week. Timing was just bad on this one."

Uneasiness grew in Maddie's stomach and didn't abate when she saw the first words of the front page headline of the other local paper. *If you can call it a newspaper,* Maddie fumed inside. It was locally considered a small-time *National Enquirer* with stories about UFOs and babies raised by goats. Sam spread the paper to reveal the full title.

Murder at Shadylawn. Possible Links to Dance Studio.

Maddie groaned. "They can't be serious. Who wrote this?" Sam handed her the paper while shaking his head.

"Someone just trying to cause a stir, I'm sure, Maddie. Just bad luck that it went to press last night. By next week, this whole thing will be over and people will be talking about some stupid reality television show or some other garbage."

Maddie looked back and forth between Sam's sneer and Dottie's distress to see if there was an underlying purpose in mentioning reality television, but their expressions seemed to correspond only to the current situation.

She then turned her attention to the by-line and sucked her breath in so quickly that Dottie grabbed her. Maddie sputtered, but couldn't even formulate the name she read on the front page.

"Renée Lambert!" Maddie finally managed to say her name, but it came out with an exclamation at the end that made it sound like she'd swallowed something wrong, sending Dottie over to her to slap her on the back a few times.

"This can't be! Renée Lambert is a nurse. Or she was anyway." Maddie had had the unfortunate experience of knowing Renée Lambert at the dance studio the previous month. A nurse at Mordon County Hospital, Renée had been revealed as both a drug user and seller. If this was the kind of reporting the *Mordon County Enquirer* supported, Maddie was glad she didn't read it.

Maddie scanned the whole article. *Sam was right, it was a load of nonsense*, she thought. The link between the village and the studio was based totally on the fact that Maddie was teaching a class on the night Floyd was murdered, and that Maddie had taught a class on a night that another student had died the month before. Maddie's name wasn't mentioned luckily, but the St. Claire Dance Studio appeared seven times in the three-paragraph article. It was as if the author had an axe to grind and knew exactly where she was going to grind it.

"Can she be held liable for this garbage?"

"Well, she doesn't name you as the teacher. That's one good thing, isn't it?" Dottie landed this last measure of support on Maddie with a squeeze of her arm. "But everyone knows and everyone's talking. I just thought you should know as quickly as possible."

"Do you mind if I take this with me?"

"Oh, sure, but, Maddie?" Sam touched the paper still in Maddie's hand as if it was contagious. "You shouldn't pay any attention to this. Garbage is what it is."

The other people Sam and Dottie had recruited to help Maddie had arrived and had gathered around the trio. Everyone kept their voices down as they started to tell Maddie what they too thought had happened.

"Floyd used to be the kindest, most gentle man you could ever come across," a plump woman named Charmaine said in a stage whisper. Maddie remembered her from the class more for her enthusiasm than for her ability. "Although he did have a certain penchant for the ladies, didn't he?"

"Well, I'd say!" Doris, a slip of a woman with a voice like a bulldozer from years of apparent smoking, added. "That rascal went for anything in a skirt. I had to put him off more times that I can tell you. Not lately though, such a shame."

Dottie nodded. "Oh, yes! He used to be so social. He used to have other friends. Remember, Sam? Floyd used to be sweet on Rebecca!"

Sam swatted at the air, his face noticeably growing red.

"Naw, he never had a chance with her." Dottie noticed Sam's reaction and turned neatly away. "Well, I suppose it's a good thing she moved down to Florida then, isn't it, Sam?"

Sam shrugged and mumbled something the rest of the group couldn't hear.

"When did he start going downhill?" asked Maddie.

"Oh, I reckon that would be about three months ago. Isn't that right?" A man named Troy spoke up and looked to the other residents clustered around Maddie, searching for agreement. Several knowing nods responded to him.

"Yep, must have been end of summer. Remember they had that barbecue out back and that circus show?"

"That's right," Charmaine agreed and nodded vigorously. "And Floyd somehow got disoriented and ended up in the ring with all the performers!"

Doris butted in again. "And that's when the turds hit the fan. He went crazy! He became irate, saying that those people were in his room and stealing his stuff when he was the one making a mess of their performance. Made a right fool of himself!"

Maddie interrupted. "I keep hearing that expression repeated—'he's always in my stuff or in my room'—but it keeps changing. Sometimes it's Floyd talking about Owen and other times it's the other way around."

"Yep, that's right. That's why they argued. They were always prowling around each other's rooms like they were looking for something the other had taken."

"Crazy as coots if you ask me. What would either of them have that would drive the other one so crazy?"

"What it is we noticed, I'll tell you, was that they seemed to be friends, but no one could tell why! They were always yipping at each other. One would say that the other one talked too loud and bothered everyone while we were trying to watch a movie and then the other would come back saying he knew where he kept *it* and was going to make him pay and all sorts of nonsense! That would drive Owen crazy and he'd get up and start shouting so they'd have to stop the movie and take both men out."

"He knew where he kept *what*?" asked Maddie.

Dottie pushed into the conversation. "Well, most people think it was about money, but that's the point. By the end, they both were talking a lot of garbage. It could have been about *anything*!"

"It was all just to pass the time. They had nothing better to do," said Sam.

Maddie looked around the group and added carefully, "Well, maybe one of them did have money."

Doris coughed, then hooted and continued in her gravelly voice, "Course they had money! We all have money! It wasn't that."

Charmaine added, "They're rich as Midas, same as anybody here. You don't get into this place without a healthy bank balance. Doris is right. They were after something *else*."

Sam wouldn't let go of his theory though. "*If* they were after anything at all. I still think they were just messing around."

"Oh, Sam, you're just sore that Floyd had Rebecca's attention."

Sam looked affronted. "That's not the way it was. And if that's the way *you* see it, I'm going." Sam stood stiffly and marched out of the room, leaving Dottie with her mouth hanging open.

"Sam, I..."

But Sam was already out the door. Dottie looked at the rest of the group, her cheeks growing pink. "I didn't mean anything, really." Doris swatted at the air.

"Course you didn't," consoled one of the women. "He's just being sensitive. Men are like that. Now I'm going to pour myself a nice G and T. Dottie, you forget about him and come over and join me."

The energy had left the group when Sam had walked out, and Maddie was left with nothing to do but thank them all and say good night, regretting the fact that she'd made the effort to come to the retirement village against Joe's orders and had come away with nothing. When the room was empty, Maddie reread the newspaper article written by Renée Lambert, *another irritable nurse,* Maddie mused, conjuring the distasteful personality of Nurse Spring easily in her mind. Re-reading the article didn't help make it any more substantial. Renée Lambert hadn't even bothered talking to the police, but had gleaned all the information in the article, it seemed, from one particular source— Nurse Sharon Spring.

Aware that someone had come into the room and fearing that it was going to be Nurse Spring, or worse, Joe, Maddie leapt into the air only to find Rolf hovering just inside the door wearing what looked like the same tuxedo he'd worn on Friday evening. Maddie had the momentary thought that maybe those were the only clothes that he owned and when she heard Berta's voice calling her husband, fully considered that Berta would enter the room in her peacock ball gown. Berta did enter, and though she was elegantly dressed, it was not in her ball gown, but an impeccably tailored suit in pale pink. However, the look on her face was anything but elegant or impeccable. She clearly looked distraught, tears in her eyes as she found Rolf now cringing against the wall. Ignoring Maddie, she reached for Rolf but he slipped further into the room.

"Rolf, darling, please let me help you! Please come back to our room!"

"You're trying to do me in, you crazy woman!"

Maddie uncomfortably made her way to the door, but as she drew close to Rolf, he whipped around to face her.

"Tell her! You know. Tell her that I don't want to go on anymore. If this is the way it's going to be, if this is what it's like to the end, I've had it! I want it to be over."

Rolf sounded lucid but his words scared Maddie and she looked to Berta who continued to draw closer to Rolf, but cautiously, like he was a wild animal she was trying to cage.

"Rolf, darling, I have a warm soup for you with crispy bread and a sausage with mustard and kraut, just like you like it." Rolf grunted. "And a cold Heineken. Come, let's go."

Rolf finally let his wife lead him out the door. As they left the room, Berta looked over her shoulder towards Maddie and the look on her face made Maddie's heart break. She hadn't been fond of the couple in the short time she'd known them, but she could clearly see the pain Berta was suffering as she faced the prospect of losing her husband.

Maddie peeked out of the room and spotted a uniformed officer she recognized walking down the hallway. She shrank back into the room as he passed, then re-emerged and quickly headed in the opposite direction. She'd congratulated herself on getting into the retirement village without running into Joe and she didn't want to mess it up now. She nipped into the ladies restroom and quickly called Craig to tell him she was ready to go and then waited discreetly until he arrived.

"Hey there! Ready to get covered in blankets again?" he said when he came upon her.

Maddie pretended to be absorbed with a text message in an effort to avoid speaking with him. His constant attention grated on her as her thoughts jumped back to Rolf and Berta. How had Rolf changed so quickly in just the last week? *Maybe he was on medication and he hadn't taken it*, Maddie mused, *just like Frank*. She didn't know anything about the man. Maybe last week Rolf was behaving abnormally and today was normal.

"Earth to Maddie. Come in Maddie!"

"What? Sorry. I was just thinking about some students of mine."

"Oh, okay then. So, do you want to get some dinner?"

"No, I don't."

"Okay. That's all right. I stopped by the Grass and Toad earlier and Ben's off tonight. We're going to grab a bite and maybe a movie."

They'd made it past the guard at the gate without seeing Joe or any other police officers Maddie recognized. Maddie looked sideways at Craig. He was tapping the steering wheel as he pushed the buttons of the CD player to get to a particular song. The sounds of Robbie Robertson came out of the speakers and he began to tap to the rhythm.

"Just picked this up at that record store on Main Street. Really good stuff there. You wouldn't think it would survive here in the suburbs."

Maddie held her breath, counted to ten then exhaled. Craig didn't notice the silence as he sang along to the song.

"Don't you want to know what I was able to learn from some of the other residents?"

"Oh, yeah, of course. But you know, maybe we can talk about it tomorrow. I'm a bit drained by the whole thing."

Maddie turned to face Craig. "Craig, yesterday and this morning it was imperative that I find out information for you. What's changed?"

"Nothing. Maddie, I appreciate what you're doing. It's just that I'm tired. I didn't realize how traumatic all this would be. Uncle Owen and I've had some really good talks, and I'm looking forward to him coming back to California with me. I'll set him up somewhere near me and this way I can have more of a relationship with him."

A little late, Maddie thought, but didn't say the words. Maybe Craig was really changing, but she had a suspicion something else was going on. What that was, she hadn't figure out yet. The Craig she once knew was emotionally constipated and this new, overly emotive man confused her. But then, people do change and Maddie knew that more than most people. Craig stopped in front of her parent's house.

"So, I'll talk to you tomorrow, right, Maddie?"

"Yes, but I have three back-to-back classes, so I won't be available until lunch."

"No problem. I think this will be a late night and I'll probably sleep in tomorrow." Craig grinned as he waved good-bye. Maddie slammed the door, angry on Paul's behalf.

Chapter Fifteen

There was no need for Maddie to have taken Sam and Dottie's copy of the *Mordon County Enquirer*. When she walked into the office the next morning, Peter was holding his own copy and waving it in front of everybody's face.

"This is libelous! It has to be. And from that woman? How does a woman who took drugs, lied to the police and was told she could never practice nursing again get a job? How can she even be working for a newspaper? Can we even *call* it a newspaper?" Peter continued to rant as he stormed into his office, throwing the paper into the trashcan as he passed Laura's desk.

"Nobody better be thinking of taking that out of there! In fact, do we have a shredder?"

Laura shook her head, rubbing her hand over the white hairs that had escaped her powerfully scented hair gel that morning.

"Then get one!" he yelled back. "I'm calling the so-called editor of that so-called paper!"

Laura looked at Maddie as Peter's door slammed closed. "I doubt anyone is taking her seriously. She's still under investigation and, from what I hear, just scraping by. I'm surprised that she's still here in Pembroke, but then, maybe they won't let her leave. You know, until after they've decided how she'll have to pay back society and all that."

Practically bouncing off the walls, Philip and Claire came into the office, each speaking over the other in an effort to be heard.

"Did you hear? There's been a murder at that old age place!" cried Philip.

"I can't believe it!" squeaked Claire. "My mother says it isn't safe here. She wants me to come back and work in Newark."

Laura rolled her eyes. "Old news, spring chickens. Not only do we know, we have firsthand knowledge." Laura pointed a pen at Maddie.

Claire gulped audibly. "You, Maddie? Dang girl, you get around, don't you?"

"Now hang on a second," declared Maddie. "I'm innocent. I just happened to be there." Both Philip and Claire looked at her apprehensively. "Honestly, I was just teaching a tango class."

"To old people?" they asked incredulously.

Maddie actually laughed. "Yes, Philip. Believe it or not, you can continue to dance even after your 50th birthday."

"Yeah, well, I'll have to take your word for that. Catch you all later." The couple left the room, Claire punching Philip affectionately on the arm as they sped out the door.

Maddie turned back to catch Laura engrossed in her image in a hand-held mirror.

"I haven't seen Frank yet. Is he coming in?"

"Oh, well, yes, he called." Laura put the mirror back in her drawer and for the first time in her life, seemed unwilling to expand on what could have been a scandal-inducing conversation opportunity.

"And? Is he all right?" Images of Frank on death's door filled Maddie's vision.

"Well, not exactly."

"Laura, what exactly is wrong with Frank? You can tell me. I'm not going to faint."

"Well, it's just that he said he had *man* problems and I don't think he really wants his private affairs discussed here at the office." Laura looked smugly at Maddie and turned back to her computer screen.

Well, that's a first, Maddie thought as she turned to leave Laura to her own devices. "If he calls, let him know I hope he gets well soon."

As she turned to leave, she heard the expected frustrated huff from Laura. Before she reached her classroom she found herself cornered by Nikki.

"Now, Maddie, just what the hell is going on here?" Maddie continued to marvel that the diminutive brunette could sound like a stand-in for Dolly Parton.

"Laura, who I'm sure is a good woman, just can't seem to give me the facts. She has, however, told me that she's worried that Frank is going to become addicted to his medication, even though he won't take it, that your reputation is going to keep you from finding a good man, and that she doesn't think she has the strength to keep it all together. She's also concerned that Cathwrynn is a pagan—though for the life of me I don't understand why that's a question—that Claire and Philip are not using birth control and that Peter is going to have a nervous breakdown. She's a very busy woman."

Maddie laughed long and hard. Nikki had been at the studio less than a month and had Laura nailed. Nikki remained fixed in front of Maddie, her hands on her hips.

"Spill it, Maddie!"

Several students walked into the hall as Nikki pulled Maddie into an empty classroom only to find Grant engrossed in the screen of his cell phone. He didn't even look up as the two women closed the door, but continued to stab at his screen.

"It has nothing to do with what happened here at the studio last month," said Maddie.

"Even though that reporter is saying it does?" asked Nikki.

"She's not a reporter. She *was* a nurse. She used to be a student here and she has an axe to grind. The only reason I'm involved at all is that I used to date the nephew of one of the men connected to the case."

Grant spoke so quietly that Maddie had to strain to hear him: "That's an unfortunate coincidence."

Maddie nodded enthusiastically when she realized that Grant had commented on her statement. "That's what I said." She faced Nikki again. "Anyway, I'm trying to help him out. Craig, my ex-boyfriend, that is. He's just..." Maddie paused mid-thought. *What was he really? Using her, probably. She knew that and she was risking her relationship with Joe by doing so.* Nikki gazed at her expectantly.

"Well, I've been able to talk to some of my students at Shadylawn and I think they have valuable information, but Joe, the police detective, won't listen to them."

Nikki looked outraged. "Clearly the police have a responsibility to listen to citizens. You must help him!" Nikki was probably remembering Craig walking into the office with his box of donuts, but continued in a slightly more restrained voice. "And make sure those people are heard."

From behind them, Maddie heard Grant sigh. "Ladies, please. I'm busy." Maddie left the room, eyeing Grant as she did so. She still hadn't heard him say more than four words at one time.

She deliberated whether she should contact Joe for the rest of the morning and made a decision after lunch. She blamed it on the conversation she'd had with Nikki and the insanely strong coffee she'd had at Vito's. With a surge of justifiable energy, she drove to his office.

"Okay, Maddie. How is it you know that Owen and Floyd were digging holes in the grounds of Shadylawn?" Joe looked surprisingly relaxed, almost uninterested in what she had to say, and that made Maddie nervous.

"And that they had something to hide?" she added.

"Yes, and how do you know that they had something to hide?"

"Do you really want to know?"

Joe's voice rose ominously with a single word. "Maddie."

Joe tilted his head, first to one side, then the other, as if stretching a kink on both sides of his neck.

"I have inside information."

"Stop right there. Inside information? Who?"

"Sam and Dottie. Students of mine."

Joe let his breath out through his nose in a slow stream. "Go on."

Maddie considered how to give Joe this piece of information. Not because she wanted to alter it, but because she didn't want to get Sam or Dottie in trouble for withholding information that could be crucial

"After class, Sam and Dottie came to me because they remembered something."

"They came to you? Well, that makes sense. Why go to one of the dozen police officers camped out at the Shadylawn Retirement Village when you could go to a dance teacher?"

Maddie tried to take the comment in stride. She knew he had a point, but the way he sneered the words *dance* and *teacher* made her spit out her next words.

"I suppose I just have a more approachable personality."

"Great. Can we just get on with this?"

Maddie told him about the *treasure hunter* and about the argument between the two men and about the dead dog. The entire time Maddie talked, Joe held his hands in a prayer position on his desk. Maddie closed her mouth.

"Are you going to write any of this down?"

"Nope." Maddie opened her mouth, but Joe shushed her. "For all intents and purposes, the case is closed."

"But, what about Owen?"

"Maddie, we have it under control."

"Can you at least tell me whether you've cleared Owen of Floyd's murder?"

"No." Maddie waited for more and when she realized that Joe had no intention of telling her anything about his investigation, she thought of how Craig had pleaded with her and stood up.

"I was just trying to help a friend."

"So I've heard."

"That's childish," she snapped.

"So is a dance teacher thinking she can solve a murder investigation better than the police!" he cried.

"Fair enough. However, Craig didn't think you would listen to him."

"Is that why he withheld information pertinent to the attempt on his uncle's life?"

"What? Joe, I didn't know that. What information? And what do you mean, his uncle's life? Floyd wasn't his uncle."

Joe looked like he regretted his last statement and rubbed the back of his neck as he spoke, "I'm not saying anything more. But now that I've told you that Craig Cavendish knows more about his uncle than he's told us, I'm asking you again to please be careful and let me do my job."

"Are you asking me to or telling me to?"

"Take it however you need to, Maddie. I'd like the same response from you either way."

She decided to change tactics. "Did you see *The Mordon County Enquirer* yesterday? Did you see the garbage that Renée Lambert is writing. Surely there must be something that you can do about that. I mean, her nonsense could be jeopardizing the case."

"Maddie. Just consider the case to be solved. I need you to go back to the studio and then back home and to get on with your life."

"Are you saying good-bye to me?" The bland expression finally fell off Joe's face, replaced momentarily by surprise, but he didn't respond.

"Can I at least ask if there's any reason Craig has to stay or can he take his uncle back to California with him?"

A strange look passed over Joe's face before he answered. "That's police business, but in case you see your boyfriend before I see him, let him know I want to talk to him."

"He's not my boyfriend."

"Whatever he is, let him know."

"Okay, I'll let him know that he's my ex-lying sack of dung and then I'll let him know you want to talk to him."

Maddie watched as Joe's eyes crinkled with a slight smile creeping up at the corners of his mouth, but she forced herself to ignore it as she reached into her pocket and pulled out what she'd found in a box in her parent's house.

"And here. This is yours. I found it in one of my old boxes." Maddie handed him a ring. She knew without a doubt that he would recognize it. It wasn't the ring he had given her when they married; she still had that one. It was his class ring, the ring his mother had bought him even though he said he didn't want it and wouldn't wear it. He'd given it to her on a silver chain and for their senior year she'd worn it around her neck calling it her third boob.

The light in Joe's eyes was immediately extinguished. Maddie was almost sorry that she'd given it back to him that way but she wasn't going to back down. Maybe he was right and they shouldn't see each other at all. In the seconds it took Maddie to wonder whether the satisfaction she felt at hurting him, even just a little, was worth it, Joe's eyes had become cold and Maddie instantly made some space between the two of them. He was always scary when he was angry, or sad. Maddie walked as calmly as she could out of his office, passed Maureen and the exasperated look on her face, and eventually out of the police station before she burst into tears.

"Joseph Padraig Clancy, you're unbelievable, you are."

"Maureen, stay out of it!"

"Oh, like that's likely to happen. And don't make that *I'm a professional* face you make. We're off the clock for the following sixty seconds."

Joe pointedly looked at his watch.

"If I watched you ten minutes, I watched you a day mooning over Maddie while we were with Gran. If you didn't look at the text messages from Maddie every chance you got, then I'll eat my hat."

"You don't know I was looking at Maddie's texts. I do have a job, you know—one that requires me to be in touch."

"They were Maddie's texts and you know it. I heard you say to Gran that she had to hold on, that you had someone you wanted her to meet. Why do you think she's still alive?"

"Your minute is up." Joe closed the door between their desks, his fists tightly clenched. He stood still for a solid three minutes before he was able to relax his grip around the ring Maddie had handed to him. He took the ring and slid it onto his finger, ridiculously pleased to see that it still fit, then thoughtfully slipped it off and put it in his top drawer before turning back to his computer screen.

"Yeah, but I just don't understand how that's going to work. I just want to see what it looks like when the man does it," said Brad.

"Brad, just think of it this way. If you continue on the same track, the two of you will separate like this!" Maddie took Carla in a practice hold and demonstrated the step. "Concentrate on maintaining your position to her and you'll actually stop her from moving forward. You see how I'm leading her naturally into my space. Unless she wants to run straight into me, she has to correct her position and then she can step over my outstretched leg. Now you just have to give her the time to do it."

Carla and Brad had started dancing with Maddie two months earlier in a group class. While the class had had its problems, namely the insincere attempts of the men in the group to actually learn the dance, now that Carla had convinced Brad to come to private lessons, they were developing good technique. Maddie watched the couple practice the step as she pondered the problem Brad had unintentionally highlighted. Maddie knew she was going to have to face it if she wanted to demonstrate the male dancer in the tango; she needed a teaching partner. She had successfully ignored the issue for several months, but she knew she'd have to address it in the new year.

Maddie had worked with a dance partner in L.A. up until she'd relocated back to the East Coast. She and Simon had worked well together and though they never had an exclusive professional relationship, they prioritized dancing together as often as they could. Maddie fantasized about finding the perfect dance partner the way that many people fantasized about finding romance, and she recognized the same depressing statistics applied to this dilemma. What with relocating, murder and rekindling a relationship with her ex-husband, she'd hardly had time to think about where she wanted to go professionally, but Brad's comment brought the reality of her situation to the forefront. A man learning to Argentine Tango often wanted to see a man do it. Finding a dance partner was another thing to add to her *to-do* list.

The competing sounds of flutes and drums from the other two studios greeted Maddie as she closed up her classroom. The flutes seemed to be coming from the room next door and Maddie could hear Cathwrynn's melodious voice as she led her JoyWicca group in the next room. From the other room, the drums subsided and Maddie heard only grunts, followed by heavy stomping on the floor. An enormous man complete with several braids that stuck out at odd angles from his head had rented the room two mornings a week for his Viking Iron Man training sessions.

Maddie found Peter at his desk in his office, his hand on the phone's receiver and a sour look on his face. Laura was nowhere in sight, presumably off having a cigarette.

"I've only just hung up the phone with Ryan Carew, *Mordon County Enquirer's* editor and publisher. Ass of a man if I've ever spoken to one. Claims Renée Lambert wrote a quality piece and it would stand. I told him my lawyer would be calling him."

"You have a lawyer?"

"No. But I'm going to have to get one." Peter peered up at Maddie from over his glasses. "Aye, well, the holiday was good. Back to the old grindstone."

Maddie smiled. "Not many couples would call the first month with a new baby in the house a holiday. You and Kristy are lucky."

"I know it. And if I forget, my better half reminds me daily."

"This might not be the time, but I was hoping I could run something by you."

"Shoot."

"I need a teaching partner. Any local suggestions?"

"Funny you should ask. I've been thinking about something these past couple of weeks waiting for Lauren Sophia to burp. Give me a couple of days."

"Oh, thanks. That wasn't exactly what I was expecting to hear you say. I'm intrigued and a little worried."

"Don't thank me yet, you may regret it." Peter bent down to pick something up from the floor. Peter frowned and held his hand out in Maddie's direction, a red and white capsule sitting squarely in the middle of his palm.

"I suspect it's Frank's. He's like a kid. When he has to take medication, he makes this big show of swinging his head back and swallowing the pills with a gulp of water. Nine times out of ten, he hasn't taken it though. Gotta run."

Maddie nodded in commiseration and left to prepare for her next class. She'd seen Frank do exactly what Peter described. No wonder the medication wasn't working.

Her next class, a group of women who'd come in the previous week for a complimentary class the week before signing up, hadn't arrived so Maddie took the time to stretch. The coupons were Peter's idea to get people into the studio to try several dances in one day. They'd loved Maddie's hour-long introduction to Argentine Tango and had asked to be taught some basic moves before they left for a cruise in three weeks time. Only after she finished stretching her hamstrings until there wasn't a centimeter between her chest and her knee, did she accept that she'd been stood up. She waited a full fifteen minutes after the class was supposed to start then closed the room up. Laura met her in the hall.

"There was a message for you on the answering machine. Not that man again. It was someone from the class you were supposed to have. They cancelled."

"Thanks, I got that much."

"No need to be snippy about it."

"I wasn't being snippy. I just would have appreciated knowing that before I waited fifteen minutes for them. Did they say why?"

Laura hesitated. "Something about how they were worried. Probably just meant the weather. And it's not even that bad today."

"I imagine they weren't worried about the weather, Laura."

"Well, yes, they did mention something about the newspaper article when I spoke to one of the women."

"When did you speak to her?"

"Oh, yesterday, but I didn't mention it because she said that they hadn't made a decision about whether to take the class or not."

"But, Laura, you should have told me! Or Peter. One of us could have talked to her. Now we've lost those students." Maddie was irate. What kind of idiot was she?

"Well, if you don't think I'm doing my job, well, then..." Laura let her sentence dwindle to an incomplete stop, but if she was expecting Maddie to placate her she was going to be disappointed.

"I didn't say you were not doing your job. I said that you should have told one of us."

Laura huffed aggressively then spun around and ripped open a file drawer.

"Well, while you're in a bad mood I might as well give you your other message," Laura said.

"I'm not in a bad mood." Maddie watched Laura's back as she continued to man-handle files into the cabinet without seeming to look at them. "What's the other message?"

"Well, I was going to tell you if you'd just calm down!" Maddie had had enough and turned to leave.

"The police called and said something about letters you wrote." Laura proceeded to use her fingers to count out each of the following words. "They were found in your ex-boyfriend's uncle's underwear drawer. Said they were racy, but he wouldn't say anything more. And I did ask. Seems like the least he could do was give you more information if he's calling to tell you something like that."

Maddie spun around. "Who was it?"

"Oh, it wasn't *your* detective. Don't worry. And how would I know?"

"I'm not worried and he isn't *my* detective. What else did he say? When did he call? Why didn't you tell me?"

"Well, I'll let you know, for *this* reason exactly. You're getting a bit snippy. I didn't want to be the bearer of bad news. Your detective can tell you himself."

"But I was just down there!" The vein in Maddie's head started pulsing and for a minute she thought she was going to faint. If letters she wrote were found in Owen's room, there was no doubt about where they came from. She sat down, aware that finding out that your ex-husband had just read private letters you wrote to your ex-boyfriend was not the news she wanted to receive from a nosy secretary at her place of work.

"I told you, he isn't *my* detective." Maddie rose slowly and left the room with Laura emitting a gentle huff and shaking her head.

"I know you did, but that doesn't change anything."

Maddie had her mobile pressed to her ear but hardly heard the ringing on the other side of the line. She'd considered several opening remarks to throw at Joe and when the phone went to his answering machine, she only looked at her mobile in surprise. *He's not even talking to me any more. Now that's mature.* She ended the call without leaving a message, then reconsidered, redialed his number and then waited through all the rings before telling him what she thought.

"Hello, Joe, it's Maddie. I was just wondering when you were going to tell me that a man who was being investigated for murder was found to have personal property of mine. Oh, wait. I'm sorry. I'm confusing you with someone I thought I was dating. Someone I thought cared about what happened to me. Someone who should have had the common decency to tell me in person this morning, three hours ago to be exact, when I was in your office, to be exact, that those letters were found in Owen Cavendish's room. My mistake."

Maddie ended the call with a feeling that something wasn't right. *What was it?* Then she realized with a start that what she felt to be so odd was that she wasn't crying. This information, this latest stab into her heart should have produced a flow of tears, but it didn't. Instead she was livid. She was furious at Joe, of course, but it didn't start with him and she knew it. Craig should have told Maddie because she knew that if her letters had been sent to Owen, then they'd come from the same place the photograph came from. After starting the engine and the heater in her car, she placed another call.

"Why the hell didn't you tell me that you sent him letters too?"

"Maddie, I..."

"What? A little titillation while he was looking at my photo? What were you thinking? Everything has changed now." Maddie wiped some spit off her phone. "Which letters were they?"

"Maddie."

"Don't bother. They were the ones that I sent you while I was in London, weren't they?"

Craig's silence was her answer. She didn't need him to confirm what she already knew. She'd spent three months dancing at Sadler's Wells during the first year of their relationship. She vividly remembered the letters she wrote during the throes of their honeymoon stage. Now she felt tears stinging her eyes. He didn't even honor their relationship enough to have wanted to save those letters.

In a small voice, Craig finally spoke, "They were photocopies."

"Shut up. Craig!"

"Look, I don't know what's wrong with me. It was stupid and insensitive. I know that now. I just wanted to make him happy. I wish I'd looked for them before the police found them. Hell, I never thought that he'd keep them."

Maddie didn't say good-bye as she ended the call.

Joe listened to the message on his mobile. He'd seen the calls come in and had chosen not to answer them. After listening to Maddie's accusations, he wasn't sorry he'd made that decision. He'd seen her with Craig and read letters she'd written to him. He wasn't delusional. He knew Maddie had had other relationships. He had too. And he didn't kid himself that she'd been any less intense with any of them than she'd been with him. But being handed letters she'd written that had been found in Owen Cavendish's underwear drawer by a junior officer with a knowing grin on his face was too much to bear.

Joe stood looking out his window at a group of high school students in flannel jackets and hunting hats erecting the town's Christmas tree in the center of Waverley Place. He'd lost his temper when he found out Officer Dunlap had called the dance studio and, unable to reach Maddie, had left a message detailing the letters with the studio secretary, a skilled gossip if there ever was one. He shouldn't have lost it with Dunlap. The fault was his. He should have talked to Maddie about the letters as soon as he found out about them. The phone on his desk rang. Seeing the light indicating it was a call coming in from the Maureen's desk, he took his time answering it.

"Maureen."

Joe's sister wasted no time. He hadn't expected her to. He'd left the original letters in her in-box with a request for copies.

"Have you lost your mind?"

He had to protect his heart, but his first priority was to the case. "No, on the contrary, I think I just found it."

He too ended the call without saying good-bye.

Chapter Sixteen

After her last class, Maddie stuck her head in the office to say good-bye even though she was depressed and just wanted to go home and crawl under the covers.

"Hey, Maddie, could you come in here for just a second?" Peter stood at the door to his office with Laura standing, conspiring at his side.

"Frank's just left and I wanted to let you know a bit about what's going on with him," said Peter.

The way Laura avoided Maddie's face told her she was holding on to the grudge. Maddie would bring up their conversation later with Peter, when they were alone. Laura gave her ubiquitous huff and exhaled.

"And about time too, I'd like to add," Laura said. Peter ignored the comment by tilting his head to the side as if confused by Laura's accusation.

Laura put his hands on her hips. "I for one think that we have to look after Frank. There's no one else standing up to the plate, is there? No children, Gloria dead."

Maddie internally congratulated herself. She knew his wife's name had been Gloria, but she commiserated with Peter's dour look.

"As I was going to say," continued Peter, "Frank has asked me to be the executor of his will and has given me power of attorney." Both Laura and Maddie gasped.

"I didn't know it was that bad!" Laura patted her chest as if she could stop the fluttering that Maddie could also feel in her own heart.

"It isn't," said Peter. "Right now he's been diagnosed with memory loss and depression and it's being managed with medication."

"You mean Alzheimer's?" asked Maddie.

"No. Not yet anyway. They're managing the symptoms but are still working on a diagnosis."

Maddie wondered how they could make sure that he took the medicine. She added: "But how? I've seen it myself, the way he pretends to take his pills."

"He and the nurses have worked out a system. They put it in his food. He knows it's there, but he conveniently forgets when they bring him an evening meal," explained Peter.

"I'm glad that he's getting his medication," said Maddie, "but I have to say, he's been saying a lot of weird things lately."

"Well," said Peter, "the nurse gave me a rundown on his medication, and she said that until they get the dosage right, it can have some strange side effects. So, we need to keep an eye out for confusion, particularly if he gets confused doing things that he normally does every day."

Maddie thought about the waterless bucket.

After Peter had left the building and Laura had busied herself in some other part of the studio, Maddie retrieved the *Mordon County Enquirer* that someone had pulled out of the waste basket. Losing students today was just one indication that the article had the potential to cause more damage to the studio's reputation than Maddie wanted to contemplate.

She reread Renée's article and swore as Laura re-entered the office with a watering can in her hand. "We don't need that kind of language here."

Maddie snickered. "I think it's exactly the kind of language we need. This paper is a joke. Look at some of these other articles. *Aliens Sighted in Boy's Choir*

Lavatory. What's that about?" Maddie flipped through the pages incredulously. "And this one! *The Mafia in Your Back yard. They're Here and They're Staying.* Now that sounds like quality investigative reporting."

Maddie nearly bowled Laura over with her next expletive. She looked up at the secretary. "Look at this!" Maddie thrust the article about the Mafia at Laura, pointing to the accompanying photo. "That man, I know him!"

Laura immediately dropped the watering can on the floor and snatched at the paper but Maddie wouldn't let it go.

"Wait! Let me read it."

"I thought you said this was a trashy paper."

"It is." Maddie turned the page back to the beginning of the article and caught her breath again as she stared at the photograph that took up the upper left hand corner of the page. Under the photograph was an article about a man found in the Passaic River with his hands in cement. Barely keeping her breathing even, she read aloud:

> The man found cemented in the Passaic River in a little used area outside the Loantaka Park between Pembroke and Mordon Hills, has been identified as Daniel Sambraus. Unlike a usual Mafia hit, this one did not end up with a dead body. Sambraus was found in ten inches of water with his hands chained and cemented to the shallow river bed, his head clear of the water by several inches. Did the mafia fail in there characteristic burial this time around? Unseasonably low water levels mean that maybe they meant for him to die. It was pure chance that he was found by retiree Richard Simpson walking his dog. Sambraus, originally from

Dorfen in the Bavarian region of Germany is 41 years old and has been remanded into custody by the Pembroke Police Department. We have been told by a reliable source that Sambraus is wanted in connection with the murder of a resident at the Shadylawn Retirement Village. Sambraus had numerous interactions with the Colombo family in Sicily where he spent several years before relocating to Atlantic City in 2000. Since then, he has been connected to several internal mafia family feuds, including the widely publicized Herara case. Daniel Sambraus has remained tight-lipped about who did this to him but those in the know don't have to guess.

Maddie had sat back down while reading the article, and when she looked up, Laura was looking intently at her.

"Maddie, what's the point?"

The point was, of course, that Maddie recognized the man in the article. She'd seen him last Friday in her Argentine Tango class. Maddie felt sick to her stomach. Daniel Sambraus looked a lot like Pierce Brosnan. Daniel Sambraus was the humble orderly at Shadylawn Retirement Village, the one who danced with all the frumpy ladies, the one who pissed Billy off enough to make him pick a fight.

Her initial instinct was to run to Joe and tell him about the article and the photo of the orderly, but she had to admit to herself that he would already know that Daniel Sambraus had been at the retirement village that evening. Joe would have interviewed people. He would have the whole thing under control. And he definitely would know that Daniel Sambraus had mafia connections. That's why he'd said that the situation was under control. She took another look at the photo and made a decision. She was going to call him anyway.

As Maddie took out her mobile phone, it began ringing.

"Maddie, it's Craig."

"Craig. I actually can't talk now. But I have something important to tell you. I just have to call Joe first." Maddie heard a sound she didn't recognize and stopped. "Craig, are you all right? Are you crying?"

"Maddie, they tried to kill Owen!"

"What? What are you talking about?"

"They found him an hour ago. A knife wound in his chest, just like the other guy. This time they didn't find the knife."

"But I thought he was under police guard. Is he all right?"

"He was under guard, but the officer must have taken a break. Luckily, a nurse walked in soon after it happened. She was able to get a doctor right away and they saved him. Seems the knife wound wasn't as deep as the other one. Maybe whoever did it got scared away before they were able to finish it."

"But this is crazy. Is Joe there?"

"The place is swarming with police. I just had to take a break. I'm going back to sit with Owen now, but I really need to see you."

Maddie didn't answer immediately, her mind trying to figure out what Joe was thinking, and wondering whether he was going to call her to tell her about the latest developments. Craig must have read something else in her silence.

"Maddie, please. I need you. I'm sorry about everything. I mean everything in California and everything earlier when we talked. I've been thinking a lot about us." Maddie, stunned into silence, didn't respond. "Maddie, I could use some support right now."

She sucked her breath in. "Of course, Craig. That's no problem. I can be there in about ten minutes."

"Thanks, Maddie."

Maddie hung up and ran out of the building without any explanation to an unimpressed Laura. As she started the car, turning the heat on full blast, her phone rang again. It was Joe.

"Joe, hi. Craig just called me. Is everything okay?"

Maddie heard the intake of Joe's breath. What followed caught her off guard. Joe's voice was alien to her.

"Maddie, under no circumstances are you to go to the Shadylawn Retirement Village. I'm going to repeat myself. You are not to go there. Do I make myself clear?"

None of the intimacies that Joe and Maddie had shared in the past month, few that they were, could be heard in his voice. Instead, the fact that he was trying to dictate what she could and couldn't do and with whom she did it rang loud and clear.

"Maddie, I want to hear you say that you heard me."

"Joe, I heard you. But Craig needs my support too. And I know you don't want to hear it, but I have to give it to him. He just asked me to come over and I'm going to."

"As long as it's not at the retirement village."

Maddie interrupted with her own growing frustration. "And I already told you, Joe, I'm teaching a class there tomorrow night and I'm not going to cancel it."

"Well, then, I'll have to cancel it for you." Several seconds of silence later, Maddie looked down at her screen to see that he had disconnected the call and she hadn't had the opportunity to ask him about Daniel Sambraus.

"Damn him, that bastard."

Maddie pulled up just around the corner from the retirement village and parked. She'd driven back to her parents' house and taken her mother's car in the hopes that Joe wouldn't recognize it. She wondered the whole way over just what she thought she was doing, knowing in her heart that there was no way she was going to get away with going into Shadylawn without bringing on the wrath of Joe, but inexplicably finding that she didn't care.

She told herself that calling Joe's office was a precaution, but really she knew she was just trying to make herself feel better. It was 5:30 and she'd noticed that his call had come from his office line. She called the main line back and was transferred to Maureen.

"Hi, Maureen, working late?"

"Actually, just leaving. Everything all right?"

"I just got off the phone with Joe but forgot to tell him something. Is he there?"

"He is but he's in a meeting and I think will be for the next hour or so. I'll leave a message for him."

"Hmmm...is the meeting there at the office? I'm coming down town anyway; I could stop by and hopefully catch him."

"Yep, here with the chief. I'll let him know."

"No, please don't. I'd like to surprise him."

Maddie hung up and drove around the corner and up to the gate. She had one hour.

At least Joe hadn't left her photograph at the guard gate with explicit instructions not to let her in. After several nervous minutes waiting to finally be told that Craig had requested her presence and she could go through, she made her way through the grounds and parked in the visitor's lot around the back.

Inside, the smells of heat and coffee and cloves permeated the air. There were several police officers walking around but none of them stopped Maddie.

Before she could get to the reception desk, Craig careened around the corner and rushed toward Maddie, hardly stopping as he threw his arms out to envelope her, sending both of them onto a sofa in the lounge. He mumbled something, but as his mouth was in her hair, she couldn't hear what he said. Finally, he broke away and Maddie instinctively looked into his eyes to see what he was thinking. Contrary to the frantic embrace, Craig's eyes seemed not panicked at all, but rather excited as his eyes roamed the room as if looking for someone.

"Is your uncle okay?"

Craig's eyes didn't meet Maddie's gaze and she instantly knew something was wrong.

"Craig, is he all right?" The panic in her voice finally drew his eyes to hers.

"Yeah, sorry, Maddie. He's stable. I can't wait to get him out of here. Detective Clancy said we can move him to another location to keep him safer." Craig pulled her by the hand off of the sofa and into a more private alcove sporting a love seat and several potted plants.

"Listen, did you talk to him? Did he say anything to you about...?" There Craig stopped, apparently stumped at how to go on.

"About what, Craig?"

Craig threw his hands up into the air and let them fall into Maddie's lap. "This. What the hell do you think?"

Maddie pushed his hands off her. "No. Contrary to your belief, I've hardly been able to talk to him and when I have it's only to be told to stay away from here, so I can't stay."

Craig's head swiveled at the sound of the elevator reaching the lobby. They both watched as the door opened and two uniformed police officers came out. Maddie slouched behind the potted plant.

"You mean, he didn't say anything about what line of inquiry they're taking."

"No, I've already said this, Craig. I can't get any information from Joe. You're Owen's nephew. You have the right to ask questions more than I do. Why don't you?"

"Look, Owen's delicate. I just don't want to be pushy."

That was one of the most insincere statements she'd ever heard come from Craig's mouth and she'd heard many. She watched as several expressions passed over his molded face, one more unlikely than the next. The first was shock, but it was quickly followed by bemusement. Then Craig put on his best wounded-puppy look, one that would have had Maddie backing down from a confrontation with him in another time and place.

"I've known you a long time, Craig. I know when you're lying."

"I have not lied about anything, Maddie. Do you think I didn't know this is a police investigation? I'm not naïve."

No, Maddie thought. *He wasn't naïve, far from it. But he was selfish and he was egotistical.*

"Craig, what information have you withheld from the police? Because I know it was enough to get Joe to consider taking you into custody for perverting the course of justice." After reading about Daniel Sambraus in the newspaper, she had a pretty good inkling as to what information Craig had withheld, but she wanted to make him say it.

"Really? Perverting the course of justice? I don't think they really use that expression anymore. You must have watched too many of those ancient British mysteries."

"Funny, Craig, really funny. I'm done." And Maddie was. She'd had a whole lot of epiphanies about her relationship with Craig in the past week, but this was the final straw. He must have read the finality in Maddie's expression because the consummate look of satisfaction on his exquisitely chiseled face melted off, ending in a look of surrender.

"I didn't say anything about it because it doesn't matter—not anymore. It's long in the past."

"Oh for freak's sake, Craig, what is it?" Maddie's stomach was churning in her growing anxiety, but she wasn't going to move until he'd spilled it.

"Owen was kind of involved with the mob."

Maddie didn't say anything. Craig's revelation wasn't a surprise, but she wasn't going to let him know that. She read Craig's indifference to his announcement as evasiveness and knew that there was no *kind of* involved with the mob. Owen had probably been in it up to his teeth. Maddie remained silent for what seemed like minutes, wanting to appear speechless in the face of this stereotypical explanation. Of course, Owen was in the mob. He lived in New Jersey. Wasn't everybody who lived in New Jersey involved in the mob? When she was in California, hadn't she been asked more times than she could count if it was true that Laundromats were actually mob fronts? After she'd watched Craig squirm for what she considered an appropriate time, she stood up.

"Right! Well, that explains it. You had to have known that Joe would have figured out that connection, didn't you?"

For an instant Craig looked truly puzzled. "No, actually I didn't. I usually find that most people conveniently don't try to figure out what they don't want to know."

"Maybe in your world, Craig, but not the real one." Maddie marveled at his apparent assumption of entitlement. "It was all a game to you, wasn't it? All cops and robbers and let's see how much I can get away with. You realize a man really died."

"Of course I do. That's why I asked you to help. I knew Uncle Owen wasn't an angel, but it was clear that someone was after him too. And I knew that once the police found out he was in the mob, they'd be prejudiced against him. I just needed a little help and then I was going to take him with me to California."

"What are you planning on doing with him, because I don't believe for a minute that you're going to take this time as an opportunity to make up for all the lost years."

Craig began to pace as he rubbed his hands together. "No, I am, Maddie. I meant it when I said that I want to get to know him. He's practically all the family I have left now."

She didn't get a chance to respond because the one voice she'd dreaded hearing rose above the ambient retirement home sounds. She hid further behind a palm. Craig heard Joe's voice too and reacted instantly.

"Don't worry, I'll distract him." Craig got up but turned back to her before leaving. "Thanks for coming, Maddie. I appreciate it."

"Shh...just get him away from here."

Craig disappeared around the corner where Joe's voice could still be heard talking to someone about surveillance tapes. Within seconds, Maddie heard Craig's voice an octave above his normal pitch.

"Detective Clancy, my uncle woke up and said he had something important to say to you." It was hard to imagine Joe believing Craig's insincere timbre, but he must have because the voices grew weak as the group rounded the corner, presumably heading to the elevators.

Maddie breathed deeply and took a peek around the corner, then scooted to the far hall leading to the frail care area where she knew there was another exit to the parking lot.

Nurse O'Neill sat at the counter of the nurse's station writing on a clipboard. Maddie was glad to see her and not her noxious boss. Somehow, she knew that Nurse Spring wouldn't have allowed her to pass through her territory. Beyond Nurse O'Neill's slender frame Maddie could see through a window and into a courtyard. Walking in a slow circle with his arm steadying someone bundled up in winter gear, Billy Holiday looked as if he were crooning to his paramour.

"He does a lot for the patients, doesn't he?"

Nurse O'Neill's head popped up, a huge smile on her face. She was laughing softly under her breath as if she'd just heard something funny.

"Yes. He gets here early and works late every day. He's saving to buy his mother a house. Isn't that sweet?"

Maddie looked at Nurse O'Neill who waited expectantly for an answer.

"I guess so."

Nurse O'Neill was ingenuous enough to beggar belief, Maddie thought, *but her innocence was certainly more welcome than Nurse Spring's brutish tactics.* Watching Billy's progress with his charge, Maddie had to admit that he looked the model employee. No one had a bad thing to say about him and that's what bothered her. A noise from further down the hall made her jump and she found Nurse O'Neill glaring at her. She was so surprised she blinked several times, sure that her eyes were playing tricks on her. Sure enough, when she looked back, the young nurse was smiling.

"Is there anything I can do for you?"

"No, no. I have to get going. I'm teaching tomorrow night though, so I'll be back."

Maddie said good night to the nurse and headed down the hall, pondering the fact that part of her wanted Joe to find her at the village after explicitly telling her not to step foot in the place. She began an internal monologue that used several choice expletives as she followed Nurse O'Neill's instructions to a door at the back of the building only to find herself face to face with a service elevator door that was at that moment sliding open. Her heart leapt into her throat as all bravado departed now that she was faced with the real possibility that Joe might walk out those doors. She was too far from the exit to make a getaway so she opened the courtyard door and closed it softly behind her.

Looking like he was enjoying every minute of it, Billy held the arm of a short woman in a white parka who resembled the Stay Puff Marshmallow Man. A bobbled hat, scarf and mittens completed her ensemble. Billy simply wore his white orderly coat with the addition of a matching Mets hat and scarf. The unlikely duo looked as if they were pretending to ice skate, Billy artfully swaying in a decent imitation of someone moving over ice, his partner valiantly trying to imitate his movement.

Maddie's conscience tugged at her as she watched the couple. Right now he certainly looked like he was going out of his way to make the lives of the residents enjoyable and, as far as the mob connection was concerned, there didn't seem any reason to think that anyone but Owen or Daniel were involved with Floyd's death. That's when she remembered the confrontation between Billy and the man she'd assumed was an orderly the night of the tango class.

Out of the direct path of the wind, she found it quite pleasant in the courtyard. Then she noticed that there were outdoor space heaters affixed to the walls hanging above them. *No expense was too much for these people,* Maddie mused.

"Well, if it isn't the tango teacher. What can we do you for?" asked Billy.

Maddie winced. "I hope I'm not disturbing you."

"Oh, not at all. We're just having a little skating under the stars. The ice is perfect!"

Maddie couldn't help but look down at the ground under Billy and his partner's feet. She raised her eyes to find raised eyebrows and a cheeky smirk.

"Please, join us. It's surprisingly fun. All you need is a little imagination. Isn't that right, Dina?"

Maddie watched as the marshmallow nodded her head and smiled up at Billy. Billy held her hand in the crook of his arm and whispered something in her ear. She nodded again and they started moving.

"We have a little more skating to do, but if you can keep up, you can join us and ask me what you want. It's about Floyd and Owen, right?"

The couple moved so slowly that Maddie had to smile. She realized with a start that it was a gift he gave to this woman. They'd reached the end of the courtyard as he stylishly steered her around an empty fountain with three cherubs sprouting out of the center of it as if continuing the circle of an ice rink.

"You know he was dying anyway. Even if he hadn't been knifed, he didn't have more than six months," explained Billy.

"What was wrong?"

"Nothing the doctor's could figure. Just getting old, ya know?"

"Yeah, I guess so."

"I'll tell you something else though." Maddie encouraged him with a nod.

"You may not care, but it's really bugging people that the police think that someone here killed Floyd then went and stabbed Owen."

"But someone here did do it."

"That's not what I mean. I mean a staff member."

"Why don't you think a staff member did it?"

"Because a staff member wouldn't knife him."

Maddie knew she was missing something, but didn't know what.

"Someone who worked here could do it so many other ways. You know—drugs and stuff. Smothering him, pushing him in a wheelchair into a lake. A knife is like, obvious."

Maddie almost laughed, but she could see Billy was serious. She glanced at Dina who remained oblivious to their conversation.

Maddie digested the information and nodded at Billy. It all made sense. Daniel Sambraus, the benign orderly was actually a mob hit man. He'd smuggled himself into the retirement village and killed Floyd. Then the mob took care of him, maybe trying to kill him or maybe they thought scaring him was enough, and now he was in police custody. Who knows what his mob connections were going to do about that. Maybe nothing.

That was it. Maddie felt let down. Somehow it was supposed to be more than that. Billy and Dina were skating as Maddie realized that she really did have to get out of there. Joe would have this all under control. If he caught her there, he'd really be angry with her and he'd have the right to be. It didn't mean she was going to cancel her class the next night but whatever feeble help she thought she could offer Craig was now over.

Billy brought his skating to a stop. "All right there, Dina! Our skating time is up. How 'bout we go and find you a hot chocolate?"

Maddie watched as he led Dina to the door and had to admit that there was something charming about Billy. Maybe she'd gotten it wrong. If she were to be honest with herself, she never really thought it was him. She just didn't like him and now she was embarrassed about her behavior.

"Thanks, Billy."

"Hey, no sweat, teach. Looking forward to your next class. See ya."

Maddie followed behind Billy and Dina, crossing the hall quickly to leave out the back door. She breathed easily for the first time in days. She'd go home and open one of her Dad's bottles of cabernet and eat a bowl of Thai red curry, another meal prepared by her mother so that she wouldn't starve. She vowed to thank her mother profusely. Assuming she could get out of the Shadylawn Retirement Village without Joe seeing her.

Chapter Seventeen

Maddie could hear Peter's voice through the closed door. "And with a final waltz to the eternal strums of Tchaikovsky, we will end class. Please change partners one more time."

The sounds of *Serenade for Strings* drifted out of the room and Maddie listened while sending a quick response to her mother's text—yet another request for a psychiatric update. She responded that she'd never felt better and that they need not hurry back. She also mentioned that she'd finished off a sizable portion of their wine collection to which her father replied that they would cancel the rest of the trip and be home within the hour. Maddie smiled as she put her phone away and the door to the classroom opened, Peter's class floating out like gazelles high on the dance of romance. Maddie greeted the few she knew and came into the classroom to find Peter giving an eager student the address of a shop that sold ballroom dance shoes.

"So, do you think I should get a pair for ballroom and a pair for Latin?"

"I love the enthusiasm but I'd recommend that you only buy one pair to start. The fact is, unless you're going to perform, the shoes are virtually the same. The differences are made up by the marketers."

"Oh, but I plan to perform. And teach!" The student added the second profession as an afterthought. Maddie caught Peter's raised eyebrow and stifled a laugh. The guy standing in front of Peter didn't look half bad. Good looking in a Matt Damon kind of way, the muscles of his biceps bulging out of his pink and green striped Izod. If his enthusiasm was anything to judge his dancing talent by, he might go far.

"And I'd like to start competing. You said that you trained for competitions here too?"

Peter nodded. "If you go down to the office, I'll be right there and I can tell you about it." The young man bounded out of the room with all the joy of a puppy let off a leash. Peter laughed after he'd had gone. "Ah, to be that young again. Between Nikki and me, Scott Tunbridge has taken ten classes in the past two weeks. I feel like he's the only person I've taught."

"Think he might burn out before Christmas?"

"I don't know. I have a good feeling about him. A little hyperactive maybe, but there's potential there."

"Reminds me a little of someone else I know."

Peter looked at Maddie in mock surprise. "What? Me? I'm much better looking. But thinking ahead about what you and I talked about yesterday? I'm thinking about *him*."

Maddie stood puzzled before putting it all together, then she was horrified. "What? Scott Tunbridge becoming my partner? Dancing Argentine Tango? Tell me you're kidding!"

"I'm not actually. I have an idea. I want to start training my own teachers. Get them proficient on all dances but have them focus on one. He'll need lessons which we'll provide for free and in return he'll assist in classes and the office and wherever else we can find use for him." Peter looked pleased with himself.

"So now we'll have a studio slave?"

"Well, that's putting a negative spin on it. I prefer to think of it as vocational training. What do you think?"

"It could work. But just to make sure we're on the same page, what is this we'll *teach for free* bit?"

"The studio will pay you as if you were teaching a group class."

Peter had taken his John Lennon glasses out of his pocket and perched them on his nose. His phone beeped and he whipped it out of another pocket, looked at the screen and grinned.

"Look! Yoko's put this up on Facebook."

He turned the screen so Maddie could see his daughter propped up in the corner of a sofa next to their St. Bernard, Dr. Faustus. *Yoko* was Peter's nickname for Kristy. Back when they were dating it was too much for their collective friends to ignore the fact that he bore a strong resemblance to John Lennon and that Kristy was Asian. While those friends never called her that after the two became a permanent couple, Peter still uses it as a term of endearment.

"Peter, before you go, I just wanted to update you on something." Peter raised his head from the screen.

"It's just that I had a conversation with Joe and he told me that I shouldn't teach at the retirement village tonight. Of course, I told him that I was going to. I just wanted you to know in case he calls here."

"He already did."

"What? When? I spoke with him this morning."

"About an hour ago. Just before I went in to teach class."

"And?"

"And, he told me that he'd asked you not to teach, that you'd disagreed with his opinion and that if I cared about your safety, I would cancel the class."

"And?"

"And, I told him that I did care about your safety and that I'd discuss this with you."

"Now wait, Peter. Joe is being unreasonable. First of all, everything looks like it's being cleared up at the retirement village. It has nothing to do with me."

Peter held his hand up. "Now, let me finish. He has a point and what I said was that I really can't in good faith cancel the class, but that I'd teach it if I had to."

"Peter, you're a great dancer, but you don't teach Argentine Tango."

"I had to make something up as I was going along, Maddie. I wasn't lying. I do care about your safety. If nothing else, I'm assisting you like I did last week."

Maddie relaxed. "That's great. I appreciate it."

"Aren't you worried at all? I mean, after what happened here during the fall, and now this. I have to admit, I'm not completely comfortable. And Kristy is at me not to go the village. The only way I could get her to calm down was to say that we needed the gig. It's too much money to stop now."

"Look, I really think Joe is overreacting because of...well, our relationship. I'm really not worried. There will be police there. Tell Kristy that."

"Anything new on Craig's uncle?"

"He's stable." Maddie didn't let on to Peter that she knew anything about mob connections. That was Joe's department.

"And how's the rest of it?" Maddie looked blankly at Peter. He returned her incredulous stare.

"The Joe, *I used to be married to you* bit and the Craig, *you broke up with me when you decided you were gay* bit and the *both men are vying for my attention in my hometown* bit. To spell it out."

Maddie burst out laughing. "It kind of sucks actually. Craig is being all clingy. Not that he's vying for me, mind you. I just think he needs the support and he's used to me being there. Joe, on the other hand, doesn't want to see me until the investigation is over."

"Sensible."

Maddie's heart thudded in her ribcage. "I think our burgeoning relationship is dead before it even started."

Peter reached out and squeezed her arm, singing some of the schmaltzy lyrics from "I'm Goin' Wash That Man Right Outa My Hair," in his own wobbly baritone.

Maddie sighed.

"I don't know which is more worrisome, that you're able to quote Nellie Forbush verbatim, or that I know it's from *South Pacific*."

"Never underestimate the power of the American musical," stated Peter. "They hold the solutions to all life's problems."

Peter left to get eager Scott sorted out with his new career as a dance teacher, as Maddie's class began to trickle in.

Later that day, Maddie argued with Joe for ten minutes to get him to relent and allow her to teach the class that night. While she knew she would teach it no matter what his reservations were, she also knew she'd feel better if he knew exactly where she stood. He finally agreed, saying that he'd both pick her up and take her home and that he'd be there for the entire class. *Well, at least I'm getting a pseudo date out of him.* However, when he arrived to pick her up at her parents' house, she realized the mistake she'd made in thinking it was anything like a date.

She'd finished getting ready and was catching up on some emails to friends back in LA, dismissing Craig's arrival in a manner she hoped sounded blasé, when she heard a car pull into the drive. After several minutes, she realized that Joe wasn't going to come to the door so she gathered her stuff. Outside, she opened the front passenger door to find Officer Rodrigues already ensconced in the seat with a cup of coffee. Her face burning, Maddie shut the door and climbed into the back.

"Officer Rodrigues will be joining us for the evening." There was a smugness in Joe's voice Maddie didn't like, and she glanced at the female officer in the front seat. Officer Rodrigues, however, sipped her coffee and remained inscrutable. Maddie recognized her from the murders at the dance studio the previous year, but the buff police officer didn't acknowledge any previous contact. Both officers simply waited while Maddie fastened her seat belt before Joe started the engine.

"Fine. We have to go or I'll be late."

"Before we get to the village, there are a couple of things I want to go over," said Joe.

"Don't say anything, please. I'm doing what you asked me to do and I just want this night to end."

"You're not doing what I asked. What I asked is that you *not* teach the class."

"Okay, let's just not talk. We're obviously going to disagree about this. I *will* teach the class. You will then drive me home. I've agreed."

Officer Rodriguez took another sip of coffee. Joe looked at Maddie in the rearview mirror. Maddie looked out the window and sighed. Joe seemed to have made a decision and flipped the radio on. WCBS still played an agonizing variety of 60s 70s and 80s cheese. *The Best of Times* by Styx was on. Maddie shook her head and chuckled.

"You've always had the worst taste in music."

Joe looked into his rearview mirror and connected with Maddie's gaze. Pulling his own gaze back to the road, he seemed to deliberate whether or to accept the parlay as Maddie toyed with a paperclip sitting on the seat next to her. She silently wondered why it was there. *Couldn't it be used to open handcuffs?* The song ended and a new one began. Finally, Joe relented and his voice was just audible out over REO Speedwagon's *I Can't Fight this Feeling Anymore*.

"Maybe so."

The song ended and they neared the retirement village. They pulled through the gate without incident, parked and Officer Rodriguez left them alone to walk up to the building together.

"Joe, I know you don't want to hear this, but.."

"Then don't say it."

"Just give me a chance."

Joe's eyes narrowed.

"Look, I just want you to know that there's nothing but friendship between me and Craig, and even that's pushing it. I really don't think that his uncle had anything to do with Floyd's death." Joe remained silent. As they got to the door, Joe opened it for Maddie and waited for her to walk through.

"You must see that now that someone's tried to kill *him,* and you must know that it was Daniel Sambraus who killed Floyd."

Joe stood with his hand on the door, remaining unnaturally silent. Without turning to Maddie, he spoke without any emotion. "First, you should have just stopped with your first statement. Second, did you pick up the expertise to pick out a criminal and solve a murder in dance school? Because if that's the case, I'll let human resources know that we've been overlooking a potential avenue for future recruitment. Third, I assume you and your so-called ex-boyfriend talked about his uncle's involvement with the mob. And fourth, for someone who feels they've solved the whole mystery, it's astonishing me that you don't understand the significance of Daniel Sambraus being in *custody* when the attempt on Owen's life occurred."

Joe walked through the door without waiting for Maddie. *I deserved that,* she thought. That and the fact that there was still a murderer on the loose should have made her just want to go home, turn off all the lights and climb into bed with a bar of dark chocolate. But she didn't. She wanted to teach her class.

Joe thought it would be harder for him to leave Maddie behind without apologizing or at least without trying to mend part of the bridge they'd broken. But it wasn't.

He felt both sick to his stomach at his own reaction and frustrated enough to want to shake some sense into her because of *her* behavior. Why the hell could she not see that there was a murderer on the loose? Her parents were right. He *would* protect her, even if it was from herself. And even if protecting her meant that he would loose her—again.

Chapter Eighteen

Joe left her in the lobby and disappeared down the hall. A beep signaled that she had a text message and she looked down to see that Peter wouldn't be able to make it after all. Kristy had a migraine. *Right, a migraine. Perfect timing.* Maddie couldn't get the idea out of her head that Kristy disliked her. Maddie continued her uncharitable inner dialogue as she peeked into the room. She wasn't trying to steal Kristy's husband, that's for sure, but she sure wished Peter were with her tonight.

The room teemed with people; more dancers had shown up than had been there the previous week. *Well, at least murder hadn't dissuaded the population of the retirement village from attending class,* Maddie thought grimly. The sound of a sultry rumba played on the sound system as Maddie searched the room for Sam and Dottie. She couldn't find them but instead found herself drawn to Berta who was looking agitated as she stood alone by a pedestal which was adorned with a vase of long-stemmed roses. Maddie instinctively looked for Rolf but didn't see him.

Maddie groaned as she watched Berta make a beeline to where she stood, rooted in the doorframe. The older woman had almost crossed the distance between them when she came to an abrupt stop mid-motion. Expecting the worst, Maddie was surprised as she watched Berta's face crumple in emotion, then fix itself into a plastic smile.

"Darling, I'm so glad you decided to come!"

Unsure what she expected to find, Maddie tentatively turned to find Rolf a foot behind her, his tuxedo as immaculate as ever. Without a word, Rolf held his hand out to his wife, and as she took it with an intake of breath, he nodded to Maddie and spoke with solemnity.

"It has been a pleasure. Please know that I will remember your kindness always." Maddie watched as Rolf held his wife elegantly in his arms. Tears were already forming in the corners of Berta's eyes, but she raised her chin and took her husband's arm. It would have been a stunningly romantic picture if Maddie didn't know that something was drastically wrong.

Rolf immediately led Berta in a dizzying set of spins that caused her feather-encased arm to swing dangerously close to Maddie, then crossed the room at a manic pace.

Maddie glanced to both sides, wondering if anyone else had seen Rolf's strange behavior, but all she noticed were dismissive expressions aimed briefly toward the couple and then dropped as the students in the class chatted with one another in what Maddie could only call a pleasantly agitated volume. She moved over to the sound system and as the rumba ended, she changed the music to an Argentine Tango. Some of the residents clapped appreciatively. Several students came up to her and she answered a series of implausible questions as she put her practice shoes on— —so many questions that Maddie suspected that several of the students were just making up bizarre reasons to talk to her.

Suddenly, a blur of motion distracted her from the two women in front of her. The couple whirling around the dance floor were so unlike the Berta and Rolf from last Friday night's Argentine Tango class that Maddie had to do a double-take. Moving out of rhythm to the music playing, Maddie would have almost accepted that they were imposters. As they drew closer to her, she could hear their unmistakable voices arguing.

"Darling, please listen to me! Let's sit down."

"I've had enough. I will dance! You're trying to stop me!"

"Darling, you need to see the doctor."

"Berta, you promised!".

"No, please, don't make me. Please, we can find another way."

"There *is* no other way. And this is the way I want it. You promised!"

"I did."

"This will also give you notoriety."

"I *thought* that's what I wanted, but I know now that it's not."

Berta's last words were swallowed in a stifled cry as they then danced out of earshot. Maddie caught the look of sheer terror on Berta's face before Rolf danced her across the floor. Berta's complexion had become an unhealthy raspberry hue as she unsuccessfully tried to keep composed. Rolf's face, on the other hand, was as serene as a sleeping baby's. While they seemed to have stopped arguing, even from across the room, Maddie could read Berta's nonverbal communication, and she was only too glad that she was not the one within range of its pain. Other dancers made way for the couple as they careened around the room. Maddie decided to stop them as they came to her side again. She didn't think they were older than 70, but she wasn't sure they'd be able to make another pass based on the colors they were turning and she was determined to defuse their destructive energy before it ruined the entire class.

"Berta, Rolf! I'm about to start class! Would you care to dance a ballroom tango before we start?" She immediately pressed a button on her iPod, then turned back to Berta and Rolf and nodded to them. Rolf continued to hold out his arm to Berta and while she hesitated, all the while looking at Maddie with a combination of frustration and embarrassment, she eventually took Rolf's hand and allowed herself to be led to the center of the room.

As they passed her, Maddie heard Rolf say, "This will make the perfect ending."

Berta nodded but Maddie noticed that it didn't look like she agreed with her husband. Her request for them to show off had done what she'd hoped it would. The anxious air that had permeated the room just moments ago had been dispelled.

Turning away briefly from the couple, Maddie caught sight of Joe in the doorway of the ballroom. He had Nurse Spring beside him, hanging on to his every word, but his eyes were glued to Maddie as he stepped back out into the hallway and closed the door. Distracted momentarily by his presence, it took Maddie a few seconds to recognize that the murmurs that normally existed in any class had escalated and were growing louder. She turned to look to where everyone else's attention seemed to be drawn and saw Berta and Rolf at the far end of the room moving through an intricate combination of *slip pivots* and *oversways,* steps more suitable to a quick-step than a tango. As several gasps stopped all activity in the room, Maddie considered that maybe the other members of the class recognized the inappropriate steps too and so it was a full ten seconds later that she realized that something was horribly wrong. recognized that something was horrifically wrong. A single piercing cry brought her focus to the far side of the dance floor.

She snapped the music off, which only spurred the entire population of the room to all start talking at once. As the source of the commotion came into view, the doors to the ballroom were flung open and a half dozen nurses, orderlies and police officers charged in, Joe at the helm.

Within the agitated crowd of students, Maddie could see Berta in her peacock dress, standing erect over the tuxedoed legs of her husband, now prostrate on the floor and jerking convulsively. Berta stood like a statue above him, her eyes fixed on the ceiling. Maddie's hand reached up to cover her mouth, trying to mask the strangled noise that threatened to erupt from her throat. She didn't succeed because the woman standing next to her reached her arm around Maddie and spoke:

"Now, dear, don't worry. This isn't your fault." But Maddie knew—somewhere deep down—that it was.

Chapter Nineteen

Once Joe reached the center of the room, he slowed down to take in the scene, so Nurse O'Neill was actually the first person to reach Rolf. As she descended to the floor next to him, a look of utter disbelief stretched across her face. She pulled something out of her pocket, looked at it, then put it back. Almost immediately, she replaced her worried expression with one of determination, and Maddie watched as she became efficient, pushing Berta who had not moved from her position standing astride her husband's chest, aside ungraciously. The nurse busily felt for a pulse and checked Rolf's breathing when Maddie heard Joe's compelling voice over the anxious murmurs.

"Please! Would everyone take a seat somewhere in this room and remain there until you hear otherwise!" Groans were heard around the room as well as cries of indignation, but most of the dance students sat themselves in chairs along the wall, too stunned, it seemed, to make any noise at all.

Rolf's body continued to jerk, but less violently and as each convulsion ebbed in intensity, Nurse O'Neill lost her efficient manner and a wild look took over her features. When Rolf grew still, it was a complete still, and Maddie understood that his life had seeped out of him, regardless of the nurse's ministrations. Nurse O'Neill remained next to Rolf, but seemed unable to behave like a nurse. Instead, she scratched at the floor next to him, sometimes connecting with Berta's unmoving foot.

208 Dead Man Dancing

Maddie looked around the room and then turned back to watch the commotion around Rolf. Another doctor, not Doctor Marlowe, but an older female physician with masses of jet-black curling hair, had arrived on the scene and had taken over next to Nurse O'Neill. Maddie now watched as the nurse lifted Rolf's hand off the floor, again and again, before emotion seemed to overwhelm her and she rose off the ground and turned towards the door. Tears streamed down her face, but Maddie couldn't help but think that she looked more angry than sad. Finding herself in the nurse's path, Maddie conscientiously stepped aside. Nurse O'Neill passed by, however, as if she couldn't even see her.

Then, from near by, Maddie heard a voice that she recognized rise above the others. She turned to find Sam and Dottie conspiring with several friends. A woman Maddie didn't know spoke up.

"And now another one! These classes get more dangerous every day. Sam, call a meeting! It's time we get to the bottom of this!" Several of the students nodded in unison toward a blonde woman wearing enormous hoop earrings.

Sam looked thoughtful and said, "At least he doesn't have a knife sticking out of him."

Dottie swatted at him. "Sam, this is serious!" Then she noticed Maddie. "Oh, Maddie! Elsie didn't really mean your classes. She just meant that, well, another person has died."

The blonde woman spoke again:

"I sure as hell meant these classes! You hear what people are saying? I came tonight just to get a look. Glad I did too!"

"*What* are people saying?" she asked, but Maddie knew the answer to that and didn't say anything as the blonde woman stood defiantly and Dottie looked sheepishly toward Rolf's body.

"Maddie, come with us. You have as much to lose as anyone here. People are dying; you're gaining a bad reputation, dear." Dottie patted her on the arm. "You don't deserve it, of course. Come with us."

Maddie had to put a stop to this. She wouldn't allow the studio's reputation to be damaged like this. But while she had to think of something to do, she had no intention of joining this old folks' crime-solving meeting. However, she didn't get a chance to state her intentions before Joe's voice bellowed from nearby. He was close enough that he probably could have whispered, but Maddie read his intention immediately.

"Maddie will *not* be joining any meeting! Maddie will be escorted home now." Joe took her none too carefully by the elbow and led her away from the gaping mouths of Sam and Dottie and the gleeful blonde.

"Joe, that wasn't my fault! I didn't say anything and there was no way I was going to meet with them."

Joe kept his hand on Maddie's elbow as he escorted her out of the ballroom and into the hallway.

"I'd like to know why you're here every time someone dies!"

Both Joe's fists were clenched and Maddie got the feeling he was only keeping them at his sides through enormous self-control. His eyes bore into her while he waited for an answer.

"Now you're sounding like all these gossiping retirees. I have no idea what you're talking about!"

Joe sighed as if having to explain a simple concept to someone over and over again.

"No, I'm sure you don't! The fact is, I don't know whether to believe you or not, but that's irrelevant right now. I want you out of here and whatever's going on in there!"

"But how could Rolf's situation have anything to do with Floyd and Owen?"

"It doesn't."

"But you still want me gone?"

"Yes, I still want you gone!"

"Okay, but .."

Joe put his finger up to Maddie's lips in what would have been a seriously sexy gesture had the wrath in his face not been there.

"It's not your concern. Do you understand me?" Joe lowered his finger and seemed about to say something when his eyes flickered away from Maddie and to something behind her.

"Mr. Cavendish! Another person I'd like to have a chat with."

Maddie swung her head around and caught the look of surprise on Craig's face. Her head swung between Joe's look of authority and Craig's growing unease. There were sides to both of these men that she wished she'd never seen and she wasn't enjoying the view.

"Well, I'll just be going now." Maddie backed away from the threatening territory war, forgetting for the moment that Joe was the one who was supposed to take her home. Maddie sighed. "You must be busy here. You don't need to take me now. I can wait in the lobby. I promise I won't budge."

"I'm not taking you. Stay!" He turned and motioned to Officer Rodrigues standing at attention in the threshold of the ballroom.

"Officer Rodrigues will drive you home." Dropping her arm, he turned abruptly and walked back the way they'd come. "This way, Mr. Cavendish!"

Craig took a second to look back at Maddie. She didn't miss his wink.

"Did he just tell you to *stay*?" Craig then pantomimed a begging dog, and when he didn't get a reaction out of Maddie, he shrugged it off. "And what's with the bad cop persona?" He pretended to shoot imaginary pistols, a sure sign that he was more nervous than he wanted to let on.

Maddie ignored Craig and followed Officer Rodrigues to Joe's car to be driven home by the silent officer. She looked forward to climbing into bed but had no such luck. As soon as she turned the lock in the door, the phone rang. She let it ring until finally it stopped, only to start again immediately. Knowing instinctively that it was her parents and that they would keep ringing until she answered or until they got transportation to take them from wherever they were in Canada to Pembroke. The image of a helicopter hovering over the train they were on, her parents, jumping off and climbing a rope ladder to the helicopter Indiana Jones-style to save their daughter made her giggle before she acquiesced and picked up the phone.

"Maddie, how'd your class go?" It was her mother with her distinctive concern sound carrying over the phone line. However, Maddie had no intention of telling her mother anything about another retiree collapsing in yet another one of her classes.

"I'm fine, just tired." And all of a sudden, she did feel tired. Tired of the sheer number of times and ways her parents asked her if she was well. *How are you? Everything all right? You doing okay, kiddo? How's it all going, honey? You feeling all right? Do you need to speak to anyone?*

And her replies were no better. *Yep, everything's great. Never been better. Nothing like a bit of murder and mayhem. Ex-boyfriends making passes at you? Ex-husbands brushing you off? No money. Job precariously balanced on the whims of a nurse turned newspaper reporter with an ax to grind. Bring it on! It all just adds to the magical, mysterious life of Maddie Fitzpatrick.*

Why hadn't she noticed this farce that she and her parents had been acting out for the past two months? Did she want it to continue this way?

"Actually, it wasn't great but I really don't want to talk about it.

"But, Maddie, what happened?"

"Mom." Maddie tried to sound determined but her mother's voice was one that Maddie knew all too well. It said that she would tell her mother what was happening and that she would feel better after. This was the mother she knew in high school. Maddie sat on the sofa and curled her legs up under herself.

"It's just that Craig being here has thrown me. I'm over him and I'm mad at him and I want to help him because. Because..."

"Because you loved him."

"Maybe. But I'm angry because he withheld information from the police and Joe thinks that I knew that and Joe won't even talk to me now."

"What information?"

"Oh, just that Craig's uncle was in the mob."

She could here the intake of breath over the phone and her father's voice in the background asking Hillary what was wrong.

"Maddie, you listen to what Joe says and stay away from the retirement village."

Maddie didn't catch the sound of horror in her mother's voice and she continued as if she hadn't heard her.

"Yes, and then there's Joe. I don't know what's going to happen with us. It's not like I moved back here expecting to get back together with him, and yet it seems I can't go a day now without wondering if he's going to call." Maddie couldn't believe that she'd admitted this intimate fact to her mother. With years of experience, Maddie knew how to keep any information regarding Joe a secret from her parents.

"And then there's the fact that another man died at Shadylawn tonight and people are canceling classes at the studio right and left, and Laura seems to have a vendetta out for me because I dared to chastise her work practices, and Frank is seriously losing his mind, and I haven't looked for an apartment."

Hillary finally burst out laughing. After a delay of ten seconds during which Maddie wondered if she'd missed something, she joined her mother. Between snorts, Maddie wiped the tears from her eyes.

"I could write the script for a soap opera, right?"

Ten minutes later, she'd hung up feeling slightly better and promising her parents to take care. After brushing her teeth, she noticed a police car parked outside her parent's house. Officer Rodrigues sat in the front seat, an insulated mug in one hand and a grumpy expression on her face. Maddie closed the curtains and went to bed. *There was no need for the police vigilance*, she reasoned. Maddie had made a decision about how her weekend was going to go and it didn't involve any ex-boyfriends or dead bodies.

Unfortunately, that wasn't exactly what happened. While Saturday morning dawned in a promising fashion and she spent the day driving from one side of Pembroke to the other looking at apartments, by Sunday morning her good intentions had faltered when she remembered that she'd left her bag with her IPod and dance gear inside in the ballroom of the Shadylawn Retirement Village.

Reversing her car out of the driveway, she made a deal with herself. This would be the last time she would go to the retirement village and then she wouldn't step foot in there again except to teach her class. She had a legitimate reason to go there now, so if Joe happened to be there she'd be able to defend herself.

Reversing out of her parent's driveway over the light snow that had fallen during the night, she wondered whether the retirement village would want to keep the classes going. Her gut instinct told her that they wouldn't—another death during another class was likely one straw too many. Only when she was actually on the road did she admit to herself that she wanted to get into the retirement village one more time because something still wasn't sitting right with her.

In her mind, Maddie re-visited each time she'd seen Rolf and Berta together. Virtually all of her experience with them had come from watching them on the dance floor. The control they executed was remarkable, but from the distress that Berta exhibited during Rolf's rapid deterioration, she sensed that these control issues extended into their non-dancing lives as well. But what bothered her the most was that Rolf had seemed to go from one end of the spectrum to the other in a matter of days. Thinking of Frank's similar behavior, she wanted to ask Nurse O'Neill if that was considered normal. She also acknowledged that Frank's behavior at the studio bore a similarity to Rolf's behavior.

There was no line at the retirement gate and after only a couple of nervous moments waiting for clearance, Maddie was let through. There was a new face behind the reception desk and Maddie told the young woman that she was there to see Berta, planning to collect her bag after she'd spoken to her.

The receptionist's bland expression was inscrutable but he gave Maddie directions to the suite that Berta and Rolf had shared. Maddie didn't know where she had gotten the nerve to lie, but was grateful to have gotten by the receptionist unquestioned. Otherwise she would have had to revert to Plan B which, though she didn't have it mapped out, would have entailed Craig getting involved.

Maddie came to Rolf and Berta's door and knocked. She didn't know what to expect: Berta wild with grief or maybe in a catatonic depression. But what she was greeted with shocked her to the core. Berta answered her knock with her hair and face impeccably made-up, her outfit crisp and clean, reminding Maddie of a Stepford wife. Berta looked momentarily surprised to see Maddie at her door, but recovered quickly and asked her in for coffee.

"I expected you to be the police."

Maddie entered, but didn't know how to respond. From Berta's resigned tone, it sounded more like the police were doing her a favor rather than issuing a command.

"You have to understand," explained Berta. "Rolf would have hated himself and me if I'd let him suffer through it. I did what he wanted."

Maddie pushed the idea percolating in her head aside. Berta wasn't really telling her what she thought she was telling her. Was she? Berta continued:

"But he wanted it. He wasn't so far gone that he wasn't able to tell me that. And we'd talked about it, of course. We knew what we expected of each other. What frightened him the most was losing control. In some of his better moments this past week he said it felt like an alien had taken over his body. He was saying and doing things that he had no control of. He said he was on the inside looking out, but he couldn't control himself. He was frightened and that made him ashamed."

Maddie didn't know what to say. She'd been brought to speechlessness on several occasions in the past week. Berta admitting to helping her husband kill himself not only stunned her into silence, but it broke her heart. She wasn't sure, but she suspected that Berta's actions would be considered manslaughter in New Jersey.

The silence between the women stretched out and then Berta rallied.

"Judge me if you want; I don't care. My life is over anyway."

"I'm not judging you, Berta. I don't know the laws about assisted suicide. I feel helpless. I didn't understand until now. But how...?" Maddie stopped in embarrassment, realizing that she'd just asked a woman how her husband had killed himself. Berta's hand fluttered into the air as if both the question and the answer were irrelevant.

"It's easy. To get the medicine needed to make one die is easy."

Maddie swallowed audibly. "How long was Rolf experiencing symptoms?"

"A week, maybe a little more. So sudden." Berta's eyes drifted to several photographs on the wall, all depicting similar scenes: Rolf and Berta dressed in ballroom competition wear, dancing, holding trophies, holding one another. Maddie felt an overwhelming sense of loss.

"It does seem extraordinary that it happened so quickly. And that he didn't want to try..."

Berta stopped Maddie short. "To see if he could be helped?" The question was asked as if Maddie were an idiot. "No! He wanted to die before he turned into a vegetable."

Maddie picked needlessly at a doily resting on the table, unable to comprehend how someone could choose to end their life after experiencing symptoms for only one week.

"I...well, if there's anything I can do for you..."

"Yes. Actually, there is. Though I'm surprised that you're the one I should tell, but I feel that I must. I've seen something happening here at Shadylawn and I suspect that it's illegal."

Maddie waited while Berta appeared to think about her next words when she heard what could only be described as a growl from the direction of the front door. Someone must have come in through the front door unseen by Berta or Maddie because when Maddie looked to Berta, the older woman had a look of horror on her face. Maddie swiveled slowly to find Nurse O'Neill looming over the both of them.

In a voice that didn't mask her fury, Nurse O'Neill spewed, "How dare you!" Nurse O'Neill's eyes had shrunk to slits, with spit actually flying from her mouth as she repeated herself over and over, her rage increasing to fever pitch.

"How dare you! You don't know what you've done! You had no right to take him. You had no right!"

Nurse O'Neill became incoherent in her wrath. As the ever-increasing volume of her voice carried out through the doorway, several people had come running to see what the problem was.

"It was you! It was you. You murdered your husband, you damn, stupid, bitch!"

Nurse O'Neill reached out her hand and slapped Berta before Maddie could react and help the seventy-year-old woman out of the path of the nurse's rage. Maddie could still hear the ring of the slap as a massive red handprint appeared on the old woman's face. Berta didn't move. She didn't even flinch. It seemed to Maddie that, like Berta had said, her life was over, she'd already left. Then Nurse O'Neill grabbed at Berta's perfectly coiffed hair. Only then did Berta try to dodge the frenzied nurse's fury.

Two orderlies who Maddie didn't recognize grabbed at Nurse O'Neill in an effort to restrain her, but she wriggled away from them and fled toward the door, screaming as she did.

"It was you! How dare you? You'll regret this! I'll never let you forget. Till the day you die, I will follow you!"

Both Maddie and Berta seemed struck dumb, but Maddie was also struck by the fact that in Nurse O'Neill's tirade, she sounded like Owen when he was raging at Floyd outside the library. The orderlies followed the nurse's flight out the doorway, one of them yelling back that he would have a nurse come immediately to check on Mrs. Rapp. Maddie turned back to Berta, who had her hand now gingerly cradling her cheek. Maddie could make out a welt in the middle of it, a residual mark of the ring on Nurse O'Neill's finger.

"Berta, is there anything I can do for you?"

Berta shook her head in three precise movements. "No, there is nothing you can do. I've done it. I will take my punishment and I will join my husband soon."

Maddie shivered though the heat was on high in the room. "Berta, please, you might be able to do something. I'm sure that someone will listen to the circumstances."

Berta stood up with a regal air. "No, I will *not* be committing suicide if that's what you mean. Unlike my husband, I'm not that brave. I will wait for my time and join him then." She paused before leaving the room, turning to gaze at Maddie.

"Thank you for the last dance, Maddie. It was the way he wanted to go. When I knew he would not change his mind, I urged him to remain here, to do the deed in private. But being in the spotlight was his life and that was the way he wanted it to end."

Berta left the living room and Maddie heard a door closing further down the hallway of the couple's suite. She took that as her cue to leave and retraced her footsteps back to the lobby where a wave of panic suddenly overtook her. Sensing she was about to faint, she sat in the empty waiting room with her head between her knees, her breath ragged as she tried to force down the unexpected emotions that were trying to claim her.

Maddie wasn't sure how long she'd been sitting there, but the next thing she knew, Joe was in the doorway of the room and he didn't look happy.

"Maddie, what the hell are you doing here?"

Maddie jumped out of her chair, nearly toppling both it and her.

"I...uh, had to collect my bag. I left it here on Friday."

Joe looked down at her clearly empty hand.

"And I talked to Berta. Her husband is dead."

Joe ran his hand through his hair. "I know. That's why *I'm* here." The way he emphasized *I'm* made Maddie squirm. She hated feeling like a truant child with him.

"It was an assisted suicide."

"Again, Maddie, I know. That's why I'm here." This time there was no emphasis on *I'm*. "Can I drive you home?"

"What do you mean, you know?"

"Berta called the police station this morning and confessed. That's why I'm here."

Maddie absorbed that piece of information. "Joe, can I tell you something?"

Joe pursed his lips. "Does it have anything to do with any of the deaths here at the village?"

"Yes."

"Then, no. Come on, I'm taking you home."

"Damn it, Joe, you're so infuriating. I could have good information and you're completely ignoring it. It could help you solve the case."

Joe threw his hands into the air at his sides. "Me? I'm frustrating? Maddie have you not stopped to consider that you are *not* a police officer, or a detective, or a private eye, or Nancy Drew! You teach dance. You write about dance. I have no idea how you do it. I don't try to do it. That would be a ridiculous fiasco."

Even Maddie had to smile at the image of Joe trying to teach a tango class.

"I know, Joe. I'm not trying to take the place of a highly trained, super successful officer of the law. I just..."

"Maddie, this isn't funny."

"I know, sorry, I just think that something is still not right. I think we've all missed something."

Joe shook his head, not in disagreement, but in exasperation. "There is no *we*, Maddie." Joe stood at the door, clearly expecting Maddie to follow him.

Maddie rose. The further she got from her conversation with Berta, the more she realized that she didn't know what she wanted to say anyway. Something was still wrong at Shadylawn, but Joe was right. There was no reason to think that she would have more insight than the police. The police knew about the assisted suicide and Nurse O'Neill's widely inappropriate behavior wasn't her problem either.

"Fine, and I don't need a ride. I drove."

"You look like you weren't feeling well. Let me drive you."

Maddie knew he was only offering to drive her because he wanted to make sure that she left. "I said no. And I meant no."

Maddie found her bag back at the reception desk, then left through the front door and walk around to the side of the building. The wind had picked up but at least it wasn't snowing again. As she reached into her bag for her keys, she felt a presence coming up fast on her left side. Before she had a chance to turn, a large object soared through the air and hit her squarely on the side of her head. She fell before she knew what hit her.

Chapter Twenty

Maddie woke with a headache she couldn't remember ever having the better of. It made her feel nauseous just opening her eyes, so after one attempt she didn't try again. She knew instinctively that she was in a hospital. The underlying hum of a working hospital is something she wouldn't forget and the sounds now brought her back to the time she'd spent at Mordon County Hospital the previous month. She knew there would be a call button to her right and without opening her eyes, reached for it. Before she found it though, a voice called out.

"Here, let me get that." It was a voice she recognized, but it took her a minute to place, so incongruous to the surroundings it was.

"Cathwrynn," Maddie whispered her name as if she were an illusion, feeling both greatly relieved and worried. Cathwrynn had reached the bed and lifted Maddie's pillow to help Maddie take a sip of water. Maddie opened her mouth but it was several seconds before she could speak.

"No, I don't want a drink. I was trying to find the call button."

Cathwrynn pushed the button to raise the bed and once that was done, lifted the glass to Maddie's lips again. "Here, have just a sip. You'll be dehydrated otherwise and then they'll have to put a drip in you."

Maddie took the required sip, then slumped back, squinting her eyes open and cringing. "Please turn off the light."

"The lights are off, Maddie."

"Then close the curtains."

"They're closed too." Cathwrynn took Maddie's hand in hers, the emotion in her voice telling Maddie she too was worried. "Maddie, you just have to rest. We're looking after you."

Her eyes still mostly closed, Maddie squinted at the woman at her side. This was the most grounded Maddie had ever heard Cathwrynn sound and that in itself was worrying.

"What happened?"

"You were at the Shadylawn Retirement Village. You were found in the parking lot. At first, they thought that you'd slipped on an icy bit of sidewalk and hit your head. There was a huge bump already forming."

"What day is it?"

"It's still Sunday. You were unconscious, but woke up in the ambulance."

Maddie couldn't remember any of the things Cathwrynn described happening. "At first, they thought I slipped? Then what did they think?"

Cathwrynn took a deep breath. "Maddie, someone hit you with a rock. It was found with blood on it and far enough away from you that they know you didn't trip."

Maddie could feel tears on her cheek but she didn't open her eyes or rub them away. "Who found me?"

"That detective. He said the two of you had been talking and that you were headed home. He'd come outside to talk to you again. Did you argue?" Maddie didn't answer. Cathwrynn seemed to float next to the bed and Maddie wasn't sure she wasn't imagining it.

"It's fortunate he had something more to say to you because he must have found you within minutes of it happening."

Two thoughts were coursing through Maddie. The first idea was that someone wanted to hurt her—maybe even kill her—and that someone had attacked her out in the open in broad daylight. Whoever it was had clearly become unhinged, making the next couple of days unpredictable and dangerous. Even Maddie knew that. She also knew that Joe was going to have a big, fat *I told you so* out of his mouth faster than she could blink. The second thought was an indulgence, but she couldn't push it aside. Joe had come out to talk to her again. *What had he wanted to say?*

"You dreamt of them, didn't you?"

"What? No." But her voice held no conviction. She had had unsettling dreams of angels and devils hovering over her as she taught a class at the Shadylawn Retirement Village. Sam and Dottie were in the dream talking to her, but she couldn't understand anything they said. Rolf and Berta were there too, floating above the other dancers in their competition outfits, the angels and devils trying to pry the couple apart. Somehow, she knew that Cathwrynn was channeling those images.

"You're staying overnight. It's just a precaution. I'll leave some friends with you." Cathwrynn hovered over the bed in silence, for the first time seeming unsure what to say. "Maddie, please try not to make a habit of this." Maddie didn't even question the identity of her so-called friends. Maddie heard the plea in Cathwrynn's request and didn't dispute her concern.

Maddie ate the toast and tea the nurse brought and turned on the television at a low volume, then spent an uneventful evening flipping through channels, painfully aware that she didn't have any further visitors.

Cathwrynn returned Monday morning and then proceeded to fret over her for the remainder of the morning, burning incense, much to the annoyance of the hospital staff, and rubbing a new concoction onto Maddie's wrists.

Maddie had suffered a slight concussion and the doctor advised a two-day break from work. Maddie had no intention of staying away from work, but she nodded her head toward the doctor, then promptly signed herself out while Cathwrynn conscientiously ignored her disregard of his professional opinion. Her parents wouldn't need to know about the incident until they returned on Wednesday and from Cathwrynn's feigned ambivalence, Maddie knew she could count on her to not say anything at the studio.

While the doctor did tell her to take it easy for the next couple of days, he also let her know that she didn't need to worry about a concussion. It turned out that the injury hadn't been so bad. Whoever had hit her had not been able to manage a hard enough blow to hurt her too badly, certainly not to kill her. What he reiterated was that someone had attacked her and that he hoped Maddie would take care of herself. On that note, Joe finally called, telling her that when she was feeling better, he would send an officer over to her house so that she could make a formal statement. He ended the call by telling her that he didn't expect to see her at the retirement village ever again.

Maddie's regular Tuesday morning class arrived in a subdued mood. She wasn't surprised in light of Rolf's death and she imagined that they were also aware of Berta's role in his suicide. She didn't know how much they knew about her own attack, but she decided not to say anything unless it was brought up. Even then, she decided to make little of it. The group in front of her today was a far cry from the usually joyful bunch and she didn't want to be responsible for causing them any more anxiety.

Maddie looked around the room for Sam and Dottie and finally found Dottie in the corner, sitting in a forlorn lump alone. Maddie put on a smile.

"Dottie, it's good to see you. Where's Sam?"

Dottie's face contorted before she straightened her shoulders. "He said he's not feeling well. I think he just couldn't be bothered."

Maddie could see that Dottie was unimpressed with Sam's abandonment of her, but she could also read real worry behind her tart remark.

"Well, it's his loss. He'll fall behind the rest of us." Dottie stood slowly, looking as if she wasn't feeling that well either.

Maddie taught the class, the most tortuous one she'd taught this group of normally enthusiastic and lively students. She kept a particular eye on Dottie who broke from the group repeatedly to sit in the corner and mope. After class, Maddie walked to where Dottie sat alone.

"I hope Sam feels better. I miss his irreverent humor." Dottie sighed but remained silent. "It's funny to think about the things that you think annoy you. You only realize you'll miss them when they're gone."

Dottie's eyes reared up. "That's it, Maddie! That's just exactly it!" Dottie shook her head as if Maddie had disagreed with her. "I promise you, it wasn't like he was hiding things from me or that I didn't notice things. You know, we've become quite close in these past months." This time tears dripped down her face and she took a handkerchief out to wipe at them.

"Just over this weekend, we went to a production of *Much Ado About Nothing* at the New Jersey Shakespeare Festival. It's one of his favorites. He recited the lines along with Benedict. I have to admit that it was a bit annoying at the time, but at least he was his normal self again. Then yesterday morning, it was like he was a different man." Dottie sniffed as she stuffed the handkerchief up her sleeve.

"Dottie, did you have an argument? Was he angry about something?"

Dottie shook her head sadly. "No, that's not it. He changed into an old person right in front of my eyes. He forgot who I was. He attacked one of the nurses. They had to restrain him. It was awful!" Dottie took the handkerchief out again and started to sob. "It was awful."

Maddie put her hand on Dottie's shaking shoulders. "I'm so sorry, Dottie."

Maddie had avoided the office when she'd arrived that morning but was unable to avoid Laura's inquisitiveness when she found the secretary waiting outside her classroom door a the end of class, a pinched expression on her face, hands on hips and foot tapping.

"Great news!" Laura made the declaration as if the news was anything but great. Still sore over last week, Maddie mused.

"Three new students for you."

"Really?" Maddie followed Laura into the office. That was good news and after last week's cancellations and today's somber class, she *was* surprised and grateful.

"Really." Laura turned back to some business she had in the filing cabinet. Maddie sighed. She'd have to work hard for this.

"Thanks, Laura, that's unexpected. And, by the way, your hair looks really nice."

Laura automatically lifted both hands to pat down her hair, but today she didn't need to. What was normally a halo of frizzy wire had today been tamed into what Maddie could only call a silky bouffant. Laura, momentarily perplexed by the disciplined state of her hair as well as the compliment, eventually waved it off.

"Finally got a product to work and now I'm kicking myself." Maddie waited. "It's a dryer sheet! Can you believe it? After all this time, and it's what my mother used to tell me to rub on my head. It's all she talked about before she died. What I say is that you should always listen to your elders." Maddie read the hidden message and shrugged. At least she'd broken the frostiness between the two of them.

"Anyway, as I was saying you have three new students, two of them first asking to make sure that you were the one who choreographed that naked tango." Laura let that piece of information settle onto the desk between them.

"I guess news travels fast out of drunken bartenders' lips."

"Well, I guess you just have to ask yourself, which is worse, losing students because they think they might die if they take one of your classes or gaining students because you're the naked tango choreographer?"

"Yeah, that's exactly what I want to be asking myself." Laura looked at Maddie from over her reading glasses, a quiver in her lips increasing as she broke out in an unfamiliar grin. Soon both women were giggling, then the giggles turned into laughs until they both had tears in their eyes and stitches in their sides. Maddie left the office lighter than she'd felt in weeks, but a boisterous voice coming out of a classroom forced her to re-evaluate her newfound enthusiasm. Craig bounded down the hallway with a group of swing dancers it appeared he had known all his life. She waited for him to notice her, but he seemed consumed with his new friends until Maddie stepped in front of him. Craig looked up, surprised and then as pleased as if he'd just been confronted with a winning lottery ticket.

"Claire and Philip are fantastic teachers! We just did a *rolling pin dip*. Can you believe it?"

As he drew closer to Maddie, the smile on his face fell.

"I'm sorry about the way everything went, Maddie."

"No, you're not."

Maddie's eyes wandered away from Craig and out the window. She watched as her next class arrived—Liam and his wife Joelle—and their fifth session with their impending wedding dance.

"I have to teach. I guess, call before you leave town."

"Okay, I will, Maddie. And I really mean it. Thanks for everything!"

Maddie turned away, leaving Craig with a complicated expression on his face. Maddie knew it all too well. He wanted to leave and get on with the rest of his life without Maddie, but he hated the idea that Maddie might think badly of him. Without looking back, she ducked into a classroom. She stood in front of the radiator warming up as an uncomfortable feeling in her gut worked its way to her hands, forcing her to repeatedly shake and squeeze them to try and dispel the tension. So much for laugh therapy.

Her class wasn't the best she'd ever taught. Both Liam and Joelle seemed uncomfortable and slipped her sideways glances every time they thought she wasn't looking. She didn't want to get more paranoid than she already felt and was about to say something when Liam spoke up.

"Look, we heard that you choreographed that dance on TV when that girl flashed her stuff."

Maddie sighed. At least it was only about that. "Yep, that was me."

"Did you mean for her to do that?"

"No, I can't say that I did."

"Then why'd you let her do it?"

The idea of containing Morgan LeRoux made Maddie want to pull her hair out and she regretted entering into this discussion in such a carefree manner. The woman who'd managed to sabotage both Maddie's television and academic careers while simultaneously winning over the American public would have been farcical if only she hadn't involved Maddie in her prank. The only luck that Maddie'd had was that the minute the episode was aired and most of Morgan had been revealed, Maddie had ducked out and laid low. She still had some friends in L.A. and they had managed some damage control.

"We didn't know you did that sort of dance as well." Maddie was so flabbergasted that she finally exploded in her second belly-shaking laugh of the day. Joelle eyed her warily and continued:

"We don't want to do anything like that at our wedding."

"No worries there. I think I can control myself."

Chapter Twenty-One

After two less than stellar classes and an unwelcome if truncated conversation with her ex-boyfriend, Maddie welcomed the end of the day. Sticking her head into the office to say goodnight, the three inhabitants of the office; Nikki her arms mid gesticulation, Laura her face sewn into her perennial pucker and Cathwrynn with eyes wide and cheeks pink, looked at her as their conversation was brought to an abrupt close. Maddie looked at each one in turn before Laura spoke up.

"Frank's having a particularly bad day. Maddie, if you've got some time, can you drop him off?"

Taking the not-so-subtle clue that they were talking about her, she didn't even pause in the doorway. "Yes, of course."

In the car Maddie passed several uncomfortable minutes getting Frank into a seat belt. Once done, he sat quietly until she thought that the entire trip would pass in silence, a prospect that would not have bothered her at all. Then, without any preamble, Frank spoke up.

"I've been thinking a lot about life, you know?"

"What about it, Frank?"

"Life and death. I never used to wonder where Gloria went to when she passed. Just knew that she was gone. I'll be gone too one day. Didn't seem to matter the what's and where's of it." Frank had his hands clasped on his lap and he started tapping his belly through his coat, a habitual movement that Maddie welcomed as it was reminiscent of the old Frank.

"But I've been thinking, like I said, and I think that what it's all about is about controlling it. Living that is. Never taking too much or too little. Controlling what you take so that it lasts. Making decisions that make it so that you can keep it going. So maybe you don't get everything you want right when you want it or things happen that seem unfair. It all comes right if you can control it. And eventually you get enough. You get what you want. That's what makes it all worth it."

Maddie slammed on the breaks. Frank jerked against his seat belt.

"Maddie, what did I say? Did I do something?" Frank looked beyond distressed. Maddie brought her hand to her mouth, then reached forward and held Frank's arm.

"That's it, Frank." Frank looked inordinately pleased until Maddie continued. "That's the thing I'm missing. Someone is controlling this thing. Why are they dying? I know that people die. Of course I do, but there's someone behind the scenes, someone with an agenda of their own."

Frank shook his head, unable to take it all in. "And they said I was going crazy."

"I'm not going crazy, Frank. Sorry, let me get you home." Maddie put the car into drive again. "I have to go back because Joe thinks it's all over. Someone was looking for something but it wasn't buried treasure. Someone wants something that Owen and Floyd, and Rolf and Berta, and even Sam and Dottie have." Maddie drove carefully now in a world of her own and though she could feel Frank's apprehensive glances, she didn't elaborate any more on the manic thoughts hopping around in her head.

"Well, if you're sure, Maddie. But it seems to me that maybe you need to go home and lie down yourself. Maybe you got hit on the head harder than you think."

She had pulled up at Frank's house and put the car in park before she turned to look at him. He sounded completely lucid now, unlike the several near near meltdowns at the studio. She breathed out slowly. Maybe he was right. Maybe she had just taken on some of his manic energy. She had gone off the top for a couple of minutes while he had been able to find his way back to clarity. She had vented and belatedly felt guilty for burdening him with nonsensical ramblings when he had enough psychological challenges of his own.

"Hmm..you may be right, Frank. Anyway, I'll think about it."

Frank looked at Maddie, then at his house and then back at Maddie again. "Why are we here?"

Startled, Maddie bit her lip. "I brought you home because you weren't feeling well, Frank."

"Oh yes, of course. Don't worry about me, Maddie. I'll be just fine. I'll see you tomorrow." Frank lumbered out of the car and Maddie watched him navigate the steep path to his door then pulled away from Frank's house unable to shake the thought developing in her head.

By the time she drove into her parent's driveway she had a headache and her heart was beating too fast. Never before in her almost thirty-four years had she thought herself capable of having a heart attack, not even when a gun had been pointed at her but she did right now. She knew who was responsible for the deaths at Shadylawn. She just needed to prove it.

Joe said that the case of Floyd's murder and the attempted one on Owen were all but solved. It was understood that they had involved with the mob and that the mob was responsible. But if it was only the mob, then why were people still dying?

Maddie knew it was a retirement home and that the people who lived there were old and would die but that didn't explain what was happening. Why had Floyd suffered from the same deteriorating symptoms weeks before he died that Rolf then suffered and now Sam seemed to be suffering?

Maddie knew. As clearly as if the one behind it all had told her exactly how it had been done. She was afraid of the realization but knew it to be true. She picked up her mobile and called Craig. She knew Joe wouldn't, or couldn't, listen to her but she had also learned enough to know that she couldn't, or wouldn't, go alone. He answered on the second ring.

"Craig, can you meet me at the retirement village?"

"What, Maddie, now? I was just heading out to drinks with Ben. I leave tomorrow, remember?"

"That's why. Please?" Craig issued a string of abnormal sighs before speaking again. "If it's important to you, I guess I can."

"It is. And thanks for making the effort." Maddie didn't hide the sarcasm in her voice. Not that Craig seemed to hear it.

"Yeah, okay. Do you want to see Owen, is that it? Remember, I'm taking him back to California with me. Well, not really. That's what we're saying. It's going to be a witness protection thing."

"All right, Craig. Listen, I don't think that you should be talking about that."

"What, do you think my phone might be tapped?"

"No, listen, I'll explain when I get there. I need to get into the village. Meet me at the dance studio in twenty minutes. Then we can drive in together."

"Maddie, are you sure? Does Joe know you're doing this? I mean, it's not like there's a mystery anymore, right? It's all been solved." Craig sounded uncharacteristically apprehensive. Maddie knew that with the precarious position Owen was in, Craig might actually have some qualms about doing something illegal.

"Right, of course, that's what I've heard. It's got nothing to do with Owen. See you in twenty minutes."

Maddie hung up feeling inordinately pleased that she'd gotten Craig to do what she wanted. Now she had to flesh out the rest of a plan.

Twenty minutes later Craig pulled into the parking lot of the dance studio. Maddie locked her car and hopped into the BMW's passenger seat.

"What, no blankets this time?"

Maddie vacillated between telling Craig what she thought in order to engage his help and using the fact that he didn't know what she was up to to catch a murderer. In the end she decided on the latter and the drive to the retirement village was carried out in almost complete silence. Contrary to Craig's questions on the phone, he didn't seem that interested in knowing what was going on. Little was said apart from Craig's initial attempt to interest Maddie in the pros and cons of a buying a vintage Golden Axe arcade game he found on-line. As soon as she heard him start in on the swordplay she tuned him out and continued her plotting.

With the murder investigation under control, the gates to the retirement village were open again and the guard was back to looking at something on his computer screen, barely offering a wave as Craig drove through. Inside it seemed that life had gone back to normal as well. The police officers that had been a permanent fixture for almost two weeks were gone, replaced by decorated trees and woodland swags. Instrumental holiday music played quietly in the background of the lobby. The marquee near the desk read the nights screening of *It's a Wonderful Life* and a meeting of the vintage car club. Craig's eyes lit up and he checked his watch.

"Hey, I might just stick my head in there. Um, if you don't need me."

Maddie wasn't sure. She had figured that Craig would be able to help physically, if she needed it, but she didn't think she would. There would be people around. This wasn't like last month when she had gone to the dance studio, alone and in the middle of the night. She hadn't made that mistake again. She let Craig know it was fine but that she still wanted a ride home. Uncharitably she couldn't help but imagine Craig flirting with some resident and ending up in someone's bed.

The receptionist in the lobby had Maddie sign into the guest book and then directed her unnecessarily to the frail care wing. Maddie's stomach tightened as she drew closer to the nurse standing, head bowed at the nurse's station. When she stood three feet from the woman, she sensed Maddie and slowly raised her head, her eye's seeming to belong to some other sort of animal.

"Hello. What do we owe the pleasure of your company for, yet again?"

Nurse Spring was still the most unlikely nurse Maddie had ever encountered and she had encountered a bad one. She had to make up something quick or she knew Nurse Spring would escort her out of the frail care area.

"Actually, I'm here to see Nurse O'Neill."

The lines on Nurse Spring's forehead first bounced in undisclosed surprised but immediately contracted to show her distrust.

"She's asked for tango lessons."

Nurse Spring looked at Maddie as if she had sprouted cauliflower out of her ears.

"I find that completely unbelievable. So much in fact that I think you are lying. Now why would you be lying?" The dangerous glint in the nurse's eye made Maddie sweat. She had to get by her. Not thinking too much or she wouldn't be able to get through with what she had to do, she bent over and let out a moan she hoped was not too theatric.

"Oh, damn." She peered up at the still inscrutable face of the nurse. Grabbing onto her stomach she continued to moan. "Cramps. They come on like this sometimes. I just need to use a toilet."

"Of course. If you turn around and go back from where you came from, you'll find one in the lobby. Good day, Ms. Fitzpatrick.."

Maddie didn't need any further incentive to leave so turned around and headed back to the lobby. There had to be another way to get to where she needed to go. As she rounded the corner she found her answer. Billy was pushing a trolley with several boxes strapped onto it.

"Billy, just the man I was hoping to run into."

Billy looked back to Maddie, his expression open as if women spouting words of adoration were a common occurrence for him.

"Hey, teach. You cool?"

"Mind if I walk with you for a minute?"

Billy looked as if he knew Maddie would come around to him eventually as he graciously beckoned with one hand and continued down the hall. As Maddie had hoped, he turned before the entrance to the frail care wing and opened a door to a service area. Maddie followed through after checking to make certain Nurse Spring wasn't lurking around the corner. Safe for the minute, she stopped.

"I just forgot something. Billy, I'll come find you in a minute. I have to get something, I mean, someone. I forgot."

"No problem, teach. No need to be nervous. I'll be ready when you are."

The grin on his face, one Maddie just last week would have taken as an egotistical leer and would have made her want to punch him in the face was today the carefree smile of a young guy making a living. The fact that he thought she was interested in him now made her laugh, rather than cringe.

"Uh, thanks. See you later."

Maddie used the emergency stairs to gain access to the second floor. There she asked an orderly where she would find the person she was looking for and followed his instructions. When she arrived in the room however, she found it to be empty. Sticking her head back out the door she called to another orderly.

"Sorry, I thought Doctor Marlowe was supposed to be in here."

"Oh, The doctor's with Sam." The orderly pointed to a door further down the hall. "Just heard Nurse O'Neill saved him. Poor guy had an obstruction and couldn't breath. I'd sure take her over that witch downstairs. Didn't hear me say that though." The orderly winked at Maddie and disappeared around a corner.

She didn't know what she thought she was going to find when she opened the door. Possibly blood, maybe screaming. Horror on the Sam's face? A maniacal laugh from the nurse? It's not what she got though. The picture before her resembled the mundane functioning of a nursing home. The nurse sat next to a bed. In the bed an elderly patient lay, eyes misted and half closed but mouth opening and closing as the nurse pushed a spoon into it.

Maddie gasped unexpectedly as she watched the spoon travel from the plate that rested on the trolley in front of the nurse to the patient's mouth, the last piece of the puzzle falling into place. The sound made the nurse turn to the door, her eyes round and questioning for a moment, then realization struck.

In those seconds, the winsome, benevolent mask that Nurse O'Neill habitually had plastered on her face fell away. Maddie wasn't sure what had elicited the change in Susan O'Neill's poise but later she understood that it must have been something in her eyes. Something that told the nurse that she knew because once Nurse O'Neill locked gazes with her, Maddie knew that she knew.

Nurse O'Neill quietly put the spoon down and Maddie instantly regretted telling Craig that she didn't need him to stay with her.

"Hello. Maddie, isn't it?"

It was the tone that Nurse O'Neill used that scared Maddie the most. Gone was the earnest, constantly put upon, congenial nurse and in its place was the monster she really was. Gone too was the whimsical, jovial appearance and instead Maddie was looking at demented eyes desperate enough to do anything. Nurse O'Neill had stood up and was walking slowly toward Maddie, her left hand behind her back. Knowing she held something potentially threatening but not knowing what it was, was the last straw. Maddie back away as Nurse O'Neill advanced across the room.

"I was just .."

"You were just what?"

"I was just leaving. Sorry to interrupt."

"Oh, you're not interrupting. I was just helping Sam with his dinner. He's been having a hard time lately. We have to make sure he keeps up his strength, don't we?" The words were the right words for a nurse to say but the intention was all wrong. Maddie had backed up as far as she could and with the wall behind her she looked furtively to her right where the weighted door had closed.

"Is there anything wrong, Maddie?"

"Not that I can think of. I'm meeting Joe Clancy here. He's the detective investigating the deaths here at the village." Maddie could imagine herself bubbly nonsensically all evening just to keep Nurse O'Neill talking.

"Why, that's funny. That yummy looking detective was just here. Said he was going back to his office. Seems like one of you is lying." Maddie didn't know whether to believe Nurse O'Neill or not but recognized the menace in her voice.

"Why?"

"Why what?" Nurse O'Neill looked honestly perplexed.

"Why do they have to die?"

The nurse barked out a laugh. "This is a retirement home. These people are old."

Maddie couldn't move any further away from the deranged nurse. "I'll scream."

Nurse O'Neill didn't blink.

"Go ahead. You'll be dead before anyone gets here. I'll be standing over you telling everyone how I tried to save you but that you had a seizure. I'm very good at getting away with this very situation."

As Nurse O'Neill finished her sentence she reached out to grab Maddie's arm with her right hand at the same time swinging her left hand in a wide arc toward Maddie. Pulling her eyes away from Nurse O'Neill's face for an instant, she spotted the syringe in the hand that was fast moving toward Maddie's shoulder.

Maddie reacted faster than she knew she could. In a single motion she ducked into a deep plié while she swung her shoulder away from Nurse O'Neill. She then stepped forward and twisted so that her opposite shoulder hit Nurse O'Neill, sending her stumbling, the syringe flying out of her hand and hitting the wall behind Maddie.

Before she could gloat at her quick reflexes, Nurse O'Neill pulled herself up and pounced, landing on top of Maddie and sending them both to the ground. She must have been able to reach the syringe because the first sting of the needle pierced Maddie's neck before she could react, instantly sending her heart into palpitations and her brain into a screwball dive to the floor with her body. She thought her eyes were open but she couldn't see anything. She tried to get her arms to react to Nurse O'Neill's abuse but couldn't feel them anymore and it was only a piercing cry from somewhere across the room that told her she was still alive.

Maddie sensed rather than felt a scurry of activity. The strongest sensation was the smell of lavender. It made her think of her grandmother and she tried to smile as she thought about joining the woman who had died when she was sixteen. A voice rose in Maddie's foggy dreams, wobbly at first but slowly gaining clarity.

"What did you give her?" There were sounds of metal hitting metal and a whooshing noise that Maddie couldn't place before she her the voice again. "You? It was you."

"Get off me." More sounds of metal crashing and a piercing scream.

"Give me that. Restrain her. I need Cogentin, now."

Maddie felt a weight lift off her chest and somewhere in the back of her head, floating around with images of her grandmother in a hula skirt, waving to Maddie with a Styrofoam fish in her hand, she heard several voices and knew they were talking about her.

"Call the police. Get doctor Marlowe now."

"No, not Doctor Marlowe."

"Shut up. Hold her until the police arrive."

Then screaming, more screaming than Maddie could bare as she slowly sensed motion around her. Finally she found she could open her eyes. Just inches from her face, Nurse Spring stared imploringly into Maddie's eyes. When she saw that Maddie responded, she let out a gasp that Maddie could have sworn was thankful. The screaming hadn't stopped and Maddie could now see that Nurse O'Neill was writhing between two orderlies.

"It was me. I saved those people. I could have saved her. It was me."

A look of sheer terror raced across Nurse O'Neill's face as Doctor Marlowe entered the room at a run. He stopped momentarily at the sight of the nurse being held by the two orderlies then immediately came to Nurse Spring and dropped to Maddie's side.

"Nurse O'Neill injected her with Stelazine. I've countered that with Cogentin."

Doctor Monroe took Maddie's hand to feel her pulse. "Good work." Another two orderlies with a gurney entered the room. "Has transport to Mordon Hills Memorial been requested?"

"Yes and the police are on their way." Maddie was lifted slowly to the gurney and found she could now see clearly. Whatever Nurse O'Neill used was fast acting but also fast disappearing. Maddie instantly remembered Sam and valiantly tried to point to him. Nurse Spring seemed to understand because she looked at Sam first with a question, then a look of alarm.

She gasped again, the full extent of Nurse O'Neill's murderous activities becoming clear to her, however her professional persona hid any emotional reaction she may have had.

"I have to attend to Sam."

Doctor Marlowe stood slowly and turned to Nurse O'Neill, and Maddie could see a look of disgust on his face from across the room. From the wildcat that Nurse O'Neill had presented to the orderlies, she deflated in front of his eyes.

"But I *am* a good nurse. *I* saved these people. *All* of them. They would have died without me. You know that. You know I'm a good nurse."

An orderly wheeled Maddie out of the room when she heard a wail that she was sure could be heard throughout the entire retirement village. As the sound of an ambulance siren grew closer, she let the tears fall from her eyes. Rolf didn't have to die but at least she had been able to help Sam.

Chapter Twenty-Two

Craig called as Maddie finished dressing, asking if he could swing by on his way to the airport. She felt a dull ache in her stomach as he pulled up to her parent's house and watched him leap out of the car from where she stood at the living room window. She could see Owen sitting bundled in coat, scarf and hat in the passenger seat but Craig made no move to get his uncle out of the car to say good-bye. With some trepidation she came to the front door before Craig could ring the bell. Her parents had returned home the day before and after the requisite explanation about her involvement in yet another murder investigation complete, they had disappeared into the back of the house for what Maddie imagined to be covert discussions regarding the sanity of their youngest daughter.

The two of them stood for a moment in silence until Maddie stepped back allowing Craig to enter.

"I can't stay. Plane leaves Newark at 10:30. I just wanted to give you this."

Craig handed her an envelope. It was thin, there couldn't have been more than one sheet inside it but the image of her long-ago love letters popped unbidden into her head. She involuntarily shuddered but took the proffered envelope.

"You don't have to open it now if you don't want to."

Craig looked as if he would like nothing better than for Maddie to open it later but she turned it over and pulled the gummed bit at the back apart. She knew instinctively that she had to end this once and for all. She didn't want some post-relationship-murder-regret letter hanging over her after he'd left. The envelope open she pulled out the single piece of paper inside it. She looked up, bewildered, then put the paper back in the envelope and thrust it at at Craig.

"I don't want any more of your money."

"Relax, it's not mine. It's Owen's money. He wants you to have it. And I didn't say anything to him, just so you know. It was his idea. I think what you did inspired him. But whatever the reason, you deserve it."

Maddie instinctively looked over Craig's shoulder to the man in the car. He didn't seem to be paying any attention to the couple on the front porch and that made her uneasy. Taking a check from this man meant taking money that could be dirty. Who knew what strings were tied to it. Craig seemed to read her very thoughts.

"No strings, Maddie. You'll never here from Owen again. Like I said, you deserve something after everything you did to help those people at Shadylawn. And if they aren't going to reward you, then let Owen do it."

I don't deserve it, Craig. I don't know him and he doesn't know me. What he saw was a sexy picture and read some letters." She didn't hide the betrayal she still felt over the letters. "The rest of it was just him reliving his nefarious days in the mob."

Craig actually laughed. "Maybe, but whatever was going on in his imagination, he found something that was worth that money. I know you and I want you to have it. If you don't, it'll only come to me anyway and you know I don't need it."

Maddie looked dubiously at Craig, wanting to take the money and run but feeling like there could still be an obligation left unsaid. Craig read her face.

"Maddie, there's nothing sinister in it. I don't know how Owen got that money and I don't care. I want you to take it and use it. I'm going back to L.A. and back to Paul. I have stuff to work out with him and I just want to know you're safe and happy."

"Thanks, Craig. I guess I'll just say thank you. I appreciate it."

"Oh, and good luck with the detective. He's hot."

"Thanks."

Not much of a chance of that, Maddie thought but kept the words and hopefully the sadness she couldn't quite shake out of her response as Craig ran back to the car. Thinking about her ex-boyfriend thinking that her ex-husband was hot, was just a little too weird.

She watched Craig drive away, probably for the last time ever and a new fluttery feeling bubbled up in her stomach. She looked down at the check for $25,000 and wrapped her arms around herself as she thought about the future, for the first time in a long time, with hope rather than anxiety.

Maddie spent the remainder of the week at home. Peter was beside himself, unwilling to forgive himself for letting Maddie risk her life again. He insisted that she stay home to recuperate but let slip that maybe there would be reason to stop by the studio on Friday afternoon. The check Craig had given her was burning a hole in her purse and she wanted to get it into her bank account so on Friday she drove downtown to run errands before dropping by the studio.

When Maddie entered the office she drew in a breath. The whole gang was there. Peter stood in his habitual stance perched against the doorframe to his office with Laura at her desk blocking the threshold to the inner sanctum. Cathwrynn sat beside Frank, the two of them looking similar in their languid expressions. Nikki and Grant sat next to one another, Nikki's feet tapping while and Grant's head was sunk to his chest as he poked at his mobile. Claire and Philip sat together in a heap by the door, fidgeting with both one another and the Luttons Laura had plastered all over the filing cabinets. Against the one free wall someone had leant two life-sized cutouts of Superman and Wonder Woman with space where the face should be so that a photo could be taken as the superheroes. Nikki beamed at Maddie.

"Just had them sitting around and thought we could use a team building experience."

She hadn't been relishing the thought of having to relate the second lethal experience in her life just a month after the first one but the fact that her team was there to support her and help remind her that she would be all right with a ridiculous bonding event was exactly what the doctor ordered. She poured herself a cup of coffee, silently thanking Peter for splurging on a new percolator and grabbed the gooiest custard filled donut she could find before being the first to step take up the Wonder Woman persona.

After everyone had a photo taken and plenty of laughs were had, seats were found and the meeting begun. Peter help up a finger, then sprinted into his office before reappearing with an outlandish trophy in the shape of a pickle with a #1 printed on it. Peter ran his hand through his hair and offered a triumphant smile.

"The first monthly St. Clair pickle award goes to Nikki Chua for her artful ability to sooth the irate dancer. I should think about hiring you as our permanent PR representative, Nikki. That was a near catastrophe averted. Thank you."

Nikki accepted the praise with a flutter of her hand. "Nothing to it. Sometimes all it needs is a little cha-cha-cha in the right direction."

Maddie raised her eyebrows to which Nikki replied. "I'll tell you later. Now, we want the story."

The room seemed to nod in unison and Peter took a seat next to Laura. "So let's start the meeting, shall we? Maddie, take it away." Maddie looked up from her coffee mug, her eyes wide.

"Don't give us that *what me* look. This ain't no business meeting. We're here for the scoop."

"All of it including the lowdown on Detective Clancy. I've been hearing things and I want some clarification." Nikki wiggled her rear back into the seat next to Grant who remained silent but held Maddie's gaze with interest. Cathwrynn tilted her head and murmured.

"Clarification arriving."

As Joe walked into the office at the mention of his name, Maddie contemplated that the whole room was in on a conspiracy.

Maddie gave Joe a self-conscious shrug and was rewarded with a pure Joe Clancy classic: a smile that started on one side of his mouth, quivered in the middle accentuating his bottom lip then gathered the rest of his mouth up in a full throttle grin. She hadn't seen one of those grins since the days he tried to convince anyone who would listen that Ireland was going to win the World Cup.

"If you don't mind, I'd like to make a public apology." Joe had everyone's attention. "Maddie, you were right and I am sorry I didn't listen to you when you told me that something was still bothering you at the retirement village." Joe put his hands on his hips as if daring anyone to contradict him. "However, I still stand by the fact that you made it sound like an episode from Murder She Wrote and in the future I'll have to give you some pointers on how to talk to an investigative team trying to catch a murderer."

Maddie choked on her donut.

"Next time? I sure hope you don't think that I'm looking for a next time." Maddie felt the word tilt and imagined that anyone looking at her could see her emotions bubbling up inside her. By the way Joe looked at her she knew he could.

Peter's gaze passed back and forth between Maddie and Joe knowingly. "All right enough of this, there's time for that later. Get on with it." Joe didn't seem to feel the need to speak so Maddie began.

"Well, I think everyone is aware that Floyd's murder was a mob hit. A mistaken one as it turns out. The hit was actually Owen Cavendish but the two men looking strikingly similar .."

Nikki nearly screeched. "But what was the mob after?"

Joe interrupted. "Federal bonds. Both Owen and Floyd were involved at various stages of illegal businesses run by the mob. We're still unravelling the case with the help of the FBI."

Maddie drained he rest of her coffee mug and continued. "I'd heard people at the police station complaining about holes being dug in the neighborhoods around the retirement village, then Sam and Dottie told me about a treasure hunter coming to the village to talk about his hobby. It seems that Floyd and Owen had taken to trying to trick each other and they would bury things that they stole from each other's rooms. So the night Floyd was murdered Daniel Sambraus confused the two men. He had impersonated an orderly, followed Floyd out of the ballroom after his attack thinking he was Owen, then later came back and killed him."

"And that's where we get interesting." Laura looked around the room at the incredulous stares. "What? Why's everyone looking like they just swallowed cod liver oil. You all know that this is the real mystery. This is the real murder."

Maddie reached for another donut and realized that everyone had stopped talking, the donut she had grabbed the object of curiosity.

"What? I'm hungry." Maddie was hungry but what she felt more than anything was an overwhelming sense of satisfaction. Everything might just be falling into place.

"Daniel Sambraus did murder Floyd Donaldson but he wasn't the one who tried to kill Owen with the knife. Mainly because no-one tried to kill Owen with a knife."

"Huh?" Philip shook his head. "I'm lost."

"It wasn't a real attempt. Nurse O'Neill stabbed Owen but not very deeply. She was then the one who conveniently found him bleeding and saved him. She didn't do it because she actually wanted to kill him. Not that way anyway. She wanted people to think that there was a murderer still on the loose so that she could continue to poison the residents of the retirement village without people questioning her."

Peter pointed to a table against the wall, presumably because there was a newspaper sitting on top of it. "And the assassin was the guy from the newspaper stuck in cement, wasn't he? But what I want to know is why Renée Lambert was writing those articles."

Joe had grabbed a sticky donut as well and spoke with a powdered sugar mustache.

"Renée Lambert is a person of interest for other reasons but other than that she plays no part in this situation. It seems she was simply being spiteful and not very clever about it. Now on top of her other problems, she and the *Mordon County Enquirer* have been slammed with a liable suit."

Peter looked vindicated. "Damn straight."

Frank who up until this point had been alternately rubbing his hands together and clapping softly, spoke up. "What I want to know is how you knew it was Nurse O'Neill."

"I saw my first clue in the newspaper even thought I didn't recognize it at the time. It was a photograph of Nurse O'Neill and Doctor Marlowe with an article welcoming them to Shadylawn."

Cathwrynn sat up with a start. "The devil."

"Oh, Cathwrynn, you don't have to be so melodramatic."

"She's not. I dreamt about her. It was Nurse O'Neill wearing the devil costume. I think my subconscious was trying to tell me something the whole time. But what was significant was that the article said that the couple had arrived three months ago, the same time that Sam and Dottie said that Floyd started deteriorating."

"Things fell into place when I drove you home, Frank. Remember?"

"What?" Frank's hands fell flat against his thighs, a look of terror on his face. "I couldn't, I wouldn't, would I?"

"It was two things really. The first was when Laura and I were speaking."

"So you mean it was me that helped you solve it, don't you? Again, I might add." Laura reached for a cigarette in her pocket only to find it empty. Presumably she forgot she'd been hypnotized. Maddie smiled benignly at Laura. She was feeling so good with Joe sitting there looking at her with, maybe awe, she wasn't even going to let Laura's ego bother her.

"Yes, Laura, it was you. You were talking about how Frank couldn't abide swallowing pills so he had worked out a system where the nurse would put the medicine in his food, then have it delivered."

"Frank nodded sagely. "That's right. Works a charm."

"But you really got me thinking, Frank. We were talking and you said something about controlling life. Taking a little, not too much so that life lasts."

Maddie looked at the desperate look on Frank's face, then at the rest of the room. Even Joe was looking at her strangely.

"Don't you see? That's when I knew that it had to be someone at the retirement village, someone with access to the residents at all hours of the day even when they were under guard. Someone who was interested in controlling the situation, making sure that the residents didn't die but were continually being brought to the brink of death before pulling them back so that they could be viewed as the hero. Or heroine as the case may be."

Maddie glanced to Joe but he didn't seem to mind her taking center stage.

"I have to admit I didn't know who it was and I kind of went after a couple of people without any real evidence." At that admittance Joe emitted a stifled laugh then brought his features back into a somber expression.

"Anyway, I wanted it to be Nurse Spring because she was so odious but there I was proven wrong again. Fact is, the woman I thought could have been a psychopathic murderer turned out to be my rescuer."

"And the other nurse, she had that disease, Munchhausen Syndrome. That's unbelievable. Here in Pembroke? Who'd have thought?"

"Well, Maddie obviously." Nikki waved a hand. "And it was worse because she was making other people sick."

Graham lifted his head. "Munchhausen by Proxy. Dastardly."

Maddie nodded.

"Turns out Nurse O'Neill conveniently followed Doctor Marlowe from Upstate New York down to Shadylawn. They continued to date, him never guessing that she was seriously ill. All she wanted to do was draw attention to herself in the hopes that the doctor would think well of her."

Joe stood up. "We're working with the police from Potsdam. They've uncovered similar cases that were never treated as homicides. The FBI has been brought in to this case too."

A somber silence followed Joe's announcement as he glanced at Maddie and made *I've got to get going* movements. Maddie stood up too and spoke to the room.

"Um, I'll be right back. I'm just going to .." Maddie made her own *I'm just going to follow Joe* movements to the knowing nods of encouragement from the room. As Maddie reached the door, Kristy came from the hall and stood in the doorway with Lauren Sophia. Peter walked over to greet them.

Kristy stood in the doorframe letting her gaze fall on Maddie before ripping it away to kiss her husband's cheek. The expression on her face was unfamiliar to Maddie. It looked like she maybe didn't feel as threatened of Maddie as much as she once had. There was still some apprehension in the look but Maddie took what she got with gratitude.

Joe had walked out into the hallway and had his coat halfway on as Maddie approached him. She resisted the urge to help him, feeling like she was all of sixteen years old again, her fingers seeming to take on a life of their own as they threatened to reach out and touch him. She stuffed her hands into her pockets.

Joe shrugged the rest of his coat on by himself. "Let's talk about something important."

Maddie's mouth grew dry. "Like what?"

"You and me." Joe took a step closer to her and Maddie's stomach felt like a zipper had just opened it up.

He kept his eye on Maddie, a habit that he had perfected in the past two weeks and reached into his pocket. Maddie hadn't pulled her eyes away from where his were boring into her so it took her several seconds to recognize what he had in his hand.

It was an envelope though he didn't offer it to her. Maddie looked between it and Joe's face, wondering what was going through his mind. As if he had been deliberating, he finally thrust the envelope toward Maddie and at the last moment, gently placed it in her hand.

"Be gentle. It's a love letter."

Maddie's breath became shallow as she recognized her own handwriting, the image of the letters she had written to Craig hovering above the actual letter in her hand. She took it gingerly, turning it over, and saw on the back flap, a lipstick kiss. She remembered putting it there. After she'd written the letter, crying the entire time she wrote from her dorm room at Berkley, she'd applied the lipstick and pressed her lips to the paper, wishing her lips were pressed against Joe. She could almost imagine that she could see the tear stains on the envelope as well. Her hands shook and she looked up at Joe to find he had stepped even closer to her, a faint smell of peppermint on his breath.

"Read it."

Maddie wasn't sure she wanted to. "I remember."

"Please, read it."

Her hands were still shaking as she took the pieces of paper out of the envelope and unfolded them. She had to step away from Joe to do so but as soon as she had spread the pages out he shortened the space between them again. She read the words, coloring as she did. She was so young and what she had written was over the top; everlasting love and soul mates. Maddie didn't think she would be capable of writing such a letter again. She stopped at the bottom of the first page.

"Keep reading."

Turning it over, she did, until she came to what she realized he wanted her to see.

Loving you is being able to take off the mask I wear every day because I know that you've already seen what's under it. There are no reasons that you should love me but I want to spend the rest of my life giving them to you.

After reading it she looked up. Joe's eyes were bright.

"I wrote this?"

"You wrote that. And it was the sexiest thing I had ever read. It still is."

"Are you for real?"

"The real deal. *We* are the real deal. Can we try again?"

"You mean, try again, again?"

"Yes, I mean try again and again and again if that's what it takes."

Maddie did the only thing possible in the situation she found herself. She turned around to the nine people watching them and told them to get lost before she wrapped her arms around the man in front of her. Joe reached down and held Maddie's face, bringing it slowly to his while his eyes never left hers. When his lips reached her Maddie felt an electric shock that made her knees buckle. She almost pulled away to delight in the sheer romantic foolishness of the moment. Could this really be happening?

As Joe's fingers moved further around her face, entangling his fingers in her hair, she knew it was happening and she knew this was exactly where she was supposed to be. Several sighs could be heard from behind them as she and Joe stumbled, lips still locked, out the door.

THE END

ABOUT THE AUTHOR

 Kate O'Connell received her BA in Theatre and History, her MA in Dance History and Criticism and her MPhil in Dance Studies. Her research focused on the Argentine Tango and, while learning about the dance, she started teaching and performing in London. She writes about Argentine Tango now, from a seaside village in South Africa, writing and dancing barefoot as much as she possibly can.

Her first Maddie Fitzpatrick dance mystery, *Dying to Dance* was published in 2014. She's currently hard at work on the third installment *Dance or Die*.

www.ingramcontent.com/pod-product-compliance
Lightning Source LLC
Chambersburg PA
CBHW050410260626
47156CB00003B/954